THE LAST PENDRAGON

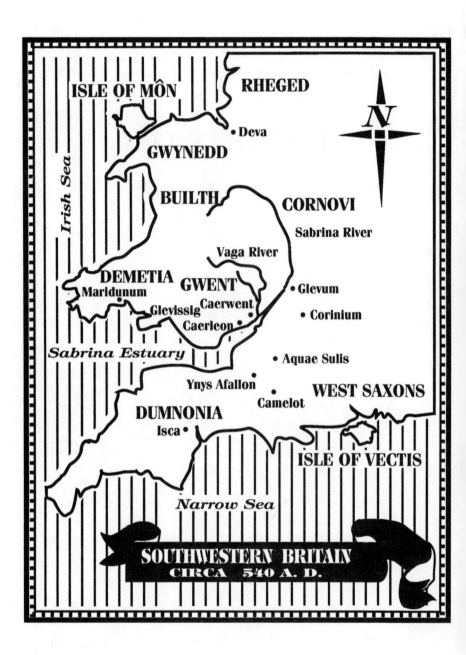

ISLE OF MÔN

RHEGED

• Deva

GWYNEDD

BUILTH

CORNOVI

Sabrina River

Vaga River

Irish Sea

DEMETIA
Maridunum

GWENT

Glevissig Caerwent
Caerleon

• Glevum

• Corinium

Sabrina Estuary

• Aquae Sulis

Ynys Afallon

WEST SAXONS

Camelot

DUMNONIA

Isca •

ISLE OF VECTIS

Narrow Sea

SOUTHWESTERN BRITAIN
CIRCA 540 A. D.

THE LAST PENDRAGON

A Novel

Robert Rice

Walker and Company
New York

Copyright © 1991 by Robert Rice

All the characters and events portrayed in this work are fictitious.

First published in the United States of America in 1991 by
Walker Publishing Company, Inc.

Published simultaneously in Canada by Thomas Allen & Son
Canada, Limited, Markham, Ontario.

Library of Congress Cataloging-in-Publication Data
Rice, Robert, 1945–
The last Pendragon : a novel / Robert Rice.
p.   cm.
ISBN 0-8027-1180-4
1. Arthur, King—Fiction.   2. Arthurian romances—Adaptations
3. Great Britain—History—To 1066—Fiction.   I. Title.
PS3568.I294L37   1992
813'.54—dc20   91-22428
CIP

Printed in the United States of America

2   4   6   8   10   9   7   5   3   1

To Linda and Joannah
for love and faith:
how can that be understood?

Prologue

Camlann

Arthur, High King of Britain, wearily glanced at the piece of broken spear in his hand and cast it aside. Shading his eyes against the dying sun, he looked down into the valley. The green turf, now smeared with red, lay torn and gouged by hundreds of horses and littered with the victims of the battle. The day had been warm, a summer day with a playful breeze that fluttered the standards of the gathered princes of Britain. It tugged at their cloaks and ruffled the manes of their horses, the kind of breeze meant for hunting the red deer or hawking in the uplands, not for dying in a nameless glen near the River Cam.

Sweat lathered the chest of Arthur's albino stallion and dripped down its legs. Its flanks heaved. The King, gray haired and blood spattered, scanned the battlefield.

At Arthur's side, the bearer of the red-dragon standard raised his war horn and sounded three sharp notes, rallying the surviving Companions for one last charge. They came to him as they could, many of them wounded, and gathered into a tight wedge behind their King: Cei of the fiery hair and fierce demeanor; Constantine, Prince of Dumnonia, Arthur's cousin and chosen successor; Rhuawn and Lucas and Gwalchmai; and the others who had remained loyal against the forces of Medraut.

Last came a dark-haired warrior riding without reins, guiding his horse with his knees and unspoken will. His shield arm was cradled in his lap and bound tightly to stem the flow of blood from his severed hand. As he galloped past the body of a slain warrior he leaned far over, gripping the sides of his horse with his legs, nearly touching the ground with his sword hand.

He seized a spear from the grip of the dead man and came back atop the moving stallion.

Curbing the horse back on its haunches, he presented the spear to Arthur with a flourish. "Even a bear cannot fight without claws, my lord."

The exhausted King looked at him with gratitude and perhaps a little awe. "They say, Bedwyr, that you could gentle the wind to ride, had you a saddle to fit her."

"No, lord." Humor gleamed behind Bedwyr's drooping eyelids. "I need no saddle."

Arthur tested the point of the spear with his thumb and returned his attention to the battlefield. Bedwyr followed his gaze. Near the river a larger band of horsemen waited for the King to carry the battle down to them, for the slope of the ground was against them. They wore the black and gold of Medraut, Arthur's son, and some carried on their shield the red-horse standard of the West Saxons.

"Ceawlin still lives," Arthur said, pointing the spear at a blond chieftain with a huge mustache and horned helmet. "There, under the red horse."

Bedwyr soothed his horse's neck with his right hand, trying to ignore the increasing dizziness from loss of blood. "He's evil, that one."

"And Medraut, see you any sign of him?" Arthur squinted against the glare.

"Aye. In the center. There." Bedwyr looked sideways at his King, who seemed to have aged a generation this day.

Arthur nodded, then turned to the other Companions. "Come, then! We'll fight such a battle that the bards will sing of it for a thousand years. For Britain!" He set spurs to his stallion and raced toward the center of the waiting rebels below.

"For Arthur!" Bedwyr drew his sword and plunged down the hill into the shadows. With hoarse shouts the rest of the warriors followed.

The clash of spear against shield rattled across the valley. Arthur's charge broke the rebel line and carried his warriors through the gap.

Unable to free his spear from an enemy shield, Arthur drew his jeweled sword, Caliburn, and wheeled to slash his way

[2]

toward Medraut. The sword flashed and shimmered, seeming to draw light from shade. Beside him Bedwyr reached the rebels' standard-bearer and hacked apart the black-and-gold flag.

The King found his son, who turned with a snarl and viciously swung his sword at his father's head. With a bell-like ring Caliburn parried the blow and for an instant the two men stared at each other, hatred in Medraut's eyes, sorrow in Arthur's. Then Medraut drove his shield into his father's face and the swords swung again.

Medraut thrust toward Arthur's stomach. At the same instant the High King's horse stumbled and the parry went wide. The thrust slid under Arthur's shield and drove deep into his abdomen. Medraut wrenched out the sword and shouted with victory, but his eyes widened as Arthur laughed. He hesitated and Arthur summoned the last of his strength to bring Caliburn down in a high arc, cleaving him between the neck and shoulder. Medraut tumbled dead from his horse.

The rebel war band, seeing their leader fall, broke and fled. Enraged but outnumbered, Ceawlin shouted threats of vengeance and led his surviving Saxons at a gallop eastward out of the valley, pursued by Constantine's warriors.

Caliburn slipped from Arthur's fingers and he slumped. He would have fallen but Bedwyr reached him, held him in the saddle, and guided him toward the trees. There he dismounted and helped the King to the shelter of a tall rowan tree, where he laid him gently on the ground. He retrieved Caliburn and slid it gently into its scabbard.

Arthur's face was ashen with the hue of death, but his eyes opened. As Bedwyr pressed his cloak against the wound to staunch the bleeding, Arthur clasped his hand weakly, holding it to the hilt of Caliburn. His voice was a whisper and the young warrior bent low to hear it.

"Here the dream dies. The gods foretold this day years ago."

"Rest you, my King. Don't try to speak."

Arthur shook his head, the movement barely visible. "Caliburn's time has ended. Know you the lake west of here?"

Bedwyr nodded, puzzled. "I know it, my lord."

Arthur paused, seeming to marshal his fading strength. Then he said: "Take the sword and cast it into the mere."

Uncertain that he had heard correctly, Bedwyr made no move to leave.

For a moment Arthur's eyes focused and he smiled at the young warrior. "You, Bedwyr, of all my Companions, have been closest to my heart. I would not have our parting come this soon, but fate wills it. Go now. I entrust Caliburn to you." His eyes closed and his hand relaxed from the Companion's wrist.

Bedwyr swallowed back the hardness in his throat. "Aye, lord." He bent and kissed Arthur's forehead, then unbuckled the King's oiled leather scabbard.

Toward them rode Lucas, Bedwyr's brother, slumped in his saddle, arms held against a crimson stain that spread outward on his tunic. He slid from his horse and stared down at the King in disbelief. "How does he?"

Bedwyr shook his head.

"They're dead," Lucas said. "All of them. Gwalchmai and Rhuawn. Cei. Even Cei. His stallion was hamstrung by Ceawlin and fell on him. All the Companions are gone."

Bedwyr scarcely heard him. "Watch over the King for me."

He mounted his war stallion and set off at a slow trot toward the marshy lake that received the waters of the River Cam. His shield arm had gone numb and he felt weak with shock. Across the high saddlebow he cradled the sword Caliburn with his right arm.

At the edge of the marsh he stopped and slid from his saddle, Caliburn gripped in his right hand. Mud sucked at his feet as he splashed through the tall marsh grass to the edge of the lake.

For a moment he stood gazing down at the great sword. Two gold serpents twined down the leather hilt. On the pommel a single amethyst gleamed purple as if it had a life of its own. Holding the scabbard between his legs, Bedwyr gently wrapped his fingers around the grip and drew Caliburn from its sheath. It warmed to his hand until it seemed to become part of his flesh.

No, he thought, I've heard Arthur wrong. He could not have meant for me to destroy this weapon. If he recovers, he'll have need of it.

He slid the blade back into the scabbard and, gripping it tightly, stumbled back to his horse. He turned the stallion and set it pounding back toward the battlefield.

As he approached the rowan tree, Bedwyr saw shapes moving in the shadows among the dead, and once heard a shriek. Looters, stealing gold and jewels from the dead and murdering the wounded. He had to move the King to safety.

Arthur lay still in the pallor of approaching death. For a moment Bedwyr did not see Lucas and he felt a flash of anger at him for leaving the King unattended. Then he saw his brother, slumped at the base of a spear. Dark blood stained Lucas's cloak and matted the grass around him.

Bedwyr slipped from his horse and knelt over Lucas. His brother's body was already growing cold. One hand gripped the spear and his sightless eyes stared down the hill, still guarding the King.

Bedwyr shut his eyes against the sting of tears. Forgive me, little brother, he thought. I shouldn't have left you.

A groan made him turn. Arthur stirred and in a faint whisper asked for water. Bedwyr took a flask from his saddle and put it to the King's lips.

After Arthur had sipped he spoke, his voice stronger. "Do not weep for your brother, Bedwyr, or for me. You can save neither. Did you obey my order?"

Bedwyr hesitated, glancing at Caliburn on his saddle. The King should not be burdened with such matters now. He would explain after Arthur regained his strength. "Aye, lord."

"What did you see?"

"See?" Bedwyr thought a moment, but remembered nothing out of the ordinary. "Only a pair of marsh fowl."

Arthur searched the last Companion's face, his gray eyes showing sadness. "You betray me as well, Bedwyr? Go now, and do as I ordered. Cast Caliburn into the mere."

The King's head fell back and his eyes closed. Another shriek sounded from the battlefield. Arthur had to be moved to safety and his wounds tended quickly or he would die. The sword would have to wait.

Bedwyr fashioned a litter from two spears and Lucas's blood-stained cloak, lashing the ends to his horse behind the saddle. Then, ignoring the pain of his mutilated arm, he dragged Arthur to the litter and set out slowly eastward.

He had no plan, only that he must find help for the King. As the horse made its way out of the valley and along a path that wound through a dark forest of beeches, Bedwyr's mind wavered on the fringes of darkness.

When awareness returned he found himself at the edge of a shallow lake, larger than the mere, with reeds growing far out into the water. In the center of the lake an island jutted from the glassy surface. Bedwyr knew it: Ynys Afallon, the Isle of Apples, sacred to Christians and Druids alike.

In the fading light a coracle made its way toward them, poled by a black-hooded figure. Another, smaller figure sat in the bow. As the boat whispered into shore Bedwyr got down from his horse, half falling, gripping the saddle to keep himself upright. The two figures stepped from the boat.

"Who are you?" He fumbled for his sword.

"Peace, Bedwyr," said the smaller figure in a woman's voice, dark and musical. "We mean you no harm. I am here to receive my brother."

"Morgan," Bedwyr stammered. "I'm sorry, lady. I didn't recognize you. How knew you that Arthur has been gravely wounded?"

She did not answer but went directly to the King and, kneeling, touched his forehead gently. "I fear you've delayed overlong, brother," she said. "My healing skills will be sorely tested." She beckoned to the hooded figure. "Come, Barinthus."

Morgan and Barinthus untied the litter and carried it toward the coracle. As they passed by Bedwyr, still leaning bewildered against the horse, Arthur opened his eyes. Caliburn glinted faintly in the twilight.

"Remember my command, Bedwyr," he murmured. "Give me your oath you will obey."

Bedwyr nodded as the world swam around him. "I swear, my lord."

Morgan and Barinthus eased Arthur into the boat and climbed in, then Barinthus began poling away from shore.

Bedwyr stumbled to the water's edge. "I would go with you."

The only response from the boat was the suck and splash of the pole lifting from the mud.

He watched the coracle float away. "I pray you, my Lord Arthur, don't leave me." He forced the words from his lips in a shout, but they came out only in a ragged whisper. "Where will I go? What will I do?"

For a moment there was only silence. Then Morgan's voice drifted back to him. "Take what comfort you can, Bedwyr. His time has passed, for now. Yet it may come again."

He watched the boat until it was out of sight. Then he sank to his knees in the mud and rocked slowly, cradling his arm in his lap, and wept.

How long he remained that way Bedwyr did not know. A clink of metal brought him back to awareness. He started and glanced wildly around for a weapon, but the noise was only the horse shifting its weight in its sleep. Bedwyr remembered Caliburn and rose stiffly, staggering until he found his balance. He pulled himself onto the horse and turned him back toward the mere by the battlefield.

Dark had fallen when he reached it, but a full moon provided enough light for him to see. He dismounted and splashed to the water's edge, Caliburn in his hand. For a moment he stood, his eyes fixed on the dark line of the far shore. Then he drew back his arm to throw the sword.

Instead, his fist opened and Caliburn slipped from his grasp to fall into the wet grass. Bedwyr's cry of anguish shredded the silence and sent echoes shivering across the lake.

"*No!*"

Two mallards took flight with a rush, their wingtips poking holes in the moonlit surface of the water.

"He may live, or there may yet come another."

Bedwyr unclasped his own sword and hurled it as far as he could into the lake. Then he bent and picked up the dripping Caliburn and walked slowly back to the horse.

Near the grazing animal an ancient bog oak survived the encroaching marsh, its gnarled shape black against the silver light. Riven by lightning in some long-past storm, the trunk had fissured and only partly healed. On impulse Bedwyr stumbled over to the tree and thrust Caliburn deep into the crack, pushing it as far as his arm could reach. Then he stepped back and looked carefully. He could see no sign of the hidden sword.

Aimlessly, consumed by pain and grief, he rode away from the lake.

PART ONE

__Irion__

ONE

The gray fortress of Caerleon rang with the clamor of shouts and curses, the snorting of horses, and the clatter of metal on wood. Inside it warriors fought a mock battle with blunt swords. One side, wearing green strips of cloth tied around their arms, slowly pressed the other side back toward the stone wall.

Leading the greens rode a young man, helmetless, whose dark hair was cut above the ears in the style Arthur had favored. His resemblance to Arthur was striking. At twenty, the soft- ness of youth had gone from his face, while training with sword and spear had hardened his arms and shoulders. But enough of the child remained in him to be delighted at the noise and sights and smells, the excitement of the mock battle.

Like a bee among blooming thistles, a small troop captain flitted back and forth between sweating warriors. "Them's shields, you bastards," he shouted, "not oat cakes! Carry them like that, the Saxons'll pick you out of your saddles like maggots out of apples."

The young man grinned. A few hundred like Gwythur, he thought, and we needn't fear the whole Saxon confederation. He dealt a stinging slap to the shoulder of a new recruit with the flat of his sword.

As the other team was driven in confusion against the wall, the troop captain let out a shrill whistle, calling the drill to a halt. Disappointed, the young man glanced at the late- afternoon sky, measuring the daylight left.

He wiped his face with a sleeve and trotted over to the captain. "Can't we go on, Gwythur?"

The captain pulled off his helmet, exposing a face as

weathered and rugged as a granite ridge. He shook his head. "They've put in a good day, Lord Irion. At least they've learned enough to ride to the latrine without falling off."

"But there's an hour of daylight left."

"The recruits are tired. When they get tired they start repeating mistakes. We've got tomorrow. And you should be wearing your helmet."

"Somebody knocked it off." Irion rubbed his head, wincing. "I guess they've learned more than I thought."

He turned his horse toward the gate and followed the weary riders out into the early spring green of the Gwent countryside. To the east the old Roman road plunged into the valley of the Usk, then ran arrow straight toward Caerwent, the capital of Gwent, eight miles away.

Up the road toward the fortress rumbled a wagon, bright blue and ornately carved, pulled by a matched team of bays. As Irion emerged, an old man seated next to the driver waved at him.

"Uncle Ynyr!" Irion shouted. He trotted his horse over to the wagon as it creaked to a halt.

Honorius, magistrate of Gwent, gathered his toga and climbed gingerly over the side, groping for the step with his foot. A breeze lifted a wisp of white hair and teased it across his bald head.

"Did you journey well?" Irion dismounted and helped his uncle to the ground.

"I'm not dead, lad, but I'm ten breaths short of it." Considering the small frame from which it emerged, Honorius's voice was surprisingly deep, like thunder trapped in a narrow valley. His Latin was pure. "When I get back to Caerwent I'm going to parboil my behind in the baths." He reached the ground and stretched, pressing his hands into the small of his back.

Irion studied his uncle with concern. Since his mother's death eleven years earlier Honorius had been his only family. "I'm glad you're home. I didn't expect you until next week."

"I didn't expect to be back until next week. But there's no point sitting in Maelgwn's mead hall twiddling my thumbs. So I left."

"King Maelgwn didn't see the need for an alliance?"

Honorius snorted. "Maelgwn doesn't see the need for his

own belly button." He smoothed back the feathery wings of hair above his ears. "Have you a moment to talk?"

"Of course. Let me turn my horse out."

"I'll walk with you," Honorius said. "I need to put some life back in my legs."

Irion's mail shirt clinked as they walked toward a rock-walled pasture that plunged down the long slope toward the river. As the old man hobbled beside him, the breeze fluttered the hem of his toga around his ankles. "The truth is, Irion," he said, "I failed. Maelgwn has no intention of agreeing to an alliance, even though we have three other chieftains committed. It won't upset him if the Saxons destroy the smaller British kingdoms one by one."

"Does he think they'll spare him?"

"He thinks he's secure in his mountains. And he would rather rule a Britain ten miles wide than serve in a Britain that extends from ocean to ocean." Honorius acknowledged Gwythur's salute as the captain rode past. "To be thirty years younger and able to ride a war-horse," the magistrate said. "Perhaps then I could forge an alliance the way Arthur did." He sighed. "But then again, I'm no Arthur."

The pain Irion felt at the mention of that name must have shown in his eyes. His uncle glanced at him and quickly changed the subject. "How goes the training?"

Irion shrugged. "The recruits are enthusiastic. There just aren't enough of them." He stopped at the pasture gate and began to unfasten the saddle cinch. "The eagles built Caerleon for an entire legion of six thousand. We rattle around in there like dried peas in a gourd."

Honorius cleared his throat. "Irion . . ." he began, and stopped.

The youth waited, watching his uncle to see if he would scratch his chin, a sure sign he was about to broach an unpleasant subject. Honorius scratched his chin and Irion repressed a smile.

"Irion," the magistrate repeated, "you know the war band has been without a tribune since Balon's death."

"Aye. But Gwythur drills them as well as Balon would have." Irion jerked off the saddle and set it on the wall. With a brush he began to curry the sweat from his horse's back.

"Perhaps," Honorius said. "But with the Saxon threat increasing daily, the war band needs a permanent leader."

"How about Gwythur?"

"Gwythur's not of noble blood. The council of elders wouldn't accept him."

Irion tried to think of someone else the warriors would follow as tribune, but he knew there was no one else as qualified as the veteran captain.

"The council meets in two weeks," Honorius said. "I'd like to place your name before them as the next tribune."

Irion stopped brushing. "Me? That's not possible."

"Why not?"

He glanced at his uncle. "You know why."

"I've watched you, my boy," Honorius said, ignoring the comment. "You're a born warrior and a natural leader. And I trust you. I need someone in that post in whom I have absolute confidence."

Irion gazed out over the river valley toward the far ridge lost in mist. During the rare moments of his childhood when he had allowed himself to dream, he had sometimes imagined being a great warrior leading the British against the Saxons. But as soon as that vision appeared, he always stifled it. He knew that he would never lead a war band. "You know the council won't accept me," he said. Bitterness lent a sharp edge to his voice.

"They will if I demand it."

"You think they'll tolerate the son of Medraut, the murderer of King Arthur, leading their warriors?"

Honorius nodded. "Most people don't hold the sins of Medraut against you, Irion. They accept you for what you are."

Irion said nothing, absently rubbing his nose, broken in a fight when he was twelve, the year he had been sent to his uncle to be raised, the year after Camlann. There had been many fights then, because everyone had taunted him, and he had usually lost. Although he could not hide the evidence of the beatings, he had never told Honorius the identity of his attackers, not for fear of worse beatings, but from shame that they had happened at all; that he had brought them on by being who he was.

But there had come a time, after one particularly painful

attack, when he swore he would never again allow himself to be beaten. Irion persuaded Gwythur, an old friend of Honorius, to teach him how to fight with his fists. Soon he excelled at it. Gwythur also taught him the basics of sword and shield, which Irion spent long hours practicing.

And the bullying had stopped, at least physically. But as he grew many of the townsfolk of Caerwent, especially the nobles, found other ways to torment him. He had learned to hide his anger when he was belittled or snubbed, often taking refuge in the barracks with Gwythur and his warriors.

"I don't agree, Uncle," he said. "Many people will never look at me without seeing my fa—Medraut. Brennus, for one."

Honorius grunted. "Brennus cannot stand and make wind at the same time. Leave him to me. He doesn't have the votes to oppose me in council." He cocked his head and looked at his nephew. "Is it the opinion of the nobles that bothers you, Irion, or are you afraid of your own ghosts?"

Irion turned away. Yes, there were ghosts. He knew he had nothing to do with his father's treason; he'd been too young even to be certain what was happening. But Medraut, people said, had been evil itself. And if his father was evil, he was the seed of evil. He had grown up waiting for the darkness to surface, wondering if he could control it when it did.

"However much a baby snake would rather be an eagle," he said, "it will still have scales when it grows up." He slapped the horse on the rump more sharply than he intended. The animal started and bolted through the gate.

Honorius raised his eyebrows. "We're not speaking of snakes. You also have the blood of Arthur, and of Uther Pendragon and of Ambrosius before him. Never forget that." He laid a weathered hand on Irion's shoulder. "I believe in you, lad. I know you have doubts about yourself, and I wouldn't ask this of you if the need weren't so great. Think it over and we can talk again later."

Irion nodded in dumb misery. He watched as his uncle hobbled back to the wagon. Medraut, he knew, had become a captain of Arthur's war band at the same age. Was it all going to happen again?

TWO

Irion and Gwythur slowed their horses to a walk as they started down the hill toward the Sabrina River. Behind them, laughing and talking, came a small company of armed warriors cloaked in the green colors of Gwent. Here the Sabrina was still wide and flecked with white foam, still more sea than river, and a rising wind carried the tang of salt. Far ahead the water narrowed, glinting like metal in the noon sun. They made their way north and east, roughly parallel to the shore as they patrolled the border of Gwent.

A new recruit, face reddened by the spring sun, shouted to a companion in front of him: "They say there's a witch lives in yonder woods who brews ale from moonlight."

"Do they, now?"

"Aye. But the drink is strong as venom on Saxon knives."

"I'll not go there," said another warrior, a man with a great hooked nose. "I'd fear the hell-hag would lay a hex on me and I'd wake up with the head of an ass."

"You already have the head of an ass," Captain Gwythur growled. "Now, stop chattering and keep a sharp eye." He glanced at Irion. "Your mood's as gray as winter, boy."

Irion had ridden most of the day in silence. From time to time he chewed on his fingernails as he struggled with his uncle's request and with his own doubts, answering questions in monosyllables or not at all. He shook his head, then shrugged. "Ride forward with me a little, will you, Gwythur?"

They nudged their horses into a trot and drew ahead of the patrol. Gwythur looked at him, waiting.

"Lord Honorius wants to name me tribune."

There was a pause, then Gwythur said, "Och! A good choice. I could think of no one better."

"I'd prefer it were you, Captain."

Gwythur grunted. "My blood's not blue enough. But I fail to see why you're gloomy."

"Should I accept?"

"Why not?"

Irion fingered the hilt of his silver-handled dagger, the only gift his father had ever given him. The fact that it had once been Medraut's embarrassed him now, but he had kept it, although he was not sure why. "Do you think the warriors would accept me?"

Gwythur's eyebrows drew together as he considered the question. "Aye. I do. They've come to know you, Irion, and they respect you. Anyway, many of them are too young to remember Medraut. They'll follow you."

They rode for a moment in silence, save for the clank of fittings and the creak of leather. Gwythur squinted at him. "There's more than that, isn't there?"

"Aye." Irion sighed. "You knew my father, Gwythur. Am I like him?"

The gnarled captain looked surprised, then thoughtful. "Medraut had a few good things about him," he said slowly. "There are times when I see pieces of him in you. But," he added, "there's more of Arthur than Medraut. You even look like your grandfather."

Irion said nothing. It was who he resembled on the inside that concerned him, not his face. He knew he could handle the job of tribune. And he had realized soon after Honorius spoke to him that he wanted it. But he was only now coming to understand why. With it, he could lead the fight against the barbarians, recapture the British land Ceawlin and his West Saxons had taken. He had even allowed himself to think about retaking Arthur's great fortress of Camelot, now used by Ceawlin as a base from which to terrorize the British to the west. If Irion could win back the fortress for the Cymry, perhaps he could clear away his father's shadow once and for all.

Gwythur halted suddenly and Irion was jerked from his reverie. The captain pointed. On the shoreline a mile ahead, a plume of smoke rose, too dark and too large to be a cooking fire. Gwythur gave a command and the patrol broke into a canter.

The track veered toward the river, winding through tall marsh grass, then up a small rise. On the other side of the knoll at the water's edge a dozen or so huts had been reduced to smoldering circles.

Gwythur raised his hand and the patrol halted. There were no signs of the raiders. Save for the black tendrils of smoke writhing up from the fishing village, nothing moved.

Irion gripped his sword hilt. "Saxons?"

The captain nodded. "It has the stink of Ceawlin."

They rode cautiously down the rise and into the village. The raiders had struck at dawn, catching the villagers still in their huts. Most of them contained charred bodies. Outside one of the houses a boy of no more than ten summers lay trampled by horses. Near his body lay a small, rusted sword, its blade pitted and useless.

Skirting the rubble of a hut, Irion's horse shied. Inside the smoking ring lay what had once been a man. His ribs had been chopped free from the backbone and spread outward.

Gwythur spat. "The blood eagle. A Saxon amusement."

"Can we catch them?" Irion trembled with anger.

"No. They came down on these folks like wolves and probably left as quick." Gwythur looked out across the brown river. "By now they're back in Camelot, proud of a good day's work."

"They could have gotten no profit from this. These people had nothing to steal."

"The profit is in killing British," Gwythur said. "And soon they will not content themselves with raiding fisher folk."

The patrol buried the bodies, then searched the area around the village, but they found no sign that the raiders had gone inland.

When they rode away from the ruins, Irion hung back, brooding on what he had seen. Ceawlin had been Medraut's ally at Camlann, and Irion remembered his father talking about the Saxon chieftain the day before Medraut left for the battle. Medraut had come to see Irion's mother at her villa in Dumnonia. He had stayed only a few hours, but his visit made a great impression on Irion—for once his father had been friendly to him. Medraut had pulled him up onto his great war stallion and taken him for a ride in the field behind the villa, boasting about his new ally, the fierce yellow-haired Saxon who would help him kill Arthur and win the High Kingship for himself.

When Medraut left he had given Irion his dagger. "Be good," he said, "or I'll cut off your ears when I get back."

Watching his father ride away, Irion had wondered if Saxons were really as terrible as he had been told. Since then he had discovered their cruelty for himself.

The rest of the day he rode alone, grim and silent. By evening he had made a decision. He spurred his horse and caught Gwythur.

The captain glanced up and Irion looked him in the eye. "I'll need your help," he said.

THREE

Irion sipped from his horn of ale and leaned back against the smooth bark of a beech tree. The wind was sharp and chilled his back even as the crackling wood fire scorched his face and hands. Off to the north other fires burned, some on hills nearby, others more distant, only bright sparks in the May Eve night.

He searched the darkness eastward for the bonfire that would be burning outside the walls of Caerwent and found it, a tiny yellow flower in the blackness. His uncle Honorius would be celebrating there, but not around the fire. He and the other elders would be feasting in the great hall, reclining on eating couches in the Roman fashion. They clung to their tradition even though their numbers dwindled each year and the hypocaust, broken now, no longer provided heat to the feast room.

Irion had always loved the festival welcoming spring. With the other warriors on duty he had eaten more than he should of roast mutton and ham and spitted duck. Now he sat and listened, drinking apple ale as his companions argued and laughed.

They seemed content, at least as content as warriors who were not fighting could be. But for Irion the shine of contentment was marred by the new line between them, the barrier that had sprung up when he had been named tribune. In spite of that, he was enjoying his new job hugely. The high point of his life had been standing in front of the council of elders taking the oath of loyalty.

Gwythur sat beside him, arguing weaponry with Hywel,

captain of infantry, a stolid giant with a chest as thick as a yew trunk. "Only a simpleton would use a sword that short," Gwythur was saying. "In your hand a Roman *gladius* looks like a table knife."

The giant infantryman rumbled to his feet, his shaved head glinting in the firelight. Bending over, he grasped Gwythur under his arms, then lifted him high in the air like a nursemaid lifting an infant. He grinned through his black beard. "Insult me, little man, but don't insult my weapons."

"Put me down, you turd-eating oaf," wheezed Gwythur. "I'll shave your beard and feed it to my horse, look you."

"Enough," Irion said. "Put him down, Hywel."

Hywel held Gwythur a moment longer, then lowered him to the ground. "I will have an apology."

Irion stood and handed him the ale horn. "Gwythur meant nothing by his remark. He's willing to apologize."

"Must I, by the gods?"

"Aye. We'll have no quarrels on Beltane."

Gwythur stared at Irion with a look that was almost a challenge. Irion met his gaze squarely. Finally, the captain broke into a slow smile and nodded. He turned and stuck out his hand to Hywel. "I meant no insult."

Hywel grunted and handed the drinking horn to the cavalryman, giving him a slap on the back with his other hand that nearly staggered him.

As they resumed their seats Hywel lifted his head like a hunting dog sniffing the wind. "Someone comes," he said.

Then Irion heard it, too: a drumming of horse's hoofs on the hard surface of the Roman road. "He's in haste, whoever he is."

They stood as the rider emerged from the gloom and made for the fire. In the light his horse's chest and neck shone with sweat. Foam flecked its mouth. As he reached them, the rider, a boy of about fifteen, reined hard and slid from his mount.

"My Lord Irion," he gasped. He looked near collapse. His face was caked with dust and grime and in one fist he carried a burlap sack covered with dark stains.

"Who are you?" Irion said.

"Niall, sir. Groom at Glevum outpost. We've been attacked. Overrun." He staggered and dropped the sack.

[21]

Irion guided the boy to a boulder and sat him down. The flames silhouetted his face, revealing streaks where tears had washed away the grime. Niall continued to talk disjointedly, as if his mind demanded he free himself of his message. "They came this morning at dawn. Took us completely by surprise." He shook his head. "We should have known. Where were the outriders? They never warned us. Only thirty of us. I'm the only one left." He looked up at Irion, eyes pleading. "They broke through. Killed everyone. But not me. They didn't kill me. I rode all day."

Irion felt his stomach twist, a cold sickness rising within him. "Who were they?"

"Saxons, lord. They wore red horses on their shields."

"How many?"

Niall buried his face in his hands. "They seemed to be thousands."

Irion knelt beside the boy and patted his shoulder. "Think carefully, Niall. It's very important that we know how many of the enemy there were."

The boy drew a shuddering breath and appeared to calculate mentally. "Perhaps two and a half hundred at start, lord. But there are some less now."

Irion nodded thoughtfully. Survivors of battles tended to count each enemy twice. The boy might be mistaken, but he would not likely err low.

Standing above them, Hywel asked, "How came you to be spared?"

Niall's glance strayed to the sack and he shivered. "Their chieftain told me to bring you a message."

"And the message?" asked Irion.

Niall pointed to the sack and opened his mouth to speak, but no words came out. Irion lifted a corner of the burlap and emptied its contents on the ground. He drew back in revulsion. From the sack rolled the severed head of a man, its teeth bared in a grimace of pain. Sugyn, the captain of Glevum outpost.

"He said to tell my war chief it was a gift to the British for Beltane," the boy said.

Irion looked at Gwythur. "Ceawlin."

"Aye," said Gwythur. "They came from Camelot itself, like as not."

Anger crackled in Irion like a gorse fire. He questioned Niall further but could get little additional information. There were no horsemen among the raiders. The chieftain had said nothing else except his name, which was Wiermund. Ceawlin himself was not with them. The boy did not know which way the raiders had gone, for they were still looting bodies as he rode away. Irion praised his courage and ordered that he be given a hot meal and allowed to rest.

Fighting panic, Irion stood. At that moment a barbarian war band looted and murdered somewhere in Gwent. Where? Was the outpost attack only a feint? If Ceawlin's entire war band invaded, how could he face them with two hundred cavalry and a handful of foot soldiers? He suddenly felt small and helpless. Standing a little apart, his captains watched him.

He took a deep breath, forced himself to be calm, and thought hard. With the outpost destroyed, nothing would stop the raiders from plundering the unprotected countryside. They had obviously planned their raid to correspond to Beltane, when the British would be sluggish from celebrating and slow to respond. No doubt they anticipated an extra day of looting before Irion's troops could reach them.

"Gwythur," he said. "How soon can you have your men ready to ride?"

"By first light, tribune."

"I need them sooner than that. The moon is four days past full. It'll rise near midnight. I want them in their saddles by the time it's up."

Hywel and Gwythur exchanged glances.

"We ride tonight?" Gwythur said. "Some of the men are going to have vine leaves in their hair, Irion."

"The Saxons are counting on just that. They think they have tomorrow to pillage our farms before we can reach them."

"A night ride is dangerous."

"Having Saxons in our backyard is more dangerous," Irion said. "There'll be light enough to see, and therefore light enough to ride. I want your men ready at midnight even if you have to strap them in their saddles."

"Aye, tribune." Gwythur saluted but remained, looking thoughtful. "Something about this business does not smell right."

"What mean you?"

"Why would Saxons warn us of their raid? It may have been days before we learned of it had they not sent Niall back with his message."

"You think perhaps they seek to draw us toward the outpost while the main attack falls elsewhere?"

"Perhaps."

"I've thought of that also. Yet we've had no reports of large hostings in the Saxon lands."

"No. And Ceawlin will not risk attacking Caerleon, at least, not yet. He prefers unarmed farmers. Still, I smell some fox trick here. Have care, Irion." He turned and stumped away.

There was no time to ponder the possibilities. Irion ordered beacons fired on hilltops from Caerwent to Malvern warning the villages and farms of their danger. From the gate tower a horn called the men to arms.

The fortress erupted as men gathered and checked weapons, threw on armor, saddled horses in grim haste. Each warrior received food for three days, to be carried on his back or in his saddlebag, for speed was the chief consideration. The supply wagons and their escort would catch them when they could.

A half hour past midnight Gwythur rode up, saluting. "Cavalry are ready, tribune. We lack only Eoin, who is bed-sick with the fire in his belly, and Dengyn, who broke his leg in training two days since."

"Form the men outside the north gate."

The warriors assembled in four squares behind squadron captains. One hundred twenty riders rode great horses, descendants of the Parthian cavalry mounts sold to the British when the legions withdrew. Bred for size and stamina, they formed the heavy cavalry, which would lead the charge into battle. Irion had divided them into squadrons of sixty, one under his command, the other under Gwythur. An additional eighty light cavalrymen, archers and swordsmen, rode small, shaggy native horses and were led by Cynlas, one of twin brothers who were Irion's best archers.

Riders sat in deep saddles with pommels and cantles that rose high in front and back to protect their bowels from spear thrusts. Hauberks of mail rings gleamed beneath their cloaks, and polished helms were slung by straps across their saddle-bows. From hooks on their saddles hung shields, kite shaped to protect the left leg, and emblazoned with the red dragon of Gwent on a green background. Long swords hung from baldrics at their left sides.

The heavy cavalry carried spears with bright, leaf-shaped heads, while the light horsemen wore three-foot bows across their shoulders. A few, such as Cynlas and Kylan, also carried long yew bows, nearly as tall as they, unstrung in leather sheaths attached to their saddles.

The faces of the warriors were grim and unsmiling, the festive mood of Beltane having evaporated like mist under an August sun. Irion faced them. "Call off! Light."

"Light formed and ready, tribune," said Cynlas.

"Heavy."

"Heavy formed and ready, tribune," Gwythur said.

"Column of threes behind the dragon."

A rider holding high the red-dragon standard trotted forward to join Irion. Spears raised like a deadly forest, they moved eastward, toward Caerwent, at a ground-eating lope.

The horses' hoofs beat a drumming thunder and the forest-green cloaks of the riders flared behind them as they swept past the walls of Caerwent. People ran out and watched silently as they rode past, women and children and old men. Some wept, knowing that no mercy would be shown them if these defenders failed.

FOUR

The cavalry reached the top of a low hill as the sky paled with the first streaks of dawn. Irion called a halt to rest the horses and eat a quick meal. They had ridden hard all night, hunched against a wind that blew thin and cold into their faces, fretting past them to cry back up the trackway to Caerwent

During most of the night apprehension had held off Irion's fatigue: worry that he was leading his warriors into a trap, uneasiness about leaving his home undefended behind him. He tried to reduce his disquiet by planning future campaigns, envisioning personal combat with Ceawlin, killing him to the cheers of his men. Then he saw himself leading an alliance of Britons against the Saxons, taking back Britain and restoring Arthur's boundaries.

But weariness and the steady rhythm of the horse had finally worn him down. In the end he had fought to keep his eyes open. Now he slid from his horse, cold and hungry and tired.

The moon was setting behind a thicket of brush and the cold light of the stars had begun to fade. As Irion's boots hit the ground Gwythur rode over, shadowy in the gloom.

"Not here, tribune," the captain said, his voice anxious. "This is not a good place to rest in the dark."

Irion looked up, surprised, then glanced around him. Not far from the trail, at the edge of vision, a cluster of dry stone circles stood dimly outlined. Waist high, most of them were open to the air, but some still wore roofs of turf. Once they had been the homes of the old, dark ones, built before the memory of any man living, unless Myrddin himself still lived.

Irion nodded. It was still night, and night was the territory of Annwn, the underworld. The dead walked, seeking men's fires to warm themselves. It would be best to stay as far from the wraiths of the ancient ones as possible. He mounted again and gave the signal to ride on.

The sun had risen when they halted once more. While the men rested, Irion sent scouts north and east toward the outpost to search for signs of the raiders. Waiting, he forced himself to eat some salt beef and a dry biscuit.

He had finished his meal when Kylan, the last of the scouts to return, galloped in and wrenched his lathered horse to a stop. One of twin brothers, Kylan was a skilled archer. His ears, and those of his brother Cynlas, stuck out at right angles beneath identical thatches of sandy hair. Pug noses and wide mouths completed their remarkable faces, the impression being of two fauns. With their skills as bowmen, Irion would have been glad to have them if they had looked like trolls.

Irion came to his feet. "Saw you any sign?"

Kylan's face twisted in disgust. "It'd be more of a challenge to track a herd of cattle. I rode to Glevum outpost and followed their trail from there. It leads west, into our farmland, then circles north."

Gwythur stumped up. "They'll be moving back toward the Sabrina today. By tonight they'll want to be safe across, before they think we can reach them."

"We may have a surprise for them," Irion said. He looked at Kylan. "How old were the tracks?"

"Made yesterday before dark. Not later."

"If they're not expecting us until evening, they may have camped nearby last night." To Gwythur he said, "Mount your men. We'll find them before they skulk back into their holes."

They splashed across a small stream and cantered east. The raiders had indeed passed that way, leaving behind a wide swath of trampled grass and debris: leather cross-garter straps, sandals, and once, the body of a Saxon raider lying mouth open, staring skyward, throat hacked open.

A short distance from the road stood a farm enclosed in a wooden palisade of pointed logs. Smoke curled from it. Irion took Gwythur to have a look.

The walls, designed for night protection against wolves,

had proven inadequate against the raiders. Splinters of broken gate lay scattered about the opening. Inside the enclosure they found storage sheds and byres and a house, front door banging in the wind.

Irion dismounted and, drawing his sword, stepped into the house. Three children, a boy and two small girls, lay heaped together on the floor, throats slashed open. The back door of the house had been kicked off its hinges. Behind the house the body of a woman sprawled on her back, naked, her face twisted in terror. A little way off a wooden milk pail lay on its side, a dark spot marking where its contents had seeped into the ground.

"Bastards!" Irion said.

He motioned to Gwythur and they returned to the troop. Without a word he signaled them forward.

They passed other farms, also pillaged. Some had been set to the torch, and these still burned. Irion knew they were closing on the raiders.

The sun was nearing its high point when Kylan came flying back to the head of the column. "I've come onto them, Lord Irion," he said. "They've stopped on the road three miles ahead to eat."

Fierce exultation swept through Irion. "How many?"

"Two hundred, plus ten or twenty. No more."

"Saw you any horses?"

"None. Only cattle they've looted. They're completely afoot."

"Show me."

Irion and Kylan cautiously rode forward. A short distance ahead the road passed between two low hills shining yellow with blooming daffodils. Here they left the trackway and climbed the hill on the right, then dismounted and crept to the top. On the road a half mile eastward of the hills a band of Saxons sprawled at ease around cooking fires, laughing and boasting as they prepared their midday meal.

Lying flat on his stomach, Irion watched them. From its size, this was obviously a raiding party, not a full-fledged invasion. Still, they outnumbered his own force. Even with cavalry he would need to surprise them. If the raiders had time, they would form a shield wall, with those in front kneeling to jab their spears butt-first into the ground, lowering their spear-heads toward the attackers. Such a deadly barricade would break any cavalry charge. But if he could keep them disorganized . . .

He looked at Kylan thoughtfully. "Come," he said. "I've an idea."

He led the scout back to the waiting troops and gathered his captains around him, then issued his orders. The cavalry he formed into two companies. One, under Cynlas, he sent to wait behind the hill from which he had just come. The other company he placed under Gwythur and sent around behind the hill on the far side of the road.

Kylan he held back. "I have something special in mind for you." As the archer listened to Irion's plan his gnomelike face broke into a grin.

Irion rode to join Gwythur, who crouched at the top of the hill watching the Saxons impassively. "If ugly could kill," Gwythur said, "we'd all be falling dead from our saddles."

They waited. As the minutes slid by Irion felt even more strongly the burden of responsibility. If he guessed wrong, many warriors under his command would die. He grasped the hilt of his sword, finding comfort in its leather grip. His hands were sweating. Beside him Gwythur glanced over.

Irion wiped his hands on his trousers. "Is it always like this, before a fight?"

Gwythur nodded. "I've never gone into battle in my life without my tunic sticking to my back."

At last Kylan appeared. From the west the redheaded scout lead a small band of archers at a trot up the road toward the raiders' camp.

As they passed between the hills a Saxon sentry saw them and shouted a warning. In the camp, men leaped up from their eating and sprang to their weapons. When they saw the size of the approaching force their alarm turned to laughter. Jeering and mocking, they gathered into a rough shield wall across the road.

Kylan led his archers forward until the raiders were just within reach of the great bows. Then he stopped in the classic archer's stance, side toward the target, feet apart. Calmly he fitted an arrow to his bowstring, drew it to his ear, and released it with a twang.

A Saxon in the front line reeled backward, shield nailed to his chest. The other bowmen shot their missiles and a dozen more raiders fell. Curses and shouts of rage rose. A few arrows flew toward Kylan but fell short.

At the top of the hill, Irion watched, smiling grimly. Another volley flew between the green cloaks and the Saxons, and more barbarians dropped. After the third volley the scant discipline of the raiders collapsed. Screaming their war cries, a small band broke away from the shield wall and charged toward Kylan's archers. The others followed, unwilling to be left out of the kill. Kylan and his bowmen turned and ran back along the road.

Irion sprinted to his horse. When the Saxons reached the gap between the hills, he signaled, and the trumpeter blew a ringing call. Spears lowered, heads tucked behind shields, the two lines of cavalry began to move, slowly at first, then faster, thundering down both hills toward the barbarians caught between.

Seeing the trap too late, the Saxons had no time to form a shield ring. Against the weight of the great horses their ranks splintered like kindling.

For Irion the battle shrank to the next foe in front of him. A squat, red-bearded man sprang up to his right, both hands swinging a heavy iron sword, more bludgeon than blade. Irion's spear tip divided the man's beard and passed through his neck, flinging him backward with a gurgling wail and a spray of blood.

Men find strange voices to greet pain and death, Irion thought. Then he forced from his mind all thought, all compassion. The willingness to kill was the price of his life.

The charge slowed, blocked by a mass of warriors shouting their hatred. Desperately, Irion urged his horse forward. Rearing and plunging, the animal fought its way deeper into the melee. At his shoulder, Gwythur kept pace, his sword arm a blur of motion.

Irion heard a call. He glanced up to see Cynlas spurring his horse toward him, stabbing downward with his spear like a dagger. Behind him surged the rest of his troop. The two companies met and Cynlas rode past with a whoop like a young recruit.

The forces crossed, emerging on opposite sides. At a signal from Irion the trumpeter blew a blast on his war horn, and they wheeled and charged again.

An iron wedge of horsemen drove into the Saxons. This time the charge scattered the raiders, save for a knot of warriors in the center protecting their blond chieftain. Into the midst of the Saxon defenders galloped Cynlas, outdistancing his troop. Irion shouted a warning, unheard in the din of battle.

The captain was soon surrounded, but fought on, an island battered by a great surf. As Irion watched, a Saxon spear caught Cynlas in the back and he sagged forward. The chieftain reached up and dragged him from his saddle.

Irion shouted to his trumpeter and the youth blew two sharp notes. The company wheeled left and fought toward the fallen captain. At the same time, Cynlas's troop reached the center and crashed into the knot of raiders. The Saxon chieftain fell, an arrow through his eye.

Seeing their leader die, the remaining raiders began to break and flee. The battle was soon over. At Irion's command the stragglers were ridden down and killed.

The tribune rode slowly back through the field as the fury of battle gradually drained away, leaving his limbs cold, his mouth tasting of ashes. He found the battered body of Cynlas where he had fallen. Next to him, eyes puffed nearly shut from weeping, sat his brother Kylan, staring into the distance.

"Can I do anything?"

Kylan looked up and shook his head.

Irion rode on, uncertain what to do next. Around him warriors wandered the battlefield, or stood in silent clusters, staring at the bodies of comrades. Some trembled as the violent fever of war left them.

Irion stopped and slid from his horse. To his surprise his left leg would not obey him and he sagged against his mount. Looking down, he noticed for the first time the smear of blood congealed around a jagged tear in his leg. He winced as the pain began.

Gwythur trotted over. "Weapons are being collected for

salvage, Lord Irion." He sounded as if he had just been through a training exercise. "Are you all right?"

Irion nodded and took a step. His head spun and he sat down abruptly. "I guess I'm torn enough to need a little mending. I feel as groggy as a hen on her night roost."

Gwythur dismounted and inspected the leg. "You've lost a lot of blood. I've seen that make even the strongest faint." He stood. "It's a deep gash, tribune, but not dangerous, if it doesn't take the rot. I'll find a surgeon."

Irion tried not to grimace as an army surgeon dressed his wound. "How many did we lose?" he asked the medicus.

"Twenty-eight dead. Twice that number wounded."

Standing above him, Gwythur nodded. "Very acceptable losses, tribune."

Not if you're Cynlas, Irion thought. Not if you're one of the twenty-eight.

Gradually the warriors gathered around. Irion limped among them, praising them, thanking them. Where it started he could not later say, but somewhere someone began chanting Irion's name, and the chant spread rapidly from man to man. Hands seized him gently and placed him on a shield, then lifted him high in the air.

In unison the warriors shouted, "Hail!" And again, "Hail!" A third time, "Hail!" The threefold tribute used by Roman troops for conquering caesars.

Astonishment turned to pleasure and Irion grinned broadly.

FIVE

Irion and his warriors reached the gates of Caerwent as the sun was setting. After the battle they had buried their dead and rested overnight before riding slowly back. Irion had sent a messenger ahead to tell Honorius of their victory, envisioning in the flush of his triumph a hero's welcome. But during the ride the exhilaration of the cavalry's salute had worn off. His leg throbbed and a vague feeling of unease had returned. Apprehension turned to alarm when he found the gates closed and barred against them.

As they halted beneath the walls, a sentry appeared in the gate tower. "Who comes?"

"It's us," Irion said. "Were you not told?"

The sentry hurried down from his tower and lifted the bar, mumbling to himself as he hauled open the heavy wooden slabs. He held a torch high as Irion rode through, peering up at him. "Lord Irion. It's glad I am to see you."

"What goes forward?"

"Lord Honorius, tribune. He's been wounded."

Cold dread touched Irion. "By whom, man?"

"I—I don't know, lord. But the council ordered me to shut the gates and be alert."

"Where is he?"

"They've taken him to Catullan, the physician."

Irion looked at Gwythur. "Have the men stand ready until I learn more of this." He kicked his tired mount into a gallop and clattered through the stillness toward the surgeon's house. As he sped through the streets he murmured quick prayers to

Nodens of the Silver Hand, to Lugh, and to the Christus that Honorius worshiped, to spare his uncle.

Catullan's surgery filled a narrow building set back from the street to make room for a crowded herb garden. Outside it, an angry glow lit the sky. As Irion drew nearer, the glow turned into a cluster of torches held by a throng of people. Faces made orange by the torchlight silently watched him climb from his horse and hobble into the building.

As he entered, smells of vinegar and herbs assailed him. On a high table in the middle of the room lay a body covered by a white shroud. Beneath a row of pegs holding bunches of dried herbs he saw Catullan. The old Roman-trained surgeon, a close friend of Honorius whom Irion had never seen smile, sat slumped on a stool.

"Is that? . . ." Irion said.

Catullan nodded. The dour medicus looked even paler than usual and his eyes were red from strain and lack of sleep.

"Does he live?"

"I did what I could, Irion." Catullan looked at him bleakly. "The arrow punctured his lung. It came out smoothly but the other lung failed. He died a few minutes ago."

Pain tore at Irion. He willed back the tears and steadied his voice. "Ah, Jesu. Why him? What did he do to anyone?"

The surgeon lifted his hand, then let it drop, leaning his head back against the wall.

Irion nodded toward the body. "May I?"

"Of course."

He went over to the table and lifted back the shroud. Honorius's eyes were closed; the furrows and creases life had etched into his face were smoothed in death. Irion's chest went hollow with a vast, dull ache; he felt as though some living part of him had been torn away. He reached down and took his uncle's hand in both of his, then bent over and kissed his forehead. "Rest you gentle, Uncle Ynyr."

He turned to Catullan. "Who murdered him?"

"A stranger. Iceni, I heard. Near dark, Honorius walked home alone from the baths and was shot from behind."

"They caught him, then?"

"Aye. A guard caught him as he was about to slip out the south gate." Catullan rubbed his eyes with his fingers.

"What reason had he to kill my uncle?"

"None that I know of."

Numb, Irion prowled back and forth beneath a hanging pewter lamp that sputtered yellow light on the walls of the surgery. He wondered what to do. The killing had the stink of a paid assassination, but he knew of no one on the council who disliked Honorius enough to have him killed. Oh, there were those who had disagreed with his uncle. Brennus was their leader, and he stood next in line to be magistrate. But a sneak killing was not his style.

"Where are they holding this Iceni?" he asked finally.

"In the guard post near the south gate, I was told."

Irion nodded and limped toward the door. "My thanks, Catullan, for trying. I will go speak with this assassin."

He rode toward the gate, a part of him numb with grief. But another part of his mind observed the situation with cold detachment, weighing the consequences of the murder against his own fate. He had been Honorius's choice of tribune, opposed by Brennus and his supporters. With his uncle gone, there might be an attempt to remove him from his new post. He resented the thought. The spark of ambition that had been kindled within him now burned hotly. He was, after all, the grandson of Arthur, the Pendragon, High King of Britain. And he had proved himself a good leader. He deserved to keep the post.

Logrin, the pompous captain of the council guard, stood outside the guard post conferring in low tones with two other guardsmen bedecked in maroon capes and ancient Roman helmets. They broke off their conversation as Irion approached.

Logrin nodded in acknowledgment. "Medraut-son." He spoke the name as if it were sour on his tongue.

"I would speak with your prisoner, Logrin," Irion said, dismounting.

"You cannot. I've sent for Brennus. He wishes to question this man first."

Irion shouldered past him. "I think even Brennus will acknowledge my right as surviving clan chief to avenge Honorius' murder." He pushed open the heavy wooden door. The guardsmen followed closely behind, but did not try to stop him.

For a moment Irion could make out nothing in the darkness. He seized a torch from the wall sconce outside the door and held it in front of him. In the far corner huddled a small man with dark hair braided in the Iceni fashion. He wore tattered, cross-gartered braccae and a filthy leather jerkin. As Irion entered, the eyes in the hatchet-thin face slitted open, glittering like small pieces of glass.

"Stand up, back shooter," Irion commanded.

The assassin said nothing, but glared at him over a small, sharp nose that gave the impression of some stealthy rodent.

"What are you called?"

Still no answer. The man shifted his position and Irion noticed for the first time an angry scar on his neck. He had seen such a mark once before, on Brath, Honorius's servant, a youth who had been a slave in one of Ceawlin's steadings and who had been rescued by the British. It was the mark of a Saxon thrall ring.

Irion spoke again, this time in the Friesian dialect he had learned from Brath. "What's your name?"

Understanding flashed in the killer's eyes, but still he stared sullenly, saying nothing.

Frustration boiled into a black rage. Irion thrust the torch into the hands of the guard behind him and seized the prisoner's jerkin, hauling him to his feet. Irion's dagger winked in the torchlight as he held it against the tip of the man's nose.

"This is a fine job you have, assassin. How many backs have you bitten with your arrows? How many throats have you slit in the dark?"

The man winced as the tip of the dagger pricked his nose, raising a drop of blood.

"Your name?" Irion repeated.

"Angarad."

"Who hired you?"

Silence. The dagger winked again and a small piece of flesh flew from the man's nose.

Angarad shrieked. "Don't hurt me." He spoke in Friesian. "Ceawlin Cerdic-son ordered me to do it. I was his thrall. Promised me freedom, he did, if I would kill the old British lord. Promised to kill me if I didn't."

Irion gripped the killer for a long moment, a breath away

from plunging the dagger into his heart. Then the glare of rage faded and he pushed him away. The assassin crumpled to the ground, cupping his hands around his bleeding nose.

Irion turned away and stumbled to the doorway, gasping for breath as he emerged into the night air. At that moment he hated Ceawlin more than he had ever hated anyone. He vowed to make the Saxon chieftain pay for his uncle's death.

Then, as the extent of his folly dawned, he stopped in his tracks. He cursed himself. The raid had been a trick after all, a diversion to distract attention from the assassination. And he had fallen into the trap. He should have known. Saxons had tried before to kill British leaders in advance of an all-out attack, to disorganize their enemies. A cold sweat broke out on his forehead. A Saxon invasion was near.

PART TWO

Bedwyr

SIX

Bedwyr pulled the woolen pillow off his head and with a groan lifted himself onto his elbow. At his movement the huge wolfhound sleeping in the corner opened his eyes and raised his ears, but did not otherwise move.

The narrow window at which Bedwyr squinted showed him gray dawn in the city of Rome. From habit he began to drag his body from the cot. Then he remembered he had no duty today, nor would he have tomorrow. He collapsed back into bed; his hand found the pillow and threw it over his head, and he drifted back to sleep. The dog closed his eyes again and snuffed a sigh.

The nightmare came: always the same, a formless blending of light and shadow, with darker figures moving in the shade, indistinct but awakening dread deep within him. Light coalesced into the shape of a giant bear and Bedwyr stood behind it watching the shadow draw nearer, unable to move, either to fight or to run. The bear limped forward to meet the onrushing shade. As the darkness engulfed it the animal blurred and faded until only its red eyes, haunted with despair, still shone. The bear cried out to him, its eyes pleading. Bedwyr shook his head in refusal. Then the shadow reached him, too, and he awoke, terrified as always, and sweating.

He must have called out in his sleep, for the wolfhound lifted his head from his paws and cocked it, puzzled. Forcing his eyes open Bedwyr lay still until his breathing slowed and the terror died. He sighed, gingerly flexing his left arm, then sat up and swung his feet onto the floor.

Last night's wine tasted sour in his mouth. Drinking it never stopped the nightmares but it dulled the fear of sleep. He rubbed his face. During the eleven years since Camlann a longing had been growing in him, a need to have peace that had become a great thirst.

The wolfhound rose and padded over, resting his head on Bedwyr's leg, a leg crisscrossed with scars, many of them white with age, some still puckered angry red. Scratching the dog's ears with long fingers, he murmured, "A couple of fang-gashed old hounds, Fergus, you and I. What's needed is to find a little farm somewhere and curl up dry and warm." The dog woofed happily. "But first we have an errand."

He stood and dressed, grimacing as his joints made their morning protest. With his right hand he fitted a leather cover over the stump of his left wrist. Peering into his polished steel shaving mirror, he rubbed his hand over a face tanned and windburned the color of bronze. Eyes that turned downward at the corners merged into deep creases engraved by years of sun glare, giving him a melancholy cast of autumn. Only the lines around his mouth betrayed the quick laughter that had won for him the hearts of Arthur and the Companions in the years of light. He shrugged. He'd shave tomorrow.

Bedwyr walked stiffly out of his sleeping cell in the officers' block into a hot, blue morning. Ignoring the praetorian kitchens where cooks boiled wheatmeal porridge, he headed for the baths to soak his body into mobility. Fergus trotted beside him.

In the undressing room he stripped off his clothing, then made his way through the steamy chambers. The splashing and shouting of Roman soldiers bounced from the stone walls and the high, vaulted ceiling. Bypassing the cold plunge he eased his body directly into the caldarium and smiled as the hot water soothed his aching muscles. On the edge the hound sat down to wait, tongue lolling in the humidity.

From an adjoining pool a centurion of another company called: "And it's just like a Brit not to know how to wash right." Bedwyr smiled again and, with a wave, sank beneath the surface.

When he came up for air the baths had become silent, save for the splash of running water. He opened his eyes. On the edge of the pool a hairy-shouldered decurion stood rigid, facing him. Near him two young recruits stood motionless, their eyes fixed in the same direction. Throughout the building, men stood to attention, some waist deep in water, others on the tiled floor, all of them naked as shorn sheep. Bedwyr threw back his head and laughed, struck by the sight of a hundred naked men standing at attention and trying to look dignified doing it.

As his laughter subsided he heard a throat clear behind him and turned. On the edge of the pool, in full uniform and polished breastplate, stood the commander of the entire Roman army: Belisarius, General of the East, Conqueror of Carthage and Rome. He was not smiling.

It was Bedwyr's turn to splash to attention.

The general motioned for them all to be at ease. "When you have a moment, centurion," he said to Bedwyr, "I would like a word." He turned and strode away.

Bedwyr quickly dressed. A guard met him at the top of the marble steps of the Pincian Palace and escorted him past the statues and columns lining the atrium, the dog's toenails clicking on the tessellated floor. They came to the huge, bronze-covered doors of Belisarius's private study, where Bedwyr ordered Fergus to stay. The giant wolfhound settled onto his haunches to inspect the guard.

Belisarius was bent over a large desk covered with maps. As Bedwyr entered he glanced up, a small man with a tightly trimmed beard, face grave and brooding. He spoke without preamble. "My sources tell me the entire Ostrogoth nation, in addition to the Burgundians, are massing here and here"—he stabbed a map with a blunt finger—"to drive us from Roman soil. Meanwhile the Emperor commands me to march north to reclaim Italia all the way to the Alps, though we are outnumbered ten to one."

He indicated a chair on the other side of the desk, poured red wine into a silver goblet, and handed it to Bedwyr. "Your resignation notice came through yesterday, Beduerus. How long have you been contracted to me?"

"Two years today, sir." He sat and took a sip of the watered wine.

The general nodded. "During that time we won the city of Rome back for the Empire and broke the siege the barbarians laid against us. Such as we have been able to do, Beduerus, we have done on the backs of our cavalry federates. The day is past when the infantry legion ruled the battlefield."

Bedwyr waited, silent. He knew the world's most powerful general did not call him into his study to seek his opinion on matters of strategy.

The Roman commander eyed him thoughtfully. "You fight recklessly, centurion. Almost as if your life means little to you."

Bedwyr set the goblet down on the desk. He felt the familiar surge of bitterness. What good was his survival when everything he had valued had been destroyed, erased as if it were no more than the tracks of small birds in the mud? But he smiled. "I've survived Saxon axes, Iberian women, and legion food, sir. I'm durable."

"Mm. Well, whatever the reasons for fighting as you do, I'm grateful. Your charge shattered the Goth shield wall and led to the breaking of the siege. I'm offering you the rank of wing tribune if you will contract for another two years."

Bedwyr blinked. "You honor me, General."

Belisarius's eyes became calculating. "As wing tribune you would receive an allotment of land when you retired."

The Old Man reads me well, Bedwyr thought. More than the rank, the lure of a few hectares of land where he could raise horses and dogs and let the world go to Uffern attracted him. He sighed. Well, maybe the small amount he had saved out of his pay would buy him that land somewhere. "You do tempt me, sir. But there's a thing I must finish that will take a journey to Britain. It's something that needs doing if ever I'm to sleep again at night."

The general studied him a moment longer, then nodded. "Well, it's no business of mine. I had to try."

Bedwyr rose to leave.

"Oh, centurion. One more thing."

He turned back warily.

"You fought with your great general, Artorius. Know you by chance one Honorius Flavian, who styles himself magistrate of Gwent?"

Ynyr of Gwent. Memories flooded through the barriers Bedwyr had so painstakingly built. "I knew such a man once, sir."

Belisarius pawed through the maps and documents on his desk, then handed Bedwyr a scrolled parchment on which the seal had been broken. "I received this communication from him some weeks since. Read it."

Bedwyr looked at the proffered parchment, filled with a sudden sense of foreboding. The general thrust it into his hands and he unrolled it.

From the loyal citizens of Britannia to Belisarius, Conqueror of Carthage and Rome and Emissary of His Majesty Justinian, Emperor in Constantinople, greetings:

Most gracious and wise General, your loyal subjects suffer from the spears and swords of the barbarians. Throughout your provinces good and loyal subjects perish and lie as fodder for dogs, or are destroyed by the flames that burn their homes. In villages and country houses, in the fields and countryside, on every road, death and slaughter threaten us. This island is smoking in one great funeral pyre. Without help we cannot long endure.

If you wish that your subjects should live, send us aid. If you desire that we should throw back the barbarians, send us arms and horses and men.

Bedwyr dropped the letter on the desk. His voice carefully neutral, he said, "Why do you show this to me?"

Belisarius's eyebrows lifted. "I thought perhaps you would be interested, since you played some sizable role in protecting the British from the Saxons."

"The problems of the British are of their own making." The words came out more harshly than Bedwyr had intended. "I have done with them."

The general gave him a long, steady look. "As you wish. But since you're returning there, I ask you as a personal favor to convey a message to Honorius."

Bedwyr hesitated, then nodded reluctantly.

"The message is simply this: Britannia, I regret, must look to itself for defense against the barbarians. We can send no aid." Belisarius picked up his goblet and carried it over to a tall window flanked by statued alcoves. Gazing out over the city, he said, "I will confess something to you. I have a dream of someday restoring the historic boundaries of the empire. Yet I know in my heart it will never be. Those years are forever gone. Your island has passed beyond the power of the empire to aid, regardless of our desires."

He strode businesslike back to the table. "And I do not decide our policies. Explain to Honorius that the Emperor looks eastward. To him, Britannia is only a shadow on the horizon. He will spare no thought, nor direct any effort, toward your island."

The general paused and extended his hand. "So. That is the way of it. Godspeed, then, Beduerus, and my thanks. You will always have a place in my personal guard should you choose to return."

Almost, Bedwyr changed his mind. Perhaps he could again bury the past and finish out his life here, fighting for money. But in his heart he knew he could no longer bear the pressure of Arthur's disobeyed order. Caliburn must be destroyed or he would have no peace. And he was sick of barbarians; sick of Goths and Vandals and Saxons; sick of what he had become fighting them. He clasped the general's outstretched hand.

The next day Bedwyr collected his last payment from the legion paymaster and rode north from the walls of Rome, toward Britain.

SEVEN

A day out of Rome, Bedwyr met a group of other mercenaries whose contracts had expired, and who traveled to Gaul to place themselves in spear service to the feuding grandsons of the Frankish King Clovis. They traveled up the west coast of Italia along the Aurelian Road, which their efforts had for the moment made secure. Westward they curved around the middle sea to the port city of Massilia, then north to Lugdunum and finally to Lutetia, which Clovis had made into his capital and renamed Paris.

As they rode through the green countryside they passed ruins of great villas formerly owned by Gallo-Roman nobles. It was a rich land, and Bedwyr found himself thinking that it would be a fine place to settle and raise horses. But a smudge of dark smoke on the horizon reminded him of the nearness of the barbarians, and he rode on.

In Paris, Bedwyr bid farewell to his traveling companions and set off along the Seine toward the coast. He reached it late on an afternoon that saw the sky turning sloe purple under great, flat-topped storm clouds. Before he could find shelter the clouds dumped their rain and scurried away, leaving behind ankle-deep mud. As he rode, the great wolfhound slogged behind him, belly matted black, growling occasionally at the mud.

A cluster of ramshackle buildings at the river mouth served as a port. Bedwyr located a dilapidated inn and went inside to learn whether any ships sailed for Britain. The sun's rays filtered through a small common room, made smoky by a turf fire. From a lean-to kitchen came the reek of fish stew.

He spoke to the innkeeper, who had just enough Latin to understand his questions. He was in luck. Yes, a ship now loading sailed for Britain. The captain's name? Caedmon, called the Crosser. No, he did not know whether he would take passengers.

Bedwyr paid for a night's lodging and saw his horse rubbed down and fed. If he found passage he would have to sell the animal for considerably less than its value, he was certain. The residents of the port enjoyed a buyer's market.

He walked to the quay. Two wooden piers jutted into the water, and at the side of each rolled a small cargo ship. One of them, squat with a short mast, looked badly built. The other promised better, with a raised cargo deck fore and aft. To Bedwyr it appeared slow but seaworthy, and he hoped this was Caedmon's ship.

Crewmen swarmed over it, mending rigging and scouring the decks, while others bustled up the pier carrying crates of pottery, amphorae of wine, and tightly bound bundles of soft-looking dyed leather. From his station near the gangplank a bald man with a ruddy, weathered face and a brown beard feathered with gray shouted instructions.

Bedwyr walked out to him, dodging crewmen. Behind him stalked Fergus, looking with deep suspicion at the water on both sides of the pier.

Bedwyr spoke to the man in Latin. "I seek the ship of Caedmon."

The man looked at him blankly and shrugged. Bedwyr tried again in Celtic. The man nodded. "I'm Caedmon."

"Are you bound for Britain?"

Caedmon's eyes narrowed. "Who's wanting to know?"

"My name is Bedwyr ap Gruffydd. I need passage. I can pay."

Behind them a cask thudded onto the pier and the captain looked up. "Two men to a cask!" he shouted. "Is it I have to tell you everything?" He turned back to Bedwyr. "I take no one on board, crewman or passenger, who cannot handle a sword. This is sea wolf water."

"I know how to use a sword, if necessary," said Bedwyr.

The captain looked him up and down. "Aye. I believe it.

Well, then perhaps I'm bound for Britain. Where on that suffering island do you go, and what's your business?"

"My business is none of yours. But I go to Gwent as a start."

The captain grunted, his eyes flickering with amusement. "Fortunate. Gwent's the only place I make port in these times. I meant no discourtesy, but it's not uncommon for pirates to plant one of their number on board a merchant ship to take the crew from behind, while his murdering cohorts board her."

He scratched at his beard, then nodded once. "Och! I'll carry you. You've not the look of a pirate. Though," he glanced at Bedwyr's missing hand, "it seems you've looked at no few battles from the inside."

After brief but intense haggling they agreed upon a fare, but it cost Bedwyr an extra silver coin for the dog's passage.

Caedmon said, "We sail at dawn. Without you, if you're not here."

As Bedwyr turned to leave, a glint of sunlight caught his eye. From the open sea a low-bellied ship plowed into the bay. Its square black-and-saffron-striped sail lay furled, and at the ship's sides sixteen pairs of oars dipped and flashed rhythmically. As it drew closer Bedwyr could see the swing of the rowers' arms. A man stood at the stern holding the steering oar; another leaned over the prow, from time to time casting a weighted sounding line overboard to read the depth of the water. After each reading he shouted in a guttural tongue.

As they neared the quay the helmsman put the steering oar hard over and the ship swung slowly around in a half circle to the far bank. The crew shipped oars that glistened with water, and men jumped over the side, splashing ashore with mooring lines.

Caedmon's face turned grim. "Sea wolf. A Saxon pirate."

"In a Gaulish port?" Bedwyr said. "Do they think to attack you here?"

"No. They make port from time to time, here and in other places. They're like all ships, needing water and food, and to make repairs. Peaceful enough, so long as they're here. If they looted every port they made they'd soon run short of places to refit." Caedmon spat into the water. "But mark you, they'll note our presence. Once we leave the quay we're fair catch."

"Will you stay in port, then, until they sail?"

"No, for they can outwait us. We sail tomorrow still." The captain looked at Bedwyr from under bushy eyebrows. "Have you repented your wish to sail with me?"

Bedwyr shrugged. "I'm not so good a swimmer as to try the narrow sea."

Caedmon laughed. "Aye, you'll do. I have a trick or two that may throw the sharks off our tail." He squinted at the sky. "There'll be fog tomorrow, I'm thinking. Be here an hour ahead of dawn."

Bedwyr made his way down to the ship in near-total darkness. He had slept fitfully with evil dreams, and a nameless feeling persisted, a sense that he was alone in a universe of oppressive gods. With a whining yawn, Fergus stopped at the bottom of the gangplank and refused to board until Bedwyr stroked his head and crooned into a drooping ear.

As they stepped on deck, they were challenged quietly by the watch. "Who comes?"

"Bedwyr ap Gruffydd."

"They're here, cap'n. Punctual as an unpaid money-lender."

Caedmon murmured some orders, and the crew hauled in the plank and cast off mooring ropes. Once away from the pier, twelve pairs of oars slid out from uncovered oar ports and dipped quietly into the water. They moved like a ghost ship through the bay, with no sound but the hiss of water against the hull, and the faint splash of the oars.

After a time dawn drifted out from the shore, revealing a glassy sea. Astern, Bedwyr saw nothing but a wake of bubbles. With the dawn came fog, white mist that draped over the ship and thickened, until Bedwyr felt as if he were packed in damp sheepswool.

The ship, heavily laden and designed more for sailing than rowing, moved slowly. Caedmon stood at the steering oar, turning it slightly from time to time, and Bedwyr wondered how he could navigate in the fog. He questioned the watch, who leaned over the bow, peering ahead.

The man flashed a gap-toothed grin. "That's why he's

named the Crosser. Caedmon can find his way across the narrow sea when no one else dares."

They rowed and listened by turns. A long stroke, and the crew lay back on the oars for a count of seven, then another stroke. Between strokes they listened for the sound of other oars in the fog, or men talking, but the only sound they heard was the slap and gurgle of water under the hull.

The fog still showed no sign of lifting when Bedwyr heard Caedmon call softly, "Make sail."

The crew shipped oars and several scrambled to run up the square sail. Moments later Bedwyr felt a puff of breeze on his face, and soon the sail snapped and billowed as it filled with a southeast wind. The breeze shredded the fog, sending rags of mist drifting past his face like cool cobwebs. Ahead he saw open water. They were out of the bay.

As they rounded the point running toward open sea, the roll of the ship became deeper, the wind grew stronger, and they ran free before it. Southward, Bedwyr heard the boom of the surf and saw tiny waves break white on the dark line of the shore.

He climbed onto the raised stern, where Caedmon gripped the steering oar, his face serene. "Have we lost them, think you?"

"Aye. They'll not follow us out here. Saxons are coast crawlers, hugging the shorelines. They fear the open water." He peered at Bedwyr, his eyes crinkling in amusement. "You've not sailed before, I'm thinking."

"Once, only." Bedwyr smiled. "I crossed the narrow sea the other way some years since. A storm hit us and I was sick the whole voyage."

Caedmon chuckled. "That's the way of it with most land lovers, at first. But if they sail enough, they come to know the pleasures of a sea voyage."

"If they don't drown first."

Caedmon patted the steering oar with a horny hand. "No. Treat her right and *Brigit* will do right by you."

As if she heard them, the sturdy ship grew playful, flinging spindrift over her bow into the faces of the crew.

The wind continued favorable and they made good speed. Late the next afternoon Bedwyr saw in the distance the cliffs of Dumnonia. On the morning of the third day they rounded Land's End, making toward the Sabrina estuary. The voyage passed so pleasantly that even Fergus, who had spent the first day lying grumpily against the mast, began to walk cautiously around the deck with Bedwyr, nose snuffling the salt spray.

They had just climbed the ladder to the stern deck when a shout came from the watch: "Ship to starboard! Running hard!"

Bedwyr swung around to see a longship coming from the southeast, high prow carved into a dragon's head. Its bows split the sea, flaring translucent green waves along its sides. A long row of multicolored shields lined the gunwales, and above them heaved a square sail, emblazoned with a black sea serpent. It raced down on them, swollen sail straining in the wind.

"By the Wind and the Sea!" Caedmon's face turned gray.

"Can we outrun them?" Bedwyr said.

The captain shook his head. "Not possible. That's a Northman longship. She'll do ten knots."

The longship closed on them, sun and sea sparkle flashing off swords and spears. A man stood at the stern oar and three men in the prow, heads turned their way.

"Prepare to be boarded!" Caedmon shouted.

The crew pulled weapons from beneath the rowing benches. Caedmon swung the steering oar hard over, and the *Brigit* shuddered, heeling sharply. Behind them the Norse ship matched the maneuver and drew closer.

Bedwyr could see the Northmen lining the gunwales, huge, grim warriors in horned helmets, who watched the *Brigit* with hungry eyes. They carried weapons of every kind and size; their chieftain, a red-bearded giant, fingered a throwing ax.

Standing on the stern deck, Bedwyr strapped his shield to his handless arm, buckling the leather thongs tightly. As the longship closed to within a spear's throw, its crew struck the sail and it glided alongside. Long-handled boat hooks reached out and grappled the *Brigit* to the Norse ship.

The pirates leaped over the side, and the *Brigit*'s deck, already crowded with armed crewmen, disappeared in a chaos of bodies and clashing weapons. A Northman slashed at the rigging and the sail collapsed onto the deck, burying three crewmen.

The Northmen outnumbered the *Brigit*'s crew by half, but

sailors as well-armed as these surprised them, for they took as their usual prey unarmed and defenseless ships, or coastal villages. Still, they drove Caedmon's crew back and laughed fiercely at the sport offered.

Caedmon plunged into the thick of the fighting, leaving Bedwyr on the stern deck, alone, save for the great wolfhound at his side. Silently Bedwyr waited, watching the fighting below. Fergus growled, hackles raised, listening for an order from his master.

Then a Northman brandishing a war hammer scrambled up the ladder.

"*Sic!*" Bedwyr said.

Fergus launched himself at the raider's throat, and they crashed to the deck below.

Out of the melee a throwing ax spun toward him and Bedwyr dodged. The ax flew past his ear like an angry goshawk and buried itself in the rail behind him.

The horn-helmeted chieftain bounded onto the deck, following his ax. He grinned, spat, and drew his sword, then came in hard, thrusting his shield into Bedwyr's face, trying to knock him off balance. Bedwyr ducked under the shield and parried the expected jab to his belly.

The chieftain was strong and fought with brutal skill. For Bedwyr, time slowed. His enemy's movements seemed languid, dreamlike. He heard no sound but the hiss and clang of sword on shield, and he studied the huge Northman's reactions as he swung and thrust, circled and parried. Then Bedwyr saw his weakness. The man threw his weight too far forward onto his toes when he lunged, and recovered slowly.

Bedwyr drew back and lowered his sword a little, enticing the thrust. The chieftain lunged and Bedwyr swung his sword up and down on the man's neck. The Northman fell like a stone.

Below, the raiders saw their leader fall and hesitated. Bedwyr waded into the fighting, his sword cutting a murderous arc ahead of him. Man and weapon became one entity, a ravening messenger of death. Five more of the raiders fell.

Astonished, the survivors broke off their attack and leaped for their ship. Dying in battle promised passage to Valhalla, but living guaranteed they would plunder again another time. They hacked the grappling hooks in two and the boats drifted apart. Throwing their weapons aside, the Northmen scrambled to hoist the sail, and the great dragon prow turned and knifed away into the sea.

On the *Brigit* the only sounds were the wind whistling softly through the rigging and the groan of a wounded crewman.

Fergus padded over to Bedwyr and sank down on the deck. Blood dripped from a wound on the dog's shoulder, and he licked it. Bedwyr kneeled to inspect the wolfhound, running his hands over the rough coat. There was only one wound, the gash in the shoulder, and it did not look deep.

Finished with his inspection, Bedwyr looked up to see the crew staring at him in awe. Caedmon limped over to him, holding his right thigh where a sword had nicked it.

"Who are you?"

Surprised, Bedwyr answered: "My name hasn't changed since I gave it to you at the pier. Bedwyr ap Gruffydd."

Understanding, then fear, spread across the captain's face. "By the Eight Winds of Heaven! You're Bedwyr Mawr. The Great One!" He spread three fingers of his right hand behind him in the sign against enchantment. "But you were killed at Camlann."

Alarmed, the crew backed away. "He's a demon or a wraith!" said one.

"Demons can't cross water," the captain said. But he looked uncertain as to whether Bedwyr was indeed a ghost.

"And dogs cannot abide wraiths," said Bedwyr. He fondled Fergus's ears and the hound thumped his tail on the deck. "I'm as alive as you are, Caedmon."

Caedmon hesitated, then grinned in relief and nodded. He turned to the crew. "This is Lord Bedwyr of the Companions."

A cheer rose from the crewmen, and Bedwyr felt his face redden. "No. No lord of yours, Caedmon. Nor of any man. Only a tired cavalryman who needs to clean his sword."

Caedmon watched him silently for a moment, puzzled, as Bedwyr wiped the blood from his sword with a rag. Then the captain limped away to appraise the damage.

Three crewmen had died in the battle, and eight of the raiders. The survivors stripped the bodies of the Northmen of valuables and heaved the men over the side. Caedmon ordered their jewelry be given to the wives or kin of the dead sailors, whose bodies they wrapped in sailcloth and weighted in preparation for submergence.

The crew looked expectantly at Bedwyr, as their battle leader, to say some words of comfort over the bodies. He turned away and looked out at the empty sea. Knowing no comfort for long years, he had none in him now to give others.

Caedmon sensed his distress and spoke in his stead. "The spirit's voyage through life is but a short journey to the harbor of Gwynved, where it will feast and dream through time beyond counting." He praised the skills of each of the crewmen, and invoked for Dai, who had followed the Christian religion, the name of Simon Peter, the fisherman.

As he spoke, waves lapped idly at the ship's sides, and she rose and fell with the swells. The pilot worked the steering oar to keep her bow into the wind.

Bedwyr looked at the bodies and saw only death. He too had once believed that his spirit would feast and dream after death. Arthur had believed in the Christian heaven. But his Christ had deserted him, as the old gods had abandoned Bedwyr and Britain.

The funeral over, the crew set about making repairs to the *Brigit*. Rigging mended, decks scrubbed clean of blood, she soon moved again, sailing up the Sabrina estuary. Gulls wheeled above the mast as they sailed up the Usk on the tide.

Ahead, Bedwyr saw the massive walls of Caerleon. He was back in Britain, but he knew he was not home.

Part Three

<u>Caerleon</u>

EIGHT

As he sat with his gashed leg propped up on a stool, Irion studied a parchment scroll, frowning. Another refusal of alliance, this one from Gereint of Demetia. The day after his uncle's death Irion had sent a courier galloping to Maridunum with an urgent request for help, calling upon Gereint to remember his earlier promise to Honorius for aid in the coming campaign against Ceawlin.

He'd sent messages to the other British kingdoms as well, but every message that he sent, every plea that he made, had been unsuccessful. Where his uncle by patient statecraft had succeeded in extracting tentative promises of help from several kingdoms, Irion received encouragement from none, and brusque refusals from most. It was as if the shadow of Medraut clung to his name, a shadow the clans shrank from in disgust.

He sighed, missing Honorius's wisdom and guidance. Still, he had to do what he could to prepare Gwent for the coming Saxon invasion, even if he had to act alone. Preparation would be much easier if only he could have advance warning of Ceawlin's plans. He . . .

Irion stood abruptly and the chair toppled over with a crash. That was it! Warning! If he could place a spy inside Camelot they would at least be forewarned. And if he had proof of imminent attack, perhaps the British would see reason.

A sharp rap sounded on the door. It burst inward and Gwythur came into the room, his flinty eyes lit with pleasure. "Bedwyr is in Caerwent."

Irion forced his thoughts away from his problems. He looked blankly at the captain for a moment, then grasped his meaning. "Bedwyr? You mean Bedwyr Mawr, the Companion?"

"The same. Staying at the Eagle, I'm told."

"But I thought he was killed in Gaul some three years since."

"Nah." Gwythur chuckled. "He's been reported killed in most lands of the known world. But he's come back to Gwent."

"Are they certain it's Bedwyr?"

"Aye. There are many who know him in these parts."

Bedwyr! Irion remembered his first glimpse of the famed warrior riding in a victory parade at the head of the Companions, directly behind Arthur. Medraut had also ridden in that parade, but Bedwyr shone brighter than any of the others, save the High King himself. He'd seemed as tall as a beech tree.

Irion smiled at Gwythur. "You've spoken often of him."

"That I have. He was the finest warrior of the Companions, and a good man, besides. I fought with him at Bassus, in Caledonia."

"I remember."

"Aye." Gwythur beamed. "That was a battle! It came soon after the allied kings chose Arthur to lead their armies against the Saxons. Their choice threw Heuil, son of Caw of Orkney, into a huff and he made common cause with the Picts north of Hadrian's Wall. We met them in the lowlands near the River Bassus."

Gwythur picked up the heavy chair with a scrape and sat, lost in reminiscence. "Honorius sent me with a troop of cavalry to aid Arthur. We ended up attached to Bedwyr's new command. That fight raged for most of the day. Finally, we split off Heuil's war band from his Pictish allies on the other side of the river. Arthur took Heuil, and the Picts fell to us. They locked themselves into a shield ring, but Bedwyr never charged it. He led us leftwise around the ring, like wolves circling a flock. Never since have I seen such a swordsman."

Gwythur laughed. "He peeled the shield ring like an onion. And what I remember most clearly, By the Three! is that he sang! Some mountain song as wild and triumphant as a paean. If only we had him leading the British now . . ."

They stared at each other, both thinking the same thought.

"Is it possible?" asked Irion.

"I know nothing of what he does in Caerwent," Gwythur

said, "but it's in my mind he may be willing to do such a thing."

Irion jumped to his feet and paced, grinding his fist into his palm. "By the Mother of all living! This could be the key, Gwythur. All the kingdoms and clans respect him. If he led an alliance against Ceawlin, even Maelgwyn would not dare hold back."

Gwythur nodded. "I'd wager a trained falcon against a turnip on it. Shall we see if Arthur's Right Arm remembers an old ally?"

Bedwyr answered their knock and let them into his small sleeping room. A bench stood against one wall, a bed covered with a gray woolen blanket opposite it. Between them, a window open to the courtyard framed a square of bright green in the limewashed white of the room. On a three-legged table below the window an earthenware washbowl steamed with hot water.

As Irion and Gwythur stepped in, a huge wolfhound rose and padded over to inspect them, sniffing each of them in turn, then went back to his corner and sat on his haunches. Bedwyr looked smaller, older than Irion remembered, and he had lost his left hand. But he still wore the same dignity and strength.

"Rumors grow wings in Caerwent," Bedwyr said, eyeing the two visitors warily. "I've only just arrived, and I'm about to wash the travel dust from my face before attending to business."

"Forgive us our impatience," said Gwythur. "I heard the Hero of Bassus had come back to Gwent, and I was overanxious to see an old friend."

Bedwyr peered at Gwythur for a moment, then a smile spread across his face. "Gwythur! As the gods see me in cowhides! How fare you?" He stuck out his hand.

"Well enough," Gwythur said with a grin, clasping the outstretched arm. "I was not certain you would remember after long and long."

"How could I forget that rockslide of a face? We melted the Pict shield ring like wax, you and I." Bedwyr eyed the little captain's uniform. "Still leading charges, eh?"

[61]

"Aye, still. But under a younger tribune. I've brought him for you to meet. This is Honorius's nephew, Irion."

Bedwyr turned to Irion, still smiling. His drooping eyes opened slightly, revealing shock, quickly suppressed.

Gwythur saw the recognition and laughed. "So! You see it, too. He has the look of his grandsire about him, has he not? And many of his qualities, as well, though he's green as grass."

Bedwyr gave Irion a puzzled look, full of appraisal.

Irion bowed slightly. "I'm honored, Lord Bedwyr. All my life I have heard people speak of you. Even my father held you in respect."

"Your father?"

Irion felt himself redden. "My full name is Irion ap Medraut."

A shadow fell across Bedwyr's face, and all warmth drained from it. He did not extend his hand. Irion felt a cold wall of ice rise between them.

Bedwyr turned back to Gwythur. "For your sake, old friend, I extend whatever hospitality this bare room provides. Sit you down and tell me what mischief you've gotten into these eleven years. Forgive me if I make use of this hot water as you talk, before it grows cold. Luxuries are not to be scorned in these times."

Ignoring Irion, he stripped off his tunic. Gwythur looked at the youth nervously and sat down on the bench. After a moment's hesitation, Irion did the same.

While Gwythur warmed to his account of life since he had last seen Bedwyr, the wolfhound rose and ambled over. He paused before the captain, presenting his enormous head to be petted, then went to Irion and looked up at him with a vast, friendly grin. As Irion fondled his ears the dog stuck his gray muzzle in his lap and blew out a sigh of contentment.

Bedwyr plunged his scarred arms up to the elbows into the steaming water, and bent over the bowl, washing his face and neck. He made an occasional comment as Gwythur told him of the reawakening Saxon lands, of Ceawlin and his terror inflicted from Camelot, and of their efforts to form an alliance against the Saxons.

"But you," Gwythur said, as he wound down. "Tell us where you've been these past years, and what you do now in

Britain. We've heard many accounts of you from one land or the other, even tales of your death. Not true, seemingly."

"Seemingly." Toweling dry his neck, Bedwyr smiled. "My adventures pale compared with yours, friend, so I won't bore you with them. But I've been most recently in Rome fighting for Belisarius. I'm here now, in part, to deliver a message from him to your Honorius. How fares the old magistrate?"

Irion and Gwythur exchanged glances.

"You would not have heard," Irion said. "My uncle is dead. An assassin hired by Ceawlin, the Saxon, killed him."

Bedwyr sank onto the bed. "Dead by Medraut's ally?" He stared at Irion for a long moment, then looked back to Gwythur. "For that I am sorry. Honorius was a staunch ally, and a friend. Who is his successor?"

"Brennus Turpilius Flavian."

"Then I'm charged to deliver my message to him. As you are tribune," he added reluctantly, glancing at Irion, "it concerns you as well." He repeated Belisarius's words of regret, and denial of help from Rome.

Irion shook his head. "If Rome would send even one legion, we could hold off the Saxons forever."

"Rome cannot spare even one legion," said Bedwyr shortly. "She herself is unable to hold back the barbarians."

Gwythur edged forward on the bench. "There may be a way for us to resist the Saxons, even without help from Rome."

Bedwyr turned to him, surprised. "What mean you?"

"You well know the independence of the British clans," Gwythur said. "Honorius tried long to build an alliance against Ceawlin, without success. Now that Irion is tribune, he . . ."

Irion interrupted softly. "I'm beside you, Gwythur. You need not speak for me as if I were in outermost Thule." He stopped petting the hound's ears and the dog gave him a firm but friendly nudge with his nose.

As if noticing the dog for the first time, Bedwyr spoke to him. "Fergus. To me." The hound ignored him and returned his head to Irion's leg.

"We need your help, Lord Bedwyr," Irion said simply. "Without it, we will fall, and the barbarian wind will blow through our towns and farms. With you, we can yet drive them back. Our failing is our inability to unite. Perhaps we cannot see beyond the selfish interests of our own small kingdoms. For whatever reason, we've had no leader since Arthur who can forge us into one nation."

He hesitated, searching for the right words. "Many of the clans would join us, I think, were Maelgwyn of Gwynedd, the most powerful, to join. But he waits in his mountains, toying with us, hoping that we will be eaten one by one by Ceawlin's wolves. Then he thinks to come down and destroy the Saxons and claim the High Kingship. But he is wrong. Even he is not strong enough, alone, to defeat Ceawlin and his Saxon allies."

While Irion talked, Bedwyr looked out the window, his face remote.

"With you leading the alliance, Maelgwyn would not dare hold back, as he did when Arthur was chosen warlord, for he saw Arthur made High King after his victories. If you lead, he will join us. Lord Bedwyr, we are in our autumn. Unless a leader comes forward to unite us, there will be no spring. We need your help."

Outside the open window, sparrows quarreled noisily. Finally Bedwyr stirred. "When I was young, I believed—we all believed, we Companions—that we could unite Britain under a High King. It seemed so obvious to us that the land would be stronger, her people better protected, under one ruler. We were right. Arthur made this a land of peace. But the British do not want unity. They prefer to bicker and play out their intrigues. So we found at Camlann."

He looked at Irion. "For me, Britain ended that day, eleven years since. Now their troubles—your troubles—are no longer mine. I've had a sackful. I have no interest in joining your fight."

He rose. "Cousins, I give you good morning. I have much to do. Gwythur, old friend, seeing you lightens my heart. I'm sorry your errand is in vain."

Gwythur stood, looking at his old friend in dismay. "What's happened to you, Bedwyr? You listen to the troubles of your countrymen, and tell me that you have no interest in us? Is there no fight left in you?"

"What has fighting gained us? The barbarians have won." Bedwyr's voice was bitter.

Gwythur looked confused, then clamped his mouth shut.

Irion fumbled for words to say that would change Bedwyr's mind. The darkness of his father's shadow clearly chilled Bedwyr's heart, and with it, the only hope for Gwent. He felt ashamed.

Rising, he said, "I would not have you turn away from us because it's the son of Medraut who seeks your aid. If you cannot forgive me for being who I am, I'll leave and play no part in this fight."

Bedwyr looked at him coldly. "One does not easily forgive the murder of one's king. Do what you will. I'll not help you."

Irion was stunned. "But I am not my father."

"Are you not?" Bedwyr opened the door.

Feeling that the stain on his soul must be obvious to everyone, Irion followed Gwythur from the room.

NINE

Whistling, Hywel carried his bowl of barley cake and milk carefully to the table where Irion and Gwythur ate their morning meal. Gwythur looked up, face lumpy with grouchiness. "Stop sounding like a tree full of birds!"

"What ails you?" Hywel sat next to him. "You look like a dog with a sore nose."

"Your snoring kept me awake most of the night."

"I do not snore," said Hywel, indignantly. "I breathe with conviction."

"You snore," Gwythur said. "And my ears are still ringing to prove it."

Hywel ignored him and finished his breakfast. As he tilted up his bowl to drain the last drops into his mouth, Kylan walked in, bow unstrung in his hand, his faunlike face puckered into a frown. Since his brother's death he remained irritable as a spring bear, avoiding the other warriors when possible. He gazed about the crowded mess hall and, seeing Irion, came over.

"Lord Irion, I would speak with you a moment."

His food untouched, Irion had been going over in his mind things he might have said that would have persuaded Bedwyr to help them. He glanced absently at Kylan. "Of course."

"Outside."

Gwythur and Hywel exchanged glances. Puzzled, Irion followed the young archer. They stepped into a soft morning, with a few clouds above them that hurried east on a wind too high to feel.

"I heard you seek someone for a mission," Kylan said as

they walked in the direction of the practice field. "I'll have a go at it."

"You're volunteering?"

"So I'm telling you."

"But you don't even know what the mission is, Kylan bach."

"It's no hard thing to guess, lord. You need someone who speaks Saxon, and he'll be risking his life. You want a spy in Camelot, true?"

"Aye. But I didn't know you spoke Saxon."

"I grew up within five miles of a Jute steading. We learned Jutish out of self-defense. I can make myself understood by Jutes, Angles, and Friesians alike."

Irion scratched his chin. "This is a matter of some size. The one who takes the job is like to suffer an unpleasant fate."

"We will all suffer an unpleasant fate if I do not."

He looked at the archer thoughtfully. "I'm sorry about your brother, Kylan. It was an evil thing. This would have nothing to do with avenging his death?"

"No."

They reached the field and Irion pointed to a target a hundred yards away. "How many arrows out of five can you get into the ring?"

Kylan strung his bow and loosed five arrows in rapid succession. All hit in the center of the ring. Irion took the bow and tried. Two of the five found the ring, the other three missed.

"Bowmen who have your eye are rare as mermaids," he said. "We need you here."

Kylan scowled. "Horsedung." They looked eye to eye. "You know I'm your man, lord. Never have I disobeyed an order, nor will I endanger myself without need. I'm begging you. Please give me this mission. If you do, you will not regret it."

Irion studied him. The youth was tough and battle hardened. With his red hair he could pass for a Jute; such warriors seemed common enough at Camelot. He knew Kylan would follow his orders, and he possessed the patience of a gravestone.

He handed back the bow with a sigh. "The job is yours."

Six days later a keg-loaded oxcart groaned to a stop in front of a hovel, and Kylan climbed down. Above him loomed Camelot Hill, crowned by its great timber rampart. He had persuaded the drayman to carry him from Isca to Camelot by offering to guard the cargo of ale in place of the regular guard, killed in a tavern brawl.

The driver began to unload the kegs, looking at Kylan hopefully. Ignoring him, Kylan picked up his bow and sauntered into the building. Mercenaries did not perform menial labor. Wearing a threadbare brown cloak and deerskin braccae bleached and stained by weather, at least he looked the part of an unemployed warrior.

The dark room of the tavern-brothel stank of peat smoke and sour ale. Crude tables and stools sprawled randomly around an open pit hearth, now cold, below a smoke hole in the thatched roof. At one end a row of cowhides covered the entrances to small cubicles.

This early, the place remained deserted, save for a slovenly tavernkeeper with a running nose who shambled out of a lean-to kitchen at Kylan's shout. He wore a scar across an empty eye socket, and he carried a slop bucket in one hand. His one eye stared at Kylan suspiciously.

"A beer and something to eat," Kylan said in Jutish.

"Let's see your money."

He pulled from his cloak a crude bronze brooch and held it up. With a grunt the man waddled to the open doorway and heaved out the slops, then disappeared back into the kitchen. Kylan settled at a table to wait. Sooner or later, he knew, Saxons coming off duty from the fortress would find their way down here.

After a short time the tavernkeeper came back, carrying a bowl of beer and a platter on which sat a charred hunk of some kind of meat.

"What is that?" Kylan asked.

The man grinned through green, broken teeth. "Mutton." He held out his hand for the brooch, and when he got it, became talkative. "Little early, ain't it?" he said in Friesian, nodding at the beer. "Ulfang catch ye, he'll cut your guts out, like them other two last week."

"Other two?"

"Drinking on watch."

"I'm not on watch. I'm not in spear service to Ceawlin. Yet. Is he hiring?"

Another grin. "How not?" The man jerked his head at one of the covered cubicles. "New slave girl. Have a go at her? Tight as a new scabbard."

Kylan fought back a wave of anger. "No." He tried to keep his voice casual.

The tavernkeeper shrugged and waddled away.

The beer tasted sour, and husks of barley floated in it. With his dagger Kylan carved off a piece of the meat and tried to chew it. Whatever it was, it was not mutton, and he gave up.

Four bowls of beer later a group of Saxons wandered in, jostling and laughing. They took over two tables in the center of the room, and the tavernkeeper lumbered back and forth refilling bowls and ale horns. More men streamed in, and before long the room became crowded, noisy, and hot.

Near Kylan sat three Friesians, grumbling about their duty schedule. One of them, a beefy blond with a beard that owls could nest in, pulled a pair of white dice from a pouch at his belt.

"Carved these meself," he boasted. "They's knucklebones of a Briton. Let's have a game."

His drinking mates stared at the dice, and one made the sign against enchantment. "Not me," he said. "They're magicked. Ye always win."

Kylan pulled off a bronze armband and tossed it onto their table. "That says I can beat ye."

All three looked over at him, noticing him for the first time. He slid his stool over to them. "Hunfirth of Jutland. Want to play?"

The blond smiled hugely and pushed the dice at him. "Guthwine of Friesia. Throw three to win."

Kylan picked up the dice. As he suspected, they were crudely weighted. He shook them in his cupped hands and threw them onto the table. Five. Fingers moved as the barbarians counted spots. They guffawed. Kylan groaned.

Guthwine tried to fit the armband around his arm, gave up, and put it on his wrist. "Try again?" he asked with a smirk.

Kylan nodded. This time he staked a tiny scrap of silver, part of a handle from a Roman wine flagon. Again he rolled five. Now in fine humor, Guthwine pushed the dice at him once more, but Kylan shook his head. Instead he ordered a round of drinks. "Better luck tomorrow," said the blond as he dropped the dice into the pouch.

"I need it." Kylan scratched the back of his head. "I ain't worked for weeks. Ceawlin need swords? I got a strong arm, and I fight as good as any."

The three exchanged glances, then laughed.

"Oh, he might," Guthwine said. "There's a few places in Dungarth's squad right now. Couple of his men hung up their axes." He wrapped his fingers around his thick neck and stuck out his tongue, crossing his eyes.

Kylan laughed with the others.

"Pay's good, too," said Guthwine. "Share of the loot and a go at the slave girls."

"How do I find this Dungarth?"

"Sometimes he comes in here." Guthwine looked around the room. "But I don't see him now. Tell ye what, since you're a friend of mine . . ." He winked at his drinking mates. "Ye buy drinks for the rest of the night and we'll let ye come with us to the fortress when we leave. That way ye can talk to Dungarth."

Kylan shrugged. "Sure. Why not?"

Sometime after midnight Kylan and the three Friesians left the tavern and staggered up the hill toward the southwest gate of Camelot, singing loudly. Guthwine waved his torch in time to the song. Kylan acted as drunk as the others, and sang even louder.

They reached the gates, closed and barred. Guthwine pounded on them.

"Who is it?" An irritated sentry peered out from the gate tower.

"Ye know us, Drom, ye ratbag!" Guthwine shouted. "Let us in."

"Oh, I know ye all right, Guthwine, and your two swamp lizard friends. Who else is with ye?"

Guthwine looked at Kylan in surprise, as if he had forgotten he was there. Kylan smiled stupidly.

"Oh, him." The blond turned back to the sentry. "He's all

right. Just some spear looking for work. Taking him to Dungarth."

"Tonight?" The sentry shook his head. "Dungarth won't like that. He's asleep. This one'll have to stay in your barracks till morning."

He signaled someone behind the gate and one of the huge wooden slabs creaked inward a few feet. Guthwine grunted and led the way through.

Kylan followed the others as they wove among long, low halls, looming black beyond the torchlight. The night air of the fortress hung still and fetid with the reek of herded humanity and beasts. Ahead, Guthwine stopped at a doorway, fumbled for a moment with the latch, then stepped inside.

As he entered, Kylan saw layers of straw running the length of the building along both walls. On top of the straw men sprawled, sleeping.

"Find your own spot," mumbled the blond. He yawned and ambled off down the aisle to his sleeping space.

Kylan had time to locate a place between two barbarians before the torch went out. Wrapping his cloak around him, he sank down on the straw. By morning, he thought with a sigh, he'd be lousy as a hedgehog.

TEN

"But why can't I move my sorcerer?"

Irion looked up from the tally list of usable weapons gleaned from the Saxon raid. At the other end of the table Gwythur was trying to teach Hywel the game of *fidchel.*

Gwythur picked up an alder-wood game piece and waved it under the huge infantryman's nose. "Because, you idiot, my archer's ready for him."

Through the open window Irion heard hoofbeats. He pulled himself to his feet and squinted against the setting sun to see Logrin, the captain of the council guard, climbing down from his fat bay mare.

Irion was suddenly wary. "Bid you good evening, Logrin," he said as the man entered.

The guardsman gave him a condescending smile, plucked a scroll from his belt, and handed it to him. Without a word he turned to leave.

Irion unrolled the message and read

To Irion ap Medraut: By vote of the council of elders your services as tribune are no longer required, and you are hereby removed from command of the army of Gwent.

It was signed by Brennus Turpilius Flavian, magistrate.

Stunned, Irion hurried after Logrin and grabbed the bridle of his horse. "Tell me the why of this! The council notified me of no meeting."

Logrin shrugged. "It was a council decision. You're not a member of the council."

"God's body, man! Do I not have a right to argue my case?"

[72]

"If you find fault with the decision, take it up with Lord Brennus. Now, if you will permit me?" He looked pointedly at Irion's hand on the bridle.

Irion let go and stepped back. "I'll do just that." He watched the guardsman ride away.

"Politics!" said Gwythur beside him. He spat. "I'm sorry, Irion."

"I'm going to Caerwent," Irion said. "This needs discussing."

Gwythur looked doubtful. "I don't think you'll turn his decision. Will grows strongest in the emptiest mind."

"I have to try." Irion limped toward the stables.

Brennus had retired by the time Irion knocked on the brass-covered door of his *mansio*. At Irion's insistence a surly houseman admitted him into the peristyle and went to wake the magistrate. After a long time Brennus tottered in, knees creaking, cane clacking over a mosaic of dolphins leaping from blue waves. His magnificent head of white hair formed a corona around a face as seamed and wrinkled as a winter-stored apple.

"Well, ap Medraut?" he snapped. "What is so confounded important it will not hold until morning?"

Irion began to regret his impatience, but there was nothing for it now except to go on. "The night's greetings to you, Lord Brennus. I ask your pardon for waking you. I've been told of the council's decision and I seek your aid in reversing it."

"Which decision is that, boy?" Brennus looked about him for a place to sit and eased himself into a gilded arm chair. He did not invite Irion to join him.

"The vote to remove me as tribune."

"Now, why should I help you change that decision? I agree with it. In fact, it was my idea."

"Have I not proven my worth as a commander?"

The magistrate looked at Irion as if he were a bad smell under his nose. "By leaving Caerwent unprotected and chasing off after some bandits? You got your uncle killed, boy."

The arrow struck home, but Irion tried to keep his face impassive. "Having troops in the barracks at Caerleon would not have prevented the assassin from sneaking into Caerwent."

"If you're telling me that you cannot defend the magistrate

with our own army," Brennus said, "then that proves my decision is right."

Irion took a breath and tried again. "There's another reason not to change commanders now, Lord Brennus. The Saxon lands are buzzing like a jostled hive. Every report brings news of more warriors arriving from Germania. Assassinating a British leader before an attack is an old Saxon trick. It's in my mind that Ceawlin will open a spring campaign against us very soon."

"Rot. I expected you to say something like that to keep your job. Even if it were true, which I do not believe, the new tribune can handle the Saxons."

"Who do you intend to name?"

"Triphun."

Anger flared through Irion like a bonfire at Beltane as he thought of Brennus's son, who passed most of his time at the Taverna of the Four Shades, leading the war band. "This is a mockery. He has no military training, and he can barely sit a horse."

Brennus stiffened. "Nevertheless. I need someone in that post I can trust."

"Have I given you any reason to distrust me?" Irion tried to keep his voice level.

"Blood will out, I say." Brennus levered himself to his feet. "I don't plan to give you the same opportunities Arthur gave your father. And now I intend to get some sleep." He wobbled out, leaving Irion alone with his anger.

Morning had come, chill and full of mist, when Irion arrived back at Caerleon. Deep in thought, he nearly collided with Gwythur as they both rounded the corner of the senior centurion's house. The rugged little captain had someone else in tow, a young man, slender as a sapling oak, wearing a dusty gray cloak and plaid kilt, black on red.

"You look like a man who fought his blankets all night and lost," Gwythur said.

Irion grunted. "I came not within fighting distance of them."

"Brennus would not be swayed?"

"No. And I have a decision to make."

Gwythur eyed him speculatively. "Well, hear this man out before you make that decision." He turned to the youth. "Tell Lord Irion what you just told me."

Young as he seemed, the messenger looked to be a veteran, with a white scar running out of his russet hair to pucker his forehead. He regarded Irion with blue eyes full of urgent trouble. "Well met, lord. My name is Vran." He spoke Cornovi Celtic. "I come from Owein of the Ravens, our chieftain."

Irion nodded. He had heard much about Owein, the Cornovi leader who fought beside Arthur in many of his famous battles. Since Arthur's death he had been a close ally of Honorius. "And?"

The youth cleared his throat, as if he were about to begin a long-prepared speech. "As you may know, lord, we Cornovi were once a large clan, spread across the belly of Britain."

"Aye."

"After Badon Hill, when Arthur forced peace on the Saxons, we prospered. There were long years of peace. Perhaps too many, for after the High King's death, when Camelot lay deserted, we made no move to occupy it and keep it in British hands. And later, when Ceawlin took it over, we were not prepared to deal with the butchery that came out of it."

"Nor were any of us," Irion said impatiently. He was in no mood for a history lesson. But the youth refused to be hurried.

"In our pride we sought no help from other British clans," he said, "and we lost much of our homeland, and many of our people. But we are learning how to fight again. My Lord Owein has gathered the people who remain into a stronghold in the hills, hidden from Ceawlin, and from there we strike as we can at the Saxons."

Irion sighed, resigned to hearing the entire story.

"For our own survival my lord keeps close watch on the comings and goings from Camelot. Five days since, as it was growing dark, a warrior of yours stumbled into our camp sorely wounded from a Saxon spear. Before he died he told us much, and asked that we deliver his warning to you."

"What was his name?"

"Berwyn, lord."

Irion and Gwythur exchanged quick, startled glances. The

[75]

dead man was one of the scouts they had sent to watch for Kylan's messages. "And the warning?" Irion said.

"Ceawlin has sent emissaries to Wessex and the Isle of Vectis. He seeks alliance with Cynric and with Wihtgar's Jutes, and he asks for a council in Cynric's camp on the day before the next full moon. Your man did not say how he got this information."

A cold knot of fear gripped Irion. Cynric was *bretwalda* of the Saxons, their most powerful chieftain. If he agreed to join Ceawlin, Gwent would be facing the entire Saxon confederation. "And what carrot does he offer Cynric to interest him in such an alliance?"

Vran lowered his head and prodded a grass tuft with the butt of his spear. "He offers Cynric the land of Gwent."

"Holy Druid Jesus! Brennus should know of this. Come with me, both of you. Vran must speak his message straight to him, for he would not believe my words. I'll ask him to delay my removal until this crisis is past, or at least choose someone other than Triphun as my replacement."

That evening a reluctant Brennus listened to the message of the Cornovi warrior, as Irion watched silently. Next to him sat his son, perfumed hair curling over the shoulders of his yellow silk tunic. The magistrate listened with apparent concern, questioning Vran on several points. For a time Irion thought he was succeeding.

But Triphun assured his father of his ability to handle the situation, and Irion sensed from the smirking glances that came his way that his replacement did not believe Vran's story. In the end, Brennus thanked them for alerting him and dismissed them. His decision would stand.

Alone, Irion rode slowly toward his quarters. Behind him a waning moon had risen above the walls of Caerwent. On impulse he turned his horse onto a narrow path leading away from the road to the north. It wound through a brush-covered gully, then up a hill into a small wood. The path became faint and overgrown, but Irion knew where it led and could have followed it blindfolded. Often as a child he had come here when he needed to escape the taunts of others, or just be alone.

When he reached a mossy boulder he turned off the path and rode down into a shallow bowl. In the center of the depression a pool flanked by willows and alders mirrored the moonlight. At the far end a spring fell from its opening in the steep hillside, a silver thread in a shining veil of mist, and plunged foaming into the pool. Near the spring's outlet stood an ancient shrine, built long before the Romans came, dedicated to the god Nodens of the Silver Hand. Now crumbling and overgrown with vines, it held for Irion a sense of peace.

He dismounted and eased himself onto a rock encrusted with lichens. From his belt he pulled his dagger and carved absently at the weathered crust. So much had changed in a few weeks. When he had last been here he'd had no thought of even becoming tribune. Now he was about to lose the position.

An idea sprang unbidden into his consciousness, the thought of riding into Caerwent at the head of the cavalry, dismissing the council, and taking command. Would the warriors follow him? He thought they would. He had earned their respect during the raid, and there were many who felt the elders were fools. Warriors normally made no attempt to hide their feelings, and he had heard much dissatisfied muttering— and some outright calls for rebellion—since Logrin had delivered Brennus's message.

Irion turned away from the idea. If he rose against the council, how then was he different from Medraut?

Sheathing the dagger he stood, then walked around the pond to the waterfall, listening to the splash of the water and the humming of insects. An owl glided silently across the water, eyes shining yellow in the moon.

But the idea would not be buried. He would be committing no treason, for he would not name himself magistrate. He would take command for only as long as absolutely necessary, until the threat of Saxon invasion was past. Then he would turn power back to the council. But on some deeper level Irion knew the difference was an illusion. And he knew that if he took this step, not only would the civil government die, so would his own self-respect. Yet perhaps he had no choice.

The next morning Irion sat alone in the study of the tribune's house, his mood gray as the clouds. A loud knock sounded at the door. In response to Irion's reluctant "Come," Hywel entered, a half dozen warriors at his back.

Irion looked up as the giant infantryman lowered his bulk into a chair across from him. "Is there a problem, captain?"

"Aye, tribune. Me and the men think so." Hywel studied him a moment, then spoke slowly, emphatically. "Ears and tail, Lord Irion, we can't allow these men to sit by and let Gwent, and what's left of Britain, be destroyed. The warriors think you should suspend the council."

Irion was not surprised. With a sigh he stood. He could delay his decision no longer. "This is a matter that needs the attention of all the warriors," he said. "Assemble the infantry on the drill field. Find Gwythur and tell him to marshal his cavalry."

As the warriors of Gwent assembled around him, Irion tried to still his doubts, to avoid thinking of the door he was closing forever. Standing stiffly in front of them, he addressed the puzzled warriors. He told them the news of Ceawlin and the Saxon alliance, and of his removal, though most had already heard it.

"Many of you feel as I do," he said, "that the council's action is unwise, that without a tried warrior to lead it, Gwent and Britain will suffer. However, the council has met for longer than the memory of any man living. Arthur encouraged it. It's not perfect, but it's one of the things that separates us from the spear-carrying animals across the Sabrina. It's rule by reason, not by the strongest. When I assumed the post of tribune, I took an oath of loyalty to the council. I cannot break that oath. I intend to turn over my staff of office to Triphun today, and become again an unranked warrior." He paused and took a breath to steady his voice. "It's been an honor to lead warriors with your courage and skill, and with whatever authority I have left, I ask that you follow the commands of Brennus and Triphun."

An undercurrent of shocked murmuring swept through the troops. Hywel strode forward. "You're saying it's better to be led to our deaths by a council of incompetents than to survive without them?"

"No. That's not what I'm saying. There are ways of changing the membership of the council, if you fault their leadership. Until then, I'll obey their orders and resign."

Irion turned and walked away in gloom. He had thrown

away his chance to avenge Honorius's death, to rid himself of the shadow of his father and win recognition as someone other than the son of Medraut. Worse, he had condemned Gwent to its doom. His decision had been as hopeless as suicide. But he could have done nothing else and lived with himself. Uncle Ynyr, he thought, I'm sorry.

PART FOUR

Caliburn

ELEVEN

Bedwyr braced his feet against the roll of the deck and tried to ignore the wolfhound's reproving stare. He could sympathize with Fergus. Even though they were only crossing the Sabrina estuary, the ferry's small size made standing on its flat deck worse than sailing on the *Brigit*. When Fergus had seen that Bedwyr intended to board it, he barked and sat down with his back to him. Not even crooning into his ear could persuade the dog to move. Only when Bedwyr suggested the wolfhound could be replaced by the brindled hound puppy they'd seen in Caerwent did Fergus give him a sour look, rise, and walk stiffly on board.

At least the horse didn't mind. The little mare he had bought in town trotted onto the deck without concern and now stood dozing, head droooping, amidships.

In Arthur's years, the ferry kept to a daily schedule between Caerwent and the mouth of the Abona River on the east side. Bedwyr had used it more than once while on the High King's business. But the ferry no longer made regular crossings, the boatman told him, because Ceawlin's war band made the Dumnonian shore unsafe. It took a bribe of nearly three times the old fare to persuade the ferryman to risk the trip.

Bedwyr felt a drop of water and looked up at the seamless mass of gray above him. So far, the rain held back, but the clouds threatened to open at any moment. He pulled his cloak tighter against the chill of the salt air. Ahead the shore grew larger, the hills and trees slipping away to his left as the ferry drifted slowly down the current.

"Mustn't use the old landing." The boatman spoke for the first time, softly. An old man, slope shouldered, he had knotted arms that still held strength. "They patrol the landing, so we must beach somewhere below it."

Bedwyr nodded. Although Dumnonia was still nominally British, its king, Cador, was powerless to stop the Saxons from raiding deep within it, and in fact paid yearly tribute to Ceawlin merely to keep his crown. Once Bedwyr was across, the danger of discovery prevented the boatman from waiting for him. He'd have to find his way back as best he could.

They neared the shore and he scanned the marshy bank. Nothing moved except the white gulls that wheeled, mewing, against the gray of the sky and a brown crane that stood tall and stiff in shallow water, turning its long neck to watch them.

Bedwyr signaled the ferryman and he guided the boat into the rushes. With a long pole, he pushed the craft through them until it bumped gently against the bank. Bedwyr led the pony onto shore and Fergus bounded after, grinning hugely as all four feet landed on solid ground. As Bedwyr turned, the ferryman was already poling away from shore.

He mounted and rode inland through the tall marsh grass until he came to a small rise, then turned southwest, following a narrow trail running parallel to the shoreline. The track led him to a clearing that held the charred outlines of a dozen or so huts. He skirted the clearing and passed on.

Without warning, the clouds opened and a curtain of rain drenched him. It hissed on the surface of the river and filled hollows in the trail with black water. Chilled, impatient to be done with his task, Bedwyr urged the pony into a trot and her sides steamed.

All that day rain fell, slow and steady. Twice he forded small rivers, through cold water up to the horse's belly. Much of his way lay through lowland marsh and he kept to the trackways, preferring the risk of meeting a Saxon raiding party to the certainty of floundering into bottomless mud if he struck off cross-country.

In the afternoon he passed below an abandoned hill fort, the site of one of Arthur's early winter camps. Without thinking, he turned and rode up the hill through a breach in the turf walls. He reined in and gazed around him. Over there had been the mead hall, where the Companions had gathered around the peat fire on winter evenings to boast and listen to Gwalchmai's harping. There, its roof caved in, stood Arthur's house, where he had lived his first winter with his new wife Gwenhwyfar. She had seemed much happier then, before Arthur became High King and she, Queen. The ruins nearest him had been the married quarters. He could still hear the happy noise, see the children and hounds tumbling about the doorways. It had been full of life then, this camp, full of promise and joyful purpose. Now nothing moved in it but a magpie scolding him from a blackthorn bush.

Disturbed, Bedwyr turned and rode back down the hill. The images of those days had come back as fresh as if he had lived them yesterday. He felt as if he had been wandering in the land of faery, where mere minutes seemed to have passed, only to return to find his family, his clan, and his King ashes for long years.

Near evening the rain turned to mist, a milky shroud that swirled head high across the trail. Through it he heard the rhythmic clop of a half dozen horses moving at a swift trot. The creak of leather and clank of iron fittings meant armed men.

Signaling Fergus to follow, Bedwyr wheeled the startled pony from the road and plunged into a small clump of willows. He whipped off his cloak and draped it over the mare's head to keep her from whinnying at the oncoming horses.

The willows did not give much cover, and an alert rider on the road would see him in spite of the mist. The horsemen passed within a stone's throw of him, heads down, intent only on reaching the dry warmth of some camp. After they passed he breathed again and rode on.

The next afternoon Bedwyr paused at the edge of a wood and looked down into a shallow valley. For hours he had seen no house, no man, no thread of smoke, no cattle. Only forest and rivers, and small glens such as this: Camlann, men called it now, the Crooked Glen. A place with little to distinguish it from a hundred other small valleys except that, eleven years ago, Arthur Pendragon had died here. To Bedwyr it still stank of blood and he would not pass through it. He turned the mare back into the trees and went around.

At the sight of the battlefield, he was suddenly flooded

with emotions and he fought unsuccessfully to quell them. If only he had been able to persuade Arthur not to fight Medraut. If only he had fought harder. His world was full of "if onlys." The vision the Companions dreamed had been nothing but illusion, spun by the gods in jest and held brightly before them to lead them on. They followed, for the sake of the dream, and were deserted. Now the meaning of their lives would be covered by the dust of the dark age to come.

The lake and the hollow tree holding the sword waited just ahead. At the edge of the wood he dismounted and tied his horse to a young alder, then walked toward the mere. Near the water's edge stood the oak, its fissured trunk exactly the same.

Bedwyr stood still, remembering. Why hadn't he thrown Caliburn into the lake, as Arthur had bidden him? He was no longer certain. It wasn't that he coveted the sword for himself; he knew it was not for him. There had seemed to be something about the sword itself, a power he felt when he held it, a sense of purpose. It was Caliburn that had driven back the Saxon onslaught, that had protected the civilization Rome had brought to Britain. Not the Empire and its corruption, but the learning of new ways; the loyalty to something larger than one's own clan; the years of peace in which farmers could till and live to harvest, merchants could trade, children could play without hiding at the sight of a stranger. To destroy it meant the light had failed, the dream had died.

Bedwyr shrugged. Well, it had died. He should have known it then. Arthur knew it. And Caliburn was only a sword. He had run from the truth long enough. He would carry out his King's final order and get on with his life.

He walked to the oak and thrust his arm into the opening, feeling for the oiled leather scabbard. His fingers gripped nothing but the spongy roughness of decayed wood.

Heart hammering against his ribs, he groped again inside the cavity. Something soft and cold and many legged squirmed under his hand and disappeared.

He leaned over and peered into the hole. He could see little. A third time he searched the crevice. It was empty. Caliburn was gone.

TWELVE

Bedwyr sat stunned. During all the nightmares and all the years of running, the possibility that Caliburn might not be waiting when he came back for it had never touched his mind. He sank to the grass, trying to think. An iridescent blue dragonfly hovered in front of him, but he did not see it. Head in his hands, he stared at the grass, but he did not see that either.

How could anyone find it? The tree grew far off any road or trackway and no farm steadings stood nearby. Scavengers undoubtedly had searched the battlefield, but they had no reason to come down here, or to look inside the tree if they did. There could be only one explanation: Someone had seen him hide the sword. But who? And how could he find him now?

At his side Fergus whined softly and put his paw on his master's arm, sensing his distress.

Caliburn must be found. Always, he justified hiding it by telling himself he did not disobey, only delayed carrying out Arthur's order. Now, clearly, his actions had lost the sword, perhaps into the hands of the Saxons.

Bedwyr forced himself to think logically. Caliburn was unique, with its hilt of twining gold serpents, its great purple amethyst set into the pommel, and the blue sheen of its steel blade. No one could use a sword so distinctive without attracting attention. If it remained in Britain someone would know of it, most likely a swordsmith, for they kept track of the creations of their craft.

In Isca there had been a smith, Waelyn by name, who had

reset the great gem for Arthur. Once, Bedwyr had known him well. If Waelyn still lived he might have knowledge of the sword. He would seek him out.

The changes eleven years had brought to Dumnonia shocked Bedwyr as he rode toward Isca. Under Arthur, the fertile countryside had sprawled with prosperous farmsteads and orchards. The High King had maintained their roads, paved their fords, and repaired their bridges. Today the peasants he passed were gaunt and ragged with a haunted look to them, as if they lived on the knife edge of want. Most fled in terror at his approach. He let them be, but watched carefully, for many looked capable of heaving a pitchfork into his back from behind a hedgerow.

The city of Isca had once thrived as a legion stronghold. A river rose on the moors to the north and flowed down past it, providing a navigable outlet to the sea, and a great road ran from it to Aquae Sulis and Corinium. Under Arthur, it had prospered again, for he rebuilt its sturdy timber buildings and made it the capital of Dumnonia. Now its walls crumbled and its gates sagged open, one of them hanging by a single rusted hinge. On the ramparts no sentries patrolled.

Bedwyr rode through the gates and gazed around him. Refuse lay everywhere, tainting the air with the stink of offal and decay. A few shabbily dressed men hurried through the crumbling streets, casting sidelong glances at him as he passed.

He stopped one of them, a man with a bloated, tallowy face, and asked him where he might find Waelyn the sword-smith. The man looked at him in fright, shook his head, and hurried away without speaking.

Puzzled, Bedwyr rode on until he saw a legless beggar propped in an open doorway of a courtyard choked with debris. In the center of the courtyard stood a statue of some god, broken off at the waist. The beggar muttered and laughed to himself, his small, bright eyes staring into the distance.

Bedwyr dismounted, walked over to him, and, kneeling, put a copper coin in the man's cup. "I seek Waelyn the smith," he said. "Can you tell me where to find him?"

The beggar went on babbling, seemingly unaware of his presence, until Bedwyr put a hand on his shoulder and looked into his eyes. "I think you are not as mad as you pretend. Does Waelyn still live?"

The bright eyes focused on him for a moment, then slid away. "Know no one by that name," he muttered. "Not safe to know things."

"He's an old friend and I need his help."

The beggar looked at the copper coin in the bottom of his cup, then at Bedwyr, who pulled out another coin, this one silver, and held it between thumb and forefinger in front of the man's face. The beggar's mouth split into a toothless smile.

"There be a smith's forge by the west wall, and the man in it used to make swords. May be the one you seek." He snatched the coin. "Though he be not likely to help you much now." He cackled and hid the coin within his rags, then withdrew muttering back into his own world.

Bedwyr rode through the city toward the west wall. Squatters now inhabited many of the gutted shops, staring sullenly from their doorways. At one corner he came upon a slave auction, a makeshift platform in the middle of the street, with a dozen women and children huddled behind a ranting auctioneer. Flanking the slaves stood two armed men in Germanic tunics with red horses painted on them and cross-gartered leggings.

Bedwyr turned into an alley. He did not think the Saxons had noticed him.

He found the smith's, part dwelling, part forge, with its back to the crumbling city wall. After tying the mare to a post, he walked through the open doorway, Fergus padding at his heel. No fire burned in the forge, and daylight filtering in from the door cast the only light.

On a granite anvil, his back to Bedwyr, sat a man polishing a short sword. A man of great sinews and bony joints, he was strongly built, though lean as a winter wolf. For a moment he continued his work as if unaware of the intrusion. Then he held up the weapon, his manner matter-of-fact.

"Lovely, eh? The smith who forged her did not forget beauty in the need for use."

"Aye," Bedwyr said. "Early Roman infantry by the look of it."

"You know your swords, sir. Peasants turn them up from

[89]

time to time with their plows. They bring them here to sell and I buy them—if not too rusted and they do not demand overmuch. I save them for our King Cador. We must all do what we can." He spoke as if reciting a piece well learned.

"I care not what you do with it," Bedwyr said. "I am not Cador's man."

The rag paused on the blade and the man cocked his head, listening. "I know that voice, or did once."

Bedwyr strode forward and laid his hand on the smith's shoulder. "Greetings, Waelyn."

The smith lifted his face and revealed the scars around sightless eyes. Below them a smile spread slowly.

"That would be the Lord Bedwyr, then. By the One! I knew you were not dead."

"How fare you?"

"Well enough. If one does not ask for too much."

At the sight of the injury Bedwyr's heart went out to his old friend. He wanted to ask him what had happened but he could not. There was an awkward silence.

Waelyn spoke, answering his silent question. "I earned the displeasure of our king." His voice now mocked the title.

"How so?"

"I refused to be his chief swordsmith. He decided I would make weapons for no one else."

"I'm sorry, Waelyn."

The smith began burnishing the blade again. "It was done a while since. Loss makes bitter wine, but sooner or later all men learn to drink it. And what draws you to Isca, lord? Men travel little for pleasure in these times."

"Business I should have finished years ago." Bedwyr sat on a tool chest, pushing aside a greasy sheepskin bellows.

Waelyn laid aside his rag and stood the sword carefully against the anvil. "First, tell me where you've been these years past, if you will, lord. We've heard little of you since Camlann."

Bedwyr told him of his years in Rome in the service of Belisarius while the smith listened in rapt silence. Finally, he asked, "Remember you Caliburn, Waelyn?"

"Remember! Do you forget the sun?" The smith sighed. "Such a sword will never be again. It could draw blood from the wind."

"Men said you had a hand in its forging."

"I? No, not I. Clever enough with iron I was, in a small way, but such skill as went into the making of Caliburn is beyond my ken. I'm proud to have been allowed to reset the stone."

"Have you heard aught of it since Camlann?"

Waelyn shook his head. "Only the same tales as everyone else. Nothing in recent years."

"Tales?"

"Aye. But after Constantine disappeared even the tales ended."

"Constantine! Constantine holds Caliburn?"

"Of course. Or at least he held it. Did you not know?"

"I did not. How came he by it?"

Waelyn scratched a bristled cheek. "I don't know, exactly. He told all who asked that Arthur gave it to him before he died, but some claimed otherwise. At any rate, everyone agreed that Arthur named Constantine his heir, and none saw reason to dispute his ownership of the High King's sword."

Bedwyr said nothing. It fit. Constantine might have seen him hide the sword, for he pursued Medraut's survivors in that direction after the battle.

"You spoke of tales concerning Caliburn. What tales?"

"Nothing one can get a grip on, really," said the smith. "Just dark rumors of evil deeds Arthur's heir performed with it. Some say the sword turned on Constantine himself, finally, and killed him."

"Do you believe that, Waelyn? That the sword is magic?"

"Magic?" The smith frowned. "Perhaps not. Save for the skill that forged it, and the unnatural color of the blade. But that may be from the source of its metal. It's no secret Caliburn was forged from a great rock that fell from the sky. That alone is magic enough."

Waelyn rose, picking up the short sword, and carried it slowly into the back of the forge. Bedwyr heard a board creak as the smith lifted it and soon he returned without the weapon.

"Why do you ask of Caliburn now, Lord Bedwyr, after all these years?"

Bedwyr stroked the wolfhound's head absently. "Those who say Arthur did not give Caliburn to Constantine are right.

As his last command the King ordered me to cast it into the lake near the battlefield. I disobeyed. I hid Caliburn rather than destroy it."

The smith nodded. "It would be ill to destroy a thing of such beauty."

"So I told myself, but it was not that. I did it for reasons that seem poor to me now. I seek to finish what I should have done then."

"Destroy Caliburn." Waelyn shook his head slowly. "What a loss. But then, perhaps Arthur foresaw rightly, after all, judging from the tales."

"How long has Constantine been gone?"

"Long. He ruled but two or three years after Camlann, or tried to. At least he did try to fight Ceawlin at first."

"And none know where he may be found?"

"Not where he may be found, nor whether he even still lives. He simply handed over his crown to his son Cador one day and disappeared. Took Caliburn with him, they say."

"Cador still rules in Dumnonia, does he not? Perhaps he would know."

Waelyn snorted. "If you call kissing Saxon hind parts ruling, aye. But I'd keep well clear of him. I doubt that he knows, and he'd not help you if he did. He's Ceawlin's man, hilt, pommel, and blade. Likely he'd turn you over to him."

"I see no other choice if I'm to find Constantine."

The smith hesitated. "There is one other who may know."

Bedwyr paused in the act of rising. "Who?"

"Elyn."

The name struck Bedwyr mute. After a long moment, he managed to say, "What has she to do with Constantine?"

Waelyn turned his face down, running his blunt fingers over the anvil. "If rumors be true, she had ample reason to try and find him, and I think that she looked. What passed between them is not clear and should come from her lips in any case."

Elyn! Her name resurrected dread, and an old, deep ache. Almost, Bedwyr preferred to be caught by Saxons than to see her. Finally, he sighed. "Where would I find her?"

"Last I heard, she survives on her family estate near the

moor, but that was some time since. The Saxons may not yet have pillaged that far. She'll be glad to see you, Lord Bedwyr."

Bedwyr stood. "I would not have had my path lead in that direction, but it seems there's no choice."

"You're welcome to lodge here," Waelyn said, "but I think you're safer away from Isca."

"Aye." Bedwyr hesitated, reluctant to leave the smith in this place. "If you wish to leave here, friend, I'll gladly take you with me."

The smith smiled a little. "I'm too old to start over elsewhere. So long as I'm careful I get on well enough." He extended his hand. "Safe roads to you, Bedwyr. Keep to the less traveled ways. An armed rider who doesn't wear the red horse will attract attention."

Bedwyr clasped the hand. "I'll take care."

He rode out the west gate, breathing deeply to expel the odor of Isca from his lungs. A rutted lane turned northward and he followed it, through a forest of stumps left by woodcutters.

Lost in thought, he saw the patrol too late. A dozen riders wearing red-horse tunics trotted over a small hill toward him.

THIRTEEN

The patrol reined in sharply as they saw Bedwyr.

It was too late to hide. He rode up to their leader, a small, hard-looking man with a glass bead hanging from one ear, and scowled.

"About time you got here," Bedwyr said. "You've cost me two days in Isca. I've been sent north. Get someone on those walls."

He pushed his mare past the surprised leader and rode on. Behind, the riders milled uncertainly and stared after him. He'd almost reached the top of the hill when the leader shouted in Friesian for him to stop. Bedwyr slapped the startled pony on the rump and they bolted for the cover of the woods.

Cursing and shouting, the patrol galloped after, closing rapidly with their swifter horses. Bedwyr gained the trees scant yards ahead of them and plunged into the green gloom of the forest, Fergus running behind.

The lane became a narrow track that wound in a bewildering pattern to avoid thickets of holly and impenetrable brambles. The bare feet of the Old People had made the path, and they had never intended it for a horse and rider. Bedwyr often had to lie flat on the mare's back to pass beneath the great branches rolling out darkly above him. Here the taller horses of the patrol were at a disadvantage and the shouts grew fainter.

The track curled and bore off in a new direction. Ahead, he heard the sound of rushing water. He trotted down a long slope, and the moss-gray oaks gave way to hazel and alder, ending abruptly at the edge of a great river. Swollen by the recent rain, it boomed and churned in spate.

Bedwyr scanned the bank up and downriver. There was no room to ride along the shoreline, for the muddy waves lapped at the alder thickets. Over the roar of the water he heard a shout and saw the patrol race down the slope a long arrow's flight behind him.

"Look's like we swim, old girl."

He slid from the mare and pulled off his boots, stuffing them into the saddlebag. His sword and baldric he lashed to the saddlebow. Seizing the reins he splashed into the cold river, bracing his legs against the surge of the current. The wolfhound stood at the water's edge.

"Fergus," he called. "To me!"

The dog raced back and forth on the bank, barking and whining as his master waded farther into the river. Finally he hurled himself into the water and began to paddle after Bedwyr.

The mare rolled her eyes in fright as the water lifted her from her feet. Bedwyr dropped the reins and began to stroke. His missing left hand made swimming difficult, and the current gripped him, carrying him several yards downstream for every yard he swam.

As they neared the center of the river the horse screamed and floundered, thrashing. Her forward motion stopped and he grabbed at the reins, trying to pull her across behind him. It was useless. Her weight made a massive anchor which the current seized and dragged down. The mare's head disappeared under the brown water. Gasping for air he let go the reins and swam for his life.

Gradually the water grew shallower and the current less strong. At last he touched bottom, stood, and slogged to the bank, where he leaned, coughing and spitting, against a willow trunk. The wolfhound scrambled onto shore and shook himself, water spraying from his wiry coat.

When he recovered his breath, Bedwyr stumbled down the bank, scanning the muddy water for the horse. There was no sign of her. She must have suffered a cramp or a twisted stomach, he thought. A shame, for he hated to see any animal suffer.

He looked across the river. Upstream the horsemen were wading into the water. Shades! Calling to Fergus he plunged into the thorn scrub that lined the shore. The briers clawed at him, ripping his tunic, slashing his face and arms.

He stumbled onto an animal track and ran along it, listening for the sounds of pursuit. Behind him Fergus padded tirelessly in an easy lope. The scrub merged into a wood of ash trees, their trunks rising straight and tall on all sides. Green light filtered through the forest canopy, and under his bare feet old leaves made a freckled yellow carpet.

Bedwyr ran. His thoughts soon narrowed to the motion of his legs, the pounding of his heart. Body on fire, his lungs labored with one will: Breathe, draw in and gasp out cool, sweet, life-giving air.

At last he stopped to rest, leaning against the rough bark of a tree, hands on his knees. Panting, the dog sat on its haunches, tongue lolling red, from the side of its mouth. When his breathing stilled, Bedwyr listened, but he heard nothing except soft woodland noises.

Taking a deep breath he started off again at a slower pace, leaving the path to weave in and out of the trees, stepping whenever possible on rocks or firm ground. Occasionally he found a fallen tree and ran along it, before jumping off and continuing in another direction.

Above him, day slid away and the light below the trees, already dim, faded into darkness. Looking for shelter, he ran down a rocky gully and into a brook, then splashed up it until he spotted a dense thicket of brush growing halfway up the slope. He signaled Fergus and climbed toward the brush, stepping carefully on outcroppings of rock.

On hands and knees he crawled into the tangle of branches and leaves, thankful at least that the branches lacked thorns. There, head pillowed on the dog's flank, he rested, then slept.

During the night he awoke to something rustling in the thicket. It proved to be only a hedgehog grunting back from a night of beetle hunting and he went back to sleep.

Full light shone on the thicket when the wolfhound roused. Bedwyr, alerted by Fergus's movement, felt the hair lift on the dog's neck as it raised its head and growled, a barely audible rumble deep in his throat. Carefully Bedwyr parted the branches just enough to see.

In the stream, two Saxons spoke together in hushed tones.

As he watched, the taller of the two gestured upstream, and the other, a wiry youth with a face as fierce as a dagger thrust, answered with a vigorous shake of his head. This one raised his eyes from the stream and scanned the hillside.

Astonished, Bedwyr felt new respect for the tracking ability of his pursuers and wonder at their determination. He saw no horses—they must have abandoned them to follow him. Instinctively he felt for his sword, then remembered he had lashed it to the mare's saddle. Stiff from yesterday's exertions and the cramped night in the brush, he could not outrun them. He froze and waited, feeling like a hare run to ground.

In the stream the men still argued. Finally the tall one drew his sword and shook it under the nose of the youth, who shrugged and raised his hands in surrender. They moved off upstream.

Bedwyr waited. When he was certain they were out of sight and hearing, he crawled from the thicket, stood, and stretched. His feet bled, his legs felt stiff. Wincing, he limped down the hill to the stream and stumbled back down it, then struck out westward, the direction, he hoped, of Elyn's villa.

At first he ran slowly and painfully, but as his muscles loosened and the soles of his feet grew numb he increased his speed, using every trick he knew to throw off pursuit and hide his tracks. He heard and saw no further sign of pursuit and he grew confident he had evaded them.

Near evening he came to a place where men had beaten back the forest and tilled the land. He recognized it as part of Elyn's family estate. The fields, once golden tan with grain, now grew to thistles and brambles.

Warily he skirted the open land, walking along the edge of the trees. At the top of a rise he stopped and looked down into a broad valley drained by a wide stream.

In the center of the valley stood a villa, a great rambling place built around two courtyards—the outer one surrounded by quarters for the farmhands, baths, sheds, and barns; the inner, smaller and more elegant, surrounded by a three-sided gallery and crisscrossed by walks. When Bedwyr had last been here there had been an upper story, half-timbered on white stucco. Nothing remained of it now but a charred ruin. The location and design made the place completely indefensible, he thought, but when built, there had been no need to make every dwelling a fortress.

This had been Elyn's home. If she still lived, she did not live here. He stood motionless watching the ruined villa and the land beyond, but nothing moved. Listening, he heard only forest sounds.

Drawn by curiosity and reviving memories he walked down the slope and through the gate. The title to the estate, a bronze tablet, still rested in the wall near the entrance. Most of the lower story yet stood, though roofless. Ivy choked the broken doorway. Bedwyr thrust it aside and entered.

Wind and rain and smoke had ravaged the elegant frescoes. Fires had been lit on the mosaic floor. Once the four columns of polished stone had supported a vaulted ceiling. Now their tops stood mutely above the walls, as if trying to look beyond the wreckage around them.

Those had been ordered, prosperous times, he thought. Elyn had made this a place of warmth and light, of friendship and music. Elyn. He pushed her memory roughly back into the corner of his mind where it had lain for long years. Those times were gone, irretrievably, and had been gone long before Camlann.

He walked through the great atrium, his footsteps echoing from the ruined walls. No voice sounded here now but the cry of birds. Fifty years more and no one would even remember what kind of life had been lived here.

Fergus had disappeared into another room exploring. As he trotted back into the atrium he froze and growled.

A voice said from the doorway, "Breathe too hard and you're dead."

Three men stood inside the door. The speaker, a dark-haired youth with small slits for eyes and a face already hardened, held a drawn bow, arrow aimed at Bedwyr's chest.

FOURTEEN

Bedwyr cursed himself for his carelessness. Then he looked closer at his captors. All three were but boys. The youngest, about ten, had a pair of disarming dimples in his cheeks and unruly hair like the feathers of a bird in a high wind.

"What right have you to come in here?" demanded the oldest.

"I mean no harm. Undraw the bow. I'm seeking someone I once knew who lived here. Her name was Elyn. Know you that name?"

The archer blinked in surprise and the younger boys exchanged glances.

"What if we did?" asked the oldest. "Who are you that we should tell you?"

"My name is Bedwyr ap Gruffydd. I'm a friend of hers from many years past."

A look of awe passed over the youngest boy's face, quickly replaced by disbelief. "You're not Bedwyr," he said. "Bedwyr was tall as a tree and fierce as lightning."

"Was he so?" Bedwyr put up a hand to rub away a smile that had started. "Perhaps the passing of years has clouded his appearance in someone's mind."

"No, sir! The Lady Elyn told me so herself."

The boy next to him jabbed him with an elbow. "Shut up, Brys!"

Brys bit his lip and scowled at the floor.

"So she does live," Bedwyr said. "Please take me to her. I have urgent business with her."

"What proof have you that you are who you claim to be?"
The eldest unbent his bow but did not lower it.

"None, except the Lady Elyn herself. She'll recognize me."

I hope, he thought. Cloakless and bootless, with grimy face and tattered trews and tunic, he looked every bit the outlaw for which the boys took him. Elyn had always been impressed by fine clothing and jewelry, and he cringed at the prospect of letting her see him like this.

"If you're Bedwyr, where are your horse and sword?" insisted the youngest.

"Lost when one of Ceawlin's patrols chased me."

Brys looked at him with scorn. "Bedwyr was no coward. He wouldn't run from anyone."

"Even Bedwyr could not defeat twelve men, alone," he said.

His three captors huddled whispering near the door, Brys casting an occasional glance at him over his shoulder. Weary, Bedwyr squatted on his heels while they talked. Finally they turned back to him.

"The lady must decide if you are who you say," said the oldest. "So we'll take you to her. But you must be blindfolded—the place of our *dun* is secret. If you're not Bedwyr, the dog will be killed, for he could find his way back."

Bedwyr sighed and stood. "Very well."

Fergus, who after inspecting the boys had sat on his haunches, tongue lolling, closed his mouth and looked up at him.

From a leather pouch the leader produced a rag and bound it tightly across Bedwyr's eyes. "Put your hands on my shoulders," he said, and when Bedwyr did so, led him from the room and out of the villa.

They walked for what seemed hours. The oldest boy, who gave his name as Beric, proved to be a good guide, walking slowly and warning of obstacles. Their path wound in a confusing pattern and Bedwyr lost all sense of direction. During most of the journey the air smelled cool and damp as if they traveled through forest.

At last they stopped and the guide turned him around twice, then pulled off the blindfold. Squinting against the late afternoon sun Bedwyr looked about him. He stood in a natural clearing surrounded by trees. Ahead of him rose a rocky hill crowned by a palisade of logs.

Beric motioned for him to follow and began climbing a narrow trail that wound up the hill. As they neared the gate a sentry hailed them from the wall.

"Ho, Beric! What have you found?"

"Someone to see the lady. Claims he's Bedwyr Mawr of the Companions."

The sentry gave a low whistle and disappeared.

Inside the enclosure a cluster of wattle bothies and byres huddled around a log hall roofed with dark, rough thatch.

"Wait here," ordered Beric, and he ran off toward the hall, scattering hens and naked toddlers, leaving Bedwyr with Brys and his older brother.

He soon came back, followed by a woman and several men. The woman who came toward him walked wand straight, holding her head like a queen. A woolen *tunica* covered long legs and a body whose lines flowed like spring water. Hair with a hint of red in the brown of it blew back from her face, a face thinner than the last time he had seen her. Her eyes, dove gray flecked with a gold that gave the sense of a fire behind them, showed a fine web of lines at their corners. Their mocking laughter of years past had been replaced by something deeper, kinder. A beauty changed by the years but not diminished.

As she approached, her eyes widened a little in recognition. Her smile was light but she watched him closely, her gaze resting for a moment on Bedwyr's maimed left arm. Self-consciously he drew it behind his back. There was no stigma attached to battle wounds, but somehow he was reluctant for Elyn to see it.

"Bedwyr, welcome," she said. "Forgive Beric and his brothers for being overzealous in protecting our privacy. We survive by staying hidden."

"The boys acted rightly. Are they yours?"

She smiled. "In a sense. We rescued them from a slave train."

Unexpectedly, she embraced him. "By the Light, Bedwyr! Is it really you? I was afraid you had died on some forsaken battlefield."

He stood awkwardly, not returning the embrace.

Embarrassed, she drew back, running her hands through her hair. "You were never one for embroidery or ornament, Bedwyr," she said, eyeing his clothes, "but neither did you wear rags when you courted me." Her tone became formal again. "There's a story here, seemingly. Perhaps we can hear it after you are rested and refreshed."

She led him to a bothy next to the log hall, where she gave orders to some of the onlookers who had gathered to gawk at him. Several of them hurried away and returned lugging a large tub of coopered beech staves, which they carried inside the bothy, while others hauled buckets filled with hot water.

"Come to the hall when you're ready," Elyn said. "Our food is simple, but we do not lack for it."

"Whatever the fare, my lady, I'm grateful. I've not eaten since yesterday's dawning."

After she had gone Bedwyr stripped off his grimy rags and climbed into the tub, lying back in the steamy warmth, letting the hot water ease his aches and bruises and soothe his torn feet. He must have dozed off, for a giggle awakened him. Behind him a young girl laid a bundle of clothing on a crude chair and hurried out, still giggling.

When the water grew cold he reluctantly climbed out and put on the clothing left for him: a tunic, breeches, a cloak of rough, blue homespun, and a pair of sandals. For these Bedwyr was thankful. He did not think his swollen feet would fit into boots. He found in the bundle as well a razor and silver looking glass, and he quelled his rumbling stomach long enough to remove the stubble of beard. In the badly broken glass, his reflection splintered like echoes from a riffled pond. Finished, he ran his hand over his chin and shrugged.

"She'll have to put up with that," he said to Fergus, curled up asleep in the corner. "I'm for food. They may even find something for a bedraggled wolfhound." The dog roused, stretched, and padded after him.

He entered the cheery mead hall, full of men and women and older children eating around a long table. Hanging mats covered the walls, and fresh rushes blanketed the floor. In a wide hearth a blazing wood fire crackled and spat sparks. Tallow candles, thick as a man's arm, burned brightly on the table.

Faces turned toward him as he entered and the loud buzz of conversation changed to excited whispers. From the head of the table, Elyn motioned to him and he took his place in an empty seat at her right hand.

A serving girl brought him a bowl of herb-scented stew with a slab of ewe's-milk cheese and a horn of beer, glancing at him to learn whether her performance was satisfactory, then stood back sucking the ends of her braids and watching him.

"To them you're a hero," said Elyn, a glint of amusement in her eyes.

"Whose fault is that?" he said.

He asked the serving girl for a scrap of meat for Fergus, and when it came, the wolfhound lay behind his master's chair, crunching the bone with an occasional growl and a glance around, to see if any rivals were sneaking up on him.

Elyn studied Bedwyr, smiling. "I thought you might like to use my brother's razor. You always were Roman in that way. I apologize for the condition of the looking glass. I don't imagine I shall ever have another."

As they ate she talked of small incidents in her daily life, cheerful things. To Bedwyr her voice was remembered music, but he muted the memory and answered politely, aloofly. In the end, however, the food and drink and friendly company worked their magic, lifting his spirits. When at last he pushed back his chair, he felt more at ease than he had in a long time.

A man sitting next to him asked him where he came from. When Bedwyr responded, other folk at the table joined in with more questions, at first hesitantly, then eagerly when they found him willing to talk about far-off places. There seemed to be no sense of position or rank among them, except that Elyn led.

During a lull Beric, his oldest captor, leaned forward and spoke eagerly. "There's a rumor, Lord Bedwyr, that King Arthur was seen riding his white stallion near Corinium a fortnight ago. And that Rome is sending three legions to aid him in driving back the Saxons."

"Arthur is dead," Bedwyr said curtly. "And Rome can send no legions at all. She herself is sorely pressed to survive."

He was about to say more: that the Saxons were too many to be stopped, that the end of civilization had come. But he caught himself. The noise and laughter in the hall died, replaced by murmuring. He frowned, angry at himself for throwing a pall over the bright cheer of the feast. To make amends he told a story about a donkey and a statue of Nero that soon had people laughing again.

After the story Elyn said: "But you stayed in Rome only two years. What of the other nine?"

"They are dark ones, lady. Their tale is not for times of warmth and cheer such as this."

She smiled. "Warmth and cheer we have in quantity, though I fear the comforts of this hall are poor compared to those I offered when last you visited the villa."

"How long since the villa burned?"

Her smile slipped away. "That is also a tale I would sooner forget. Raiders destroyed it five years since. I was not at home and so survived. But they killed my brother, Caerdin. I miss him terribly."

Bedwyr remembered Caerdin as handsome and carefree, a young man who lived for hunting and fast horses. "I'm sorry," he said.

"Caerdin always told me the villa could not be defended, if it came to that," she said. "But we foolishly thought ourselves far enough from Camelot to be safe. After the raid I wandered aimlessly about the ruins for a time. I don't remember much about those days. Gradually other folk, field hands and laborers, began drifting in, still looking to our family for protection. I finally awoke to the fact that, of our family, only I remained, so I pulled myself together and we started to rebuild our lives. We found this place and built the *dun* and make out well enough." She smiled again. "We survive."

"Indeed, you have done well," said Bedwyr.

She brightened. "Enough of serious talk. Perhaps you would favor us with a song, Bedwyr. My harp, I saved."

"I? I know only a few barracks songs. I'd rather listen to you, for there was never one who could wake the harp strings as you can."

Elyn laughed, pleased. "They can hear me anytime. Please, Bedwyr?"

He gave a mock sigh and bowed and a cheer went up in the hall. Elyn disappeared and came back a moment later with a small Celtic harp of polished willow, with shimmering strings of fine, white bronze. She placed it carefully on a stool and beckoned to him.

Bedwyr rose and, tilting the harp toward him, self-consciously struck a pose like a young bard, to the laughter of the crowd. His fingers wandered over the strings while he thought of something to play, then he launched into a well-known *gentraige*, bright and rollicking, soon taken up by his audience. He played two more songs and the hall resounded with singing.

His repertoire exhausted, Bedwyr sat down, to the protests of Elyn's folk. When they could not persuade him to return to the harp, they shouted and stamped for Elyn.

She rose, however, and held up her hands.

"Another time, good people. But now our guest is weary and I would speak with him a little before he retires."

Amid groans of dismay and good-natured grumbling the people quickly cleared the table and dispersed. When they were alone Elyn took Bedwyr to the hearth and sat him in a cross-legged Roman chair with ornately carved arms.

"A few things in addition to the harp we saved from the villa," she said as he fingered the carvings in admiration. She handed him a full horn of dark heather beer and sat across from him in a matching chair, pulling from a basket beside it a torn tunic and a needle and thread.

She smiled at his surprise. "I'm not above such things. Here everyone shares the work. And now, perhaps you'll tell me the reason for your visit. Or were you only traveling toward another place when the boys found you?" For a moment her voice held a hint of the mockery he remembered of old.

Bedwyr drank from the horn and set it on the hearth, wondering how to begin. He decided to come at the matter directly.

"Do you remember Arthur's great sword, Caliburn?"

She stiffened, the color draining from her face. When she spoke her voice sounded hard, strained. "You have become cruel, sir."

Bedwyr stared at her in amazement. "Lady?"

She looked at him as if he were a weed, then saw his bewilderment. Her expression softened a little. "You do not know? No, I can see you don't. Whatever you were, Bedwyr, you were never cruel."

She dropped her gaze to her sewing. "Why do you seek it here?"

"A swordsmith by the name of Waelyn told me Constantine of Dumnonia held the sword after Camlann. Now it seems both Constantine and Caliburn have disappeared. The smith had no idea where they might be found." He watched her work the needle through and through the woolen cloth. "He suggested I ask you, lady; that you, if anyone, have cause to know his whereabouts, though he did not tell me why. Did he do wrong to suggest it?"

She busied her hands with the sewing, jerking the needle through the cloth. Bedwyr noticed it held no thread. At last she looked up. "Your smith was right. I know where Constantine is. Or was, when I saw him several years since, and it's likely he's still there. Whether he keeps your sword, I know not. I hope it's been melted in the fires of hell."

Her anger took him aback. "Has Constantine done you harm?"

"Yes! He did me harm. He did me great harm."

She rethreaded the needle and began to sew again, pricked her finger and sucked it, then gave it up. She looked up at him, her eyes red rimmed. "I hoped I'd left it behind and forgotten, but I see that you will have it from me. Very well. You're entitled to hear it."

Clutching at the fabric in her lap she began to speak. "When Medraut . . ." She glanced at Bedwyr, then quickly away. "When my husband turned against Arthur and usurped the throne, his actions forced me to a decision. My family supported Arthur. I supported him too, Bedwyr, whatever you may think. I had to choose between my family and my husband. I chose my family. I chose Arthur. And I brought my children home to the villa to live."

She squeezed the tunic against her stomach. "I had three boys, Bedwyr, do you remember? All of them beautiful, so lithe and handsome. They wanted to be cavalry officers like you when they grew up. They admired you. We all did."

Bedwyr nodded absently. Her words had brought back memories as painful to him as Elyn's were to her. He had been admiring a hawk belonging to his brother Lucas when the messenger galloped into Arthur's camp with the word: Medraut had claimed the High Kingship and imprisoned Gwenhwyfar. The look of shock on Lucas's face still haunted him. And within a month Lucas was dead, and Arthur. Why did they die while he survived?

Elyn continued, "My father died at Camlann, you know that. Medraut also, of course. So many people died. When the war ended, my brother Caerdin and I swore loyalty to Constantine, though he was not Arthur."

She hugged herself, shivering, staring at the floor. "Constantine was a Christian, as I am—or at least he observed the Christian holidays. A year after Camlann he invited some of his supporters to Isca to spend Christmas—Caerdin and me, too, so we went. We took with us my oldest sons, Llachar and Glyn. Irion, the youngest, lay bed-sick with a fever, not serious, but uncomfortable for him to travel. So we left him at home." She smiled sadly. "He was very angry with me."

Her voice sank to nearly a whisper and the words flowed now like blood from a reopened wound. "On Christmas Eve I took my sons to Mass in the palace chapel. Afterward we stayed to pray. Only we three remained in the sanctuary when Constantine came in, dressed as a monk, which I thought odd. He would not look at me."

She stopped and Bedwyr thought she would say no more, but at last she continued. "Beneath his robe he was armed. He walked up behind my sons and drew his sword. I knew Caliburn: I remember the amethyst winking in the candlelight. When he drew the sword his face changed and his eyes became bright and strange."

Tears welled up in her eyes and without a sound spilled down her cheeks. "Then he m-murdered my sons. I could do nothing. I hit at him. I clawed him. He simply pushed me away and walked out. I suppose he thought Medraut's children a threat to his crown, but God knows they weren't."

Bedwyr stared at her, sickened. Elyn's children, too. And his disobedience of Arthur had caused the murders, as certainly as if he had wielded the sword himself.

She took a deep breath. "I held my wits together long enough to remember the danger to Irion, and I sent a servant galloping back to the villa. I learned later he arrived only an hour ahead of Constantine's men. On my orders, the servant took Irion from his sickbed and across the Sabrina into Caerwent, to Honorius, Irion's great-uncle. The servant told them we had died of a fever, also on my orders."

"That you also died?" Bedwyr said. "But why?"

She sighed. "I feared if Irion knew the truth he would come seeking Constantine one day and himself be killed. And Honorius, had he known what happened, would have felt obligated to start a blood feud with Constantine's clan, which would have meant war with Dumnonia. Under the Roman clothes, the old dear is British, after all. There was already too much war, Bedwyr, too much killing."

"And later, did you let them know?"

She lifted her shoulders helplessly. "I wanted to. But Irion was settled by then into a better life in Caerwent. What could I offer him here?"

She rose and began pacing, setting the rushes to whispering under her feet. "I said there had been too much killing. But I determined to cause one more death: Constantine's. I vowed to myself I would kill him, whatever the cost. But a short time after—after that Christmas, he disappeared. Rumor said he just renounced his throne and walked away. If anyone knew where he went, no one said. Still, I resolved to find him. So I persuaded my brother and our house guards to help me and we looked. It took months, but we found him, in Ynys Afallon, a Christian monk. A monk!" She laughed bitterly.

"I went to see him. I hid a dagger in my sleeve and went to see this murderer. Morgan would not have welcomed me had she known my thoughts."

Elyn shook her head and sat on the edge of the chair. "But I couldn't do it, Bedwyr. Constantine had lost his mind, or most of it. I don't even think he knew me. He just sat there and smiled and nodded his head when I accused him. How could I kill something like that? So I left him. As far as I know he's there still."

"I'm sorry," Bedwyr said, lost in misery. It was such an inadequate thing to say, but it was all he could think of. As he listened, his bitterness toward her drained away. He picked up the horn and handed it to her. She took it from him, cupped both hands around it and drank, then gave it back.

Silence settled on them. Elyn sat lost in her own thoughts, while Bedwyr tried to find something to offer her for solace.

At last she stirred and lifted her head. "Have I answered your question?"

"I had no knowledge of this," he said. "I would not have awakened such an evil memory. It may be of comfort to know I came lately from Caerwent. I saw your son."

Elyn's hand flew to her mouth. "Saw you Irion?"

"Aye. Though I didn't know him until he gave his name. He's a fine-looking man. Tribune of Gwent." He did not mention the help Irion sought from him, nor his refusal.

"Tribune. That's wonderful." Pride shone from her eyes. "And Honorius, how does he?"

Bedwyr hesitated. "He's been killed, Elyn. An assassin."

Her face again became grim. "Bad news on the heels of good. Who killed him?"

"The Saxon chieftain Ceawlin, I was told."

"An evil omen." Folding her sewing, she laid it in the basket and rose. "Forgive me, Bedwyr. I am tired. Will you excuse me?"

He stood. "Of course."

"You're welcome here as long as you wish to stay. Sleep well, Bedwyr." She smiled wanly and disappeared into a chamber at the end of the hall.

The next morning, when Bedwyr pushed back the hide covering and stepped through the doorway of his hut, he found Elyn already at work, talking with a group of men. The warm morning held a promise of rain. Seeing him, she left off and came over with a bright smile that held no trace of last night's shadow. Brys, his dimpled captor of the day before, tagged behind her. The boy looked up at him with shining eyes, convinced by now he was the real Companion.

"We broke fast already," she said, "but the cooks will find you something if you're hungry. I hope your sleeping quarters proved comfortable."

"They were fine." Bedwyr smiled. "Arthur always said I could sleep hanging from a peg."

She studied him. "What will you do now, Bedwyr? Will you go to Ynys Afallon?"

"Aye."

He'd intended to leave this morning, but now he dreaded setting out on the long walk. His muscles ached and his feet remained swollen and sore.

As if reading his thoughts she said, "Why not stay another day and rest? You're in no shape to be walking all that way. Besides, I'd like your advice on our defenses."

He hesitated, then yielded. "In truth, I wasn't looking forward to traveling today."

After he ate, Elyn introduced him to Cas, the captain of her small band of warriors. A tall man, too thin, with a worried expression that had made a permanent nest on his face, he limped over and greeted Bedwyr stiffly.

"While you have traveled the world, Lord Bedwyr," he said, "we've been preparing to defend our home from the man who defeated you."

Elyn shot him a warning look but Bedwyr ignored the remark. "How many trained fighters have you?"

Cas paused to think. "Twenty-four men and nineteen women. Enough to defend these walls. I designed them myself."

"Did you so?" said Bedwyr. "Yet perhaps we can improve them."

They walked around the perimeter of the palisade made of logs about eight feet tall, carved to a point on top and dug into the hill.

"Were I in charge," Bedwyr said, "I would dig a deep ditch outside these logs and pile the earth from it into a dike below. As it stands, the wall is too low and too easy to scale."

Cas's scowl faded and he looked thoughtful.

"You should also add three of four more ladders around the inside walls so that reserves can be quickly rushed to any point on the wall."

They walked back inside, Bedwyr pointing out a weakness here, making a suggestion there. Cas's hostility grudgingly gave way to a look of respect.

He turned to Elyn. "Lord Bedwyr's suggestions make

sense. With your permission, lady, I'll start on them right away."

"Of course, Cas, if you agree. I trust your judgment."

"He means well," she said to Bedwyr as she watched him limp away, "although he is overly proud. Thank you. He accepted your suggestions more easily than he would have mine."

An old man, brown and weathered, with short, bowed legs, clumped up and stood timidly at Elyn's elbow, looking at Bedwyr with reverence.

"Yes, Gwurgi?" she asked.

"It be Buttercup, missus," he said, not taking his eyes off Bedwyr. "She still got the hoosh. I looked at her this morning and she be worse. Would Bedwyr Mawr come and see her, I'm asking?"

Elyn looked at Bedwyr with an apologetic smile and spoke in Latin. "Buttercup is a nanny goat, one of our best milkers. To these folk a famed warrior like you can do anything. Would you come with me and look, to please him?"

"A goat? I know nothing of sick goats, my lady."

"It matters little. The goat will die. She has a sickness that makes her cough and refuse to eat, and there's no cure that we know. But it will comfort Gwurgi if you look."

He shrugged and Gwurgi led them to a long byre on the other side of the *dun*. Behind them came Brys, and alongside the boy trotted Fergus, inspecting the frightened chickens with interest.

The byre was dark and warm and Bedwyr smelled the stench of pig dung. A dozen hogs lay fanwise in a corner, greeting them with sulky grunts.

In a stall at the far end they found a small black goat. She stood with her legs wide apart, head drooping, turning liquid eyes to Gwurgi in patient suffering.

"Buttercup," announced the herdsman, looking at Bedwyr expectantly.

Bedwyr scratched his head and walked slowly around the nanny, pretending to study her. He had no clues to what caused her distress, and not a glimmering of what to do about it. If it were an infected wound, then perhaps. But this. Gwurgi's gaze followed him anxiously around the animal.

He tried to think of something. Anything. "Have you any vinegar?" he asked.

"Aye," said the herdsman, brightening.

Bedwyr did his best to conceal his disappointment, trying to come up with something they would not have. "What of centaury?"

Gwurgi looked dubious and Bedwyr felt a moment of hope. But Elyn, a gleam of laughter lurking behind her eyes, said, "We keep some dried centaury among the herbs. Run and get it, please, Brys."

They mixed the centaury leaves with vinegar in a bit of broken pot. Gwurgi tilted up the goat's head and Bedwyr poured some of the mixture into each nostril. He was startled when the animal broke away and sank to the ground with a gasp.

The herdsman beamed at the strong reaction, looking from the heaving beast to Bedwyr as if he were a Druid. Bedwyr would have been flattered had he not expected the goat to die instantly. Her value he calculated as equal to half his silver arm ring. He looked at the ground, he looked at the goat, he looked at the rafters—anywhere to avoid Elyn's eye.

Suddenly the goat lurched to her feet with a tremendous cough and began to eat her fodder. Gwurgi hooted with delight and thanked Bedwyr profusely.

He shrugged. "It always works."

The rest of the morning he walked with Elyn as she made the rounds of the *dun*, supervising the daily activities. He had forgotten how comfortable she was to be with, how the rightness of her fitted him like a favorite garment. He pushed back the thought.

Outside one bothy a small group of children clustered around an olive-skinned old man.

"Our school," she said proudly, and a little sadly. "We're fortunate to still have Simmias the Greek to teach them, though the barbarians burned my library. They took our memory, Bedwyr, and our children grow up ignorant in spite of our efforts. Of what use is reading if there are no scrolls?" She ruffled Brys's hair, who grimaced. "And if it will not help to hunt deer or catch fish?"

Near midday the sun slipped from behind the clouds and

they took barley loaves, slices of cold venison, and tangy heather beer outside the gate to sit by themselves on the warm south slope. The wolfhound flopped down beside Elyn, his gaze following every morsel of food into their mouths. Though his dignity did not allow him to beg, he was not above shaming humans into sharing their meal.

While they ate, Bedwyr watched the forest below them stretching away into the distance until its trees became dark fur on the rolling hills. He lay back on his elbow and smelled the scent of the earth, soothing and rich. For the moment the ghosts of his past seemed far away. There are times, he thought, to lie still on the grass and listen to nothing louder than the roots of things growing.

In the distance a strand of smoke drifted upward in the still air. Elyn saw it. "There is hardly a day without smoke in the sky from some steading going up in flames," she said. "A shadow falls over the land, Bedwyr. I can feel its chill."

"But not today," he said. "Today nothing matters but that the sun shines and the sweet air is warm."

She smiled and plucked a pale yellow primrose from the grass, bringing it to her nose. "It's wonderful to see you. It's been an age."

"Aye. I've grown old since."

"You're not old."

He shrugged, smiling. "Within a finger's width of it."

They sat in comfortable silence. Finally, he looked sidelong at her, working up courage to ask the question that nagged at him. He blurted: "Why him, Elyn?"

Her fingers stopped plucking at the flower.

"It was a lifetime ago," she said slowly. "Medraut was handsome and highborn. He would be king after Arthur. I wanted to be a queen."

She glanced at him, as if afraid he would laugh at her, but he looked at the ground. She put her hand on his. "You would have been a kind and gentle husband, Bedwyr, but you were a warrior and always would be. I wanted more, though I loved you."

He looked at her in surprise.

"And anyway," she added, "you never asked."

"I did not," he admitted. "It was because I couldn't find

[113]

voice for the words that gathered on my tongue. But you knew how I felt."

"A woman needs to be asked, Bedwyr."

"Aye. I know that now. Would it have made a difference?"

She sighed. "No. Not then. Then, my life was like a dream and I moved through it with little thought for anyone but myself. People existed to make me happy. There were feasts and music and laughter. And the villa, the beautiful rooms, and important visitors." She smiled, remembering. "My marriage feast lasted a week. I was young and it was all going to last forever."

She squeezed his hand and withdrew hers. "But you, Bedwyr, you always drove women to distraction. None of us were impervious to your charm, though I think you were never aware of it. Have there been no other women since Eneva died?"

He shrugged. "I've lain with one for warmth, or to share the rain of a winter's night. Not from love. I don't think I even loved Eneva. Marriage was a duty to be undertaken."

How could I have loved anyone after you? he thought. But he did not say it.

In the afternoon the sun disappeared again above shaggy clouds that piled on top of the forest. After the evening meal Bedwyr stood in the open doorway of the feast hall looking out at a soft, gray rain. Elyn came up behind him, stirring a breeze that brought the smell of her crushed-flower perfume.

"What see you in the rain?"

"It's full of wraiths tonight."

She drew him away from the door. "Come inside. We'll shut out the rain and I'll play for you."

She pulled the stool near the hearth and placed the harp upon it, its strings glistening in the light from the fire. Drawing it to her, she settled it in the hollow of her shoulder. For a few moments she gazed into the fire, then swept a glissando from the strings. Another followed, and from it a melody emerged, clear and lucent, bright notes that flew like sparks from the hearth toward the distant rafters.

Against the shining melody her fingers wove a hint of a darker, sadder melody, echoing the most ancient Celtic song. As he listened, the darker air swelled and grew and submerged in it the bright tune, and then it, too, died away to a murmur.

Elyn began to sing, in a voice sweet and sad, of dark fires and lost kingdoms, of dying stars and the song of the first bird. Then the harp surged again with a beauty to burst the heart, and the music cascaded over him like a silver waterfall. He stood and walked to the unshuttered window, looking out, for he felt that the shimmering notes might easily turn to tears in his eyes.

At that moment he knew she had won, and was surprised, for only then did he become aware of the depth of his struggle against her, a ghost that had lain down with him, had risen up with him, and stood ever between him and the sun.

He turned, and laying a hand on the strings to still the music, bent to her.

Once during the night he awoke with a start, sweating, and groped for his missing sword. She reached out to him and drew him back beneath the sheepskins, comforting him. Lying in his arms, she absently traced the whiteness of a faded scar on his chest. Moonlight from the clearing sky hung like a white curtain in the window, while water dripped from the thatched eaves.

"Is the song I sing worth the learning?" she asked.

He smiled. "It sang already in my memory."

"What a fool I was. From the day I knew I loved you not a day has passed that you were not moving in my heart. And when I sat alone and listened to the loom clack by the hearth on winter evenings, in my mind moved the shadow of a dark-haired warrior. To have wasted all those years."

He stilled her with a kiss. "Tonight's joy is fair payment for yesterday's loss."

They made love again, with less urgency this time, a deep wave that rolled in from the world's beginning, lifting them, washing over them and leaving them gasping.

FIFTEEN

Although his unfinished quest nagged at the corners of his mind, Bedwyr found excuses to delay leaving. He helped work on the improvements to the stockade and taught Brys and his brothers to catch trout by tickling their bellies. For the first time in long years he welcomed the nights, for he shared them with Elyn and the nightmares remained at bay.

One morning she came to him, eyes sparkling, manner mysterious. "I have a gift for you," was all she would say.

Near the cow byre Gwurgi waited, grinning, a leather bucket of grain in his hand.

Bedwyr gave her a sideways glance. "Buttercup again?"

"No, no." She laughed. "Buttercup is fine. Just come with us."

The morning shone warm and bright with a breeze that herded a few lamb's-wool clouds slowly over the *dun*. They passed through the gate and walked down the slope into the forest. A path led them to a brook, where they turned and walked upstream until they came to a natural clearing of lush grass, with dense whitethorn forming a natural barrier around it. Across the stream stretched a wood fence.

Gwurgi slid back the poles that served as a gate and motioned Bedwyr through. Then he put his fingers to his mouth and blew a shrill whistle.

At the far end of the pasture, a stallion lifted its head and looked at them, ears pricked forward in curiosity. The horse stood tall, over sixteen hands, and his coat, mane, and tail shone as white as the winter peak of Yr Widdfa. He carried himself like a ten-point stag, the curve of his arching neck marking his spirit and his pride.

Bedwyr turned to Elyn, a question starting, and she said, smiling, "No. It's not Rhyfelwr, Arthur's war stallion. But he's a full brother—by the same sire, out of the same mare, foaled the year before Camlann."

Bedwyr shook his head slowly. "I would not have thought it possible there could be another stallion so like Rhyfelwr. Does he resemble him in temperament as well?"

She nodded. "He has a great heart."

Gwurgi held the grain bucket high in the air and thumped it with his knuckles. The stallion nickered and galloped toward them, alive with the sheer joy of running, his mane and tail streaming like spindrift.

"He is the last," said Elyn, "and it's not fair to him to keep him closed in like this, alone. He's yours, Bedwyr, if you'll have him."

"If I will have him?" Bedwyr watched the stallion glide toward him. "He moves like a spirit." Watching him, Bedwyr understood why Saxons thought white horses were supernatural. He was a horse that Llyr, the Wind, would be proud to ride. "I thank you, lady, from the depth of my heart."

As he neared them the stallion slowed to a trot and danced up to Gwurgi, stretching his nose toward the grain. Elyn scooped up a handful and held it out, and the horse nibbled it delicately from her hand.

"Has he a name?" Bedwyr asked.

"I call him Ariant," she said.

"The Silver One. Fitting." He scratched behind the stallion's ears. "Is he trained?"

"Aye. He was Caerdin's favorite colt and he worked long with him, though it's some years since he's been put through his paces. Shall I have Gwurgi bring a saddle and bridle?"

Absently Bedwyr shook his head, lost in the feel of the sleek muscles under his hand as he stroked Ariant's shoulder. At the caresses and soft words the stallion's eyes glazed, spellbound, and Bedwyr sprang lightly onto his back.

The great stallion lifted his head in surprise and tensed his powerful muscles, uncertain, deciding whether to rid himself of the human on his back. Before he could act, the man guided him away from the fence and into the meadow. Ariant found himself trotting, then cantering, then in a full gallop. His heart pounded fiercely with the pleasure of running. The man sat lightly on his back and rode him as if they were one, moving with him, anticipating him.

Then the human willed him to stop and he did. He felt a cue from the man's legs that he had not felt for many seasons. He hesitated, probing the memories of his muscles for the meaning of the signal, then went up in a rearing half-turn, swinging on his hind legs and slashing at an imaginary enemy with his forehoofs.

Another cue came and the stallion remembered, wheeling and kicking out with his deadly hind legs. More signals and Ariant responded, at first uncertainly, but soon quickly and smoothly, until his muscles felt warm and sweat soaked his chest.

At last the man guided him quietly back to the fence where the other humans waited. He slid from his back and came around to his head, offering him a handful of the sweet grain. Ariant accepted it, then butted him gently in the stomach with his nose. The man understood and scratched behind his ears. The stallion snorted. He'd waited a long time.

The day came when Bedwyr could no longer ignore the nagging urgency of his task, and one evening as they sipped mead before the hearth, he told Elyn he must leave.

Her hands, running softly across the harp strings, stilled. "How soon?" she said.

"In the morning."

Silence held them for a moment, then he added, "You've not asked why I seek Caliburn, and for your forbearance I'm grateful. But I would not have this between us while we're apart."

She folded her hands in her lap, watching him.

"Eleven years since, as the King lay dying on the field of Camlann," Bedwyr said, "he placed his sword in my hand, ordering me to cast it into the mere close by the battlefield. That was the first I had touched Caliburn. In it I sensed something." He frowned, groping for the words. "Not magic, I think, but a sense of some purpose or strength. I think now that it was only the disquiet in my mind.

"I rode to the mere intending to carry out Arthur's command. But I was young, and still believed in his dream. Instead of hurling Caliburn into the water I hid it in a hollow tree, thinking, I suppose, that someone else worthy of it might yet come. Constantine must have seen me hide it and later retrieved it."

He spread his hands in a gesture of helplessness. "Had I obeyed, Constantine might not have murdered two of your sons, and the third would have grown up at your side."

She leaned forward and slid her hand into his. "You are mortal, as I am, love, and we cannot see as much as the flicker of a candle flame into the future. Decisions that are fair seeming when made may later prove ill. I will not blame you for this thing."

Bedwyr took the comfort she intended.

She smiled at him. "I would hear more about Irion before you leave. What is he like?"

"I know little about him," he said, uncomfortable. "I saw him only once." He did his best to describe the youth he had met in Caerwent, trying to conceal from Elyn the abhorrence he had felt when he looked at him.

She was not fooled. "You dislike him."

Bedwyr did not look at her. "He is Medraut's son."

"And Arthur's grandson. And my son."

"He is Medraut's son."

"Irion cannot help who his father was," she said, "any more than you or I." She gazed into the fire, her hands moving idly across the harp strings. "I think that I will travel to Caerwent when harvest is done, to see my son. There is much I would like to tell him, to make him understand."

"There is another thing you should know," Bedwyr said. "Irion seeks to unite the Cymry against Ceawlin, and he sought my help in doing so. I refused."

She stopped playing and looked at him, her face unreadable. "Why, Bedwyr?"

"The problems of the British are of their own making. I am quit of them."

"I don't believe that. I know you. You haven't changed, not

deep inside. You're bitter and hurt and you blame yourself for Arthur's defeat. It's time you forgave yourself. Then perhaps you can forgive the rest of us."

Her words nettled him. "How can you know what I feel? It's true I once fought for something more than survival, but that was a foolish dream. The barbarians have won, Elyn. I've spent a lifetime fighting them, walking in their darkness, feeling it, tasting it. When you wander that long in their world of cruelty you cannot escape its taint. Even when we defeat them in battle they win, after all, in the end."

She did not argue. When he finished she said, "Come back when you can, Bedwyr. The hearth will be desolate without you."

His anger embarrassed him. "I'll come back, Elyn, *gwyn*," he said. "I've learned that love dies hard in the heart; however you may kill it in the mind."

"Then take care. I'll still be here for you to find me."

SIXTEEN

The causeway ended at the edge of the lake and Bedwyr reined in Ariant, gazing out at the island. At his feet the water made stealthy lapping sounds as it licked the rushes.

He had ridden all day through lowland marsh, a land of lagoons and streams, of trembling bogs and stagnant pools; a land that seemed empty save for insects and water birds; widgeon that churned the water as they rose, startled, and herons that flew lumbering away from their hunting at his approach. Deep in the marsh the shallow lake lay suspended like green glass in the reeds. As he watched, the sunset kindled the water to flame.

Here Arthur had left him. Here he had promised to destroy Caliburn, and had disobeyed. He fought down a surge of guilt and anguish. For an instant he wondered if the High King, himself, waited on the island to punish him. Then he dismissed the thought. Arthur was dead.

Bedwyr gazed out over the water. From the center of the lake climbed Ynys Afallon, a tor that rose on one end to a rounded peak, then dipped downward to a gently sloping shoulder before plunging back into the water: The Isle of Apples. Across its lower slopes, wherever a foothold existed, huddled turf-roofed bothies, cells for the Christian monks. At the top of the tor an ancient grove of twisted oaks grew like a living crown. There still lived the priestesses of a belief much older than that of the Christians, for the boundaries of religion were less guarded here. And there would be Arthur's sister, Morgan, the high priestess and healer.

Bedwyr's stomach tightened. He had no desire to see

Morgan. Perhaps she was not a witch, as many said. And he did not believe she was evil; she had often helped Arthur. But there was something about her that daunted him and he had no wish to discuss his quest with her. He hoped there would be no need. Constantine was a Christian, and if he were still on the island, he would probably be found in the community of monks on the lower slopes.

Bedwyr unsaddled Ariant and removed the bridle. The stallion folded his legs under him, lay down, and rolled in the dirt of the path. Standing, he shook himself like a dog, then began to crop the coarse marsh grass.

In the reeds at the water's edge Bedwyr found a coracle partly full of muddy water. He bailed the water from it with a rush basket, then turned to Fergus.

"Keep Ariant out of trouble for me," he said, tugging at the dog's ears. "I hope to be back tomorrow."

Fergus looked up, tail wagging, not at all unhappy about staying on the shore. Bedwyr stepped into the boat and stroked with the broad-bladed paddle to move the craft into the lake.

It was nearly dark when he gave a final pull on the oar and the boat drifted into a pier that poked out from the island. Its boards creaked and complained as Bedwyr climbed onto it.

Groups of monks made their way through the dusk toward a stone building surrounded by huts. He caught up with a straggler, a gangling youth, slope shouldered beneath his robe, who mumbled as he walked, punctuating his comments by waves of his arms.

"Bid you good evening," said Bedwyr.

The monk continued his agitated muttering. Bedwyr clasped his shoulder and the startled cleric jumped and spun around with a yelp. When he saw the sword he gasped and put his hand over his mouth.

"I mean you no harm. Can you tell me where to find the Abbot Gildas?"

The monk stared at him blankly for a moment, then pointed upward. "In God's holy heaven, I'm sure. Brother Gildas died last Christmas." He peered at Bedwyr curiously. "I thought everyone knew that. You must be a foreigner. You speak Celtic well."

"I've been away. Who is your new abbot and where might I find him?"

The monk smiled and pointed upward again. Seeing Bedwyr's confusion he laughed. "No, no. Abbot Worgret is up in the abbey for compline. You may attend. But you'll have to leave that outside." He looked at the sword. Bedwyr nodded and the monk turned and hurried after the others, his robe wrapping around his ankles as he ran.

At the door of the gray stone abbey Bedwyr paused to unbuckle his baldric and prop the sheathed sword against the wall. Inside, the rows of benches looked nearly filled, mostly by robed monks, tonsured heads bowed. But Bedwyr saw many other people as well, most of them injured and seemingly bewildered.

He scanned the room but saw no one who looked like Constantine. Toward the far end a stone-pillared divider separated the chancel from the worshipers. An altar of darkened wood, on which stood a plain wooden cross painted white, occupied most of the chancel.

In front of the altar stood a man whom Bedwyr took to be Abbot Worgret. Grim and scowling, with patches of dark purple under his eyes and a bald head corrugated like a walnut shell, the abbot waited impatiently for the congregation to be settled.

Bedwyr found a space against the back wall and squeezed into it. The room felt warm and close, smelling of old wax and incense, and as the chanting droned on he closed his eyes for a moment.

He was jostled awake as the monks on either side of him rose to leave, the service over. One of them gave him a reproving look as he stepped over his outstretched legs.

Bedwyr looked around for the abbot and found him standing at the door watching the worshipers file out.

"Abbot Worgret?" He addressed him in Latin.

The abbot turned, his gaze sweeping Bedwyr from head to foot. "I am Worgret."

"My name is Bedwyr ap Gruffydd. I'm looking for a man who I believe lives here. It's a matter of great importance that I talk with him."

"There are many men living here, as you see. All of them are under the protection of the Holy Church." His scowl deepened. "Are you from over there?" He stuck his thumb in the direction of Camelot.

"No. I fought with Arthur. I seek this man only to speak with him."

"What is his name?"

"Constantine, formerly King of Dumnonia, and Arthur's heir."

The abbot's eyes flickered but his face remained impassive. "There is no one here by that name."

Something in his tone alerted Bedwyr. "He may be using his British name, Custennin ap Goreu."

Worgret gave him a black look. "One of our brothers does use that name. But he's very ill and will speak to no one from the outside. I'm sorry you've wasted a journey."

He turned away, then paused as if remembering his obligation to travelers. "All the guest cells are full but you may spend the night here on one of the pews if you wish." He strode out the door.

Bedwyr rubbed the back of his neck in frustration.

From the chancel a voice said, "He's not as bad as that, truly. Only he does not like warriors."

He turned to see a monk watching him with amusement. The man looked powerfully built, with a kind, round face full of old regrets and a brown beard grizzled with the frosts of the years. Bedwyr looked closer.

"Cethrum!" he cried, delighted. "Is it you, then?"

He went to the chancel and embraced him. "I wouldn't have recognized you with your new haircut. I never imagined you in a place like this."

The monk patted his tonsured head, smiling. "Where better for Arthur's priest to stay out of trouble than in a monastery? Is it well with you, Bedwyr?"

"Well enough. Aye."

"I thought . . ." the priest began.

"That I was dead?" Bedwyr smiled. "You're in good company."

Cethrum studied him for a moment, beaming, then seemed to remember his task. He turned and resumed snuffing out the candles, wetting his thumb and forefinger and pinching the burning wicks.

"Worgret becomes grouchy when we waste candle wax," he said. "But then, Worgret is usually grouchy about one thing or another. I think it's his digestion."

He looked over his shoulder at Bedwyr. "There's no need to sleep on a pew. My cell is small but there's room for two, and my pallet is softer than the wood of these benches."

Bedwyr declined but Cethrum insisted. "You'd be doing me a service by taking my bed, for the abbot rightly urges us to subdue the comforts of the flesh. The ground will do my spirit good."

Before putting out the last candle he touched the burning wick to a small lantern, setting it glowing. "Come," he said and lumbered through the aisle toward the door, his walk the rolling gait of an autumn-fattened bear.

Bedwyr retrieved his sword from the wall and followed. Ahead he heard the flap of Cethrum's sandals and saw the lantern flash and wink as it swung in his hand. The lantern stopped at a hive-shaped mud hut and disappeared inside.

Stooping, Bedwyr pushed aside the door covering and found himself in a tiny, windowless cell, barely large enough for him to stand upright. A single straw pallet served as furniture. On one wall a shelf held a few simple items, and a cloak hung from a peg nearby. Against the wall leaned a hazel-twig broom for sweeping the dirt floor.

Cethrum stuck the lantern in a niche in the wall and sat cross-legged on the pallet, and Bedwyr did the same.

"I'm sorry we cannot offer you better lodgings," the priest said. "The island is filled with refugees and we're as cramped as toes in a tight boot. We take all we have room for, but still we must turn some away."

"Peasants burned out by Ceawlin?"

"Aye. Most of them. As things worsen in Britain they flee to monasteries, trusting in God's protection."

"And will your God protect Ynys Afallon from the Saxons, think you?" Bedwyr asked.

"Perhaps it's more the lake that protects us," Cethrum said with a smile. "Ceawlin ignores us because we're not worth the trouble to him, and he knows we have nothing here worth taking. Also, I think he fears Morgan."

The priest suddenly grinned white in the gloom. "God's

Breath, Bedwyr. Seeing you again is like rain on wilted lettuce. Start at the beginning and tell me where you've been since Camlann?"

Once again Bedwyr told of his time with Belisarius. They talked far into the night while the lantern flickered, casting moving shadows on the ceiling.

When Cethrum's questions finally stopped, Bedwyr stretched out his legs and crossed them, leaning against the wall. "And you, my friend," he said, "you never seemed one for the cloistered life. How came you here?"

Cethrum gathered his beard into one hand and stroked it thoughtfully. "In truth, the isolation begins to wear on me, and I sometimes feel it's time to move on. But when I came here I needed rest. I'd been wandering through Britain since Camlann, completing my work, and was worn from traveling."

"Completing your work?"

"Aye." The priest peered at him. "I would speak of it to no one but you, Bedwyr, or one of the other Companions, if any were left." He hesitated. "Remember how you carried the King from the field that evil day?"

Bedwyr frowned at the mention of it. He saw in his mind the blood-stained litter made from cloaks and spear shafts, Arthur lying on it pale in death. "I remember as if divided from it by only one night's sleep," he said. "Would that I could forget. Why do you speak of this?"

"Arthur's fall began the death of Britain," said the priest. "I knew it then as clearly as I see you here now. We slide into long years of barbarism, whose end no man can see."

He heaved himself up and began pacing, his bulk cramming the cell. "Arthur was all the common folk of Britain had, Bedwyr. After he fell, who did they have left to think of them? When the barbarians slaughtered their kin and burned their steadings, what could they cling to, to give them hope?"

He glanced at Bedwyr. "That sounds odd, I know, coming from a Christian priest. But to the peasants, the teachings of the Christ still sit lightly on top of their ancient beliefs, and provide little comfort for this life."

His head scraped the ceiling, bringing down a shower of dust and thatch, which he ignored. "I don't know if I did right before God, but I feel in my heart He will understand. An idea came to me. I spread the tale that King Arthur did not die, that Morgan put him into a deep sleep, and that he rests in a cave in the Hollow Hills beneath Camelot, waiting until the need of his people is great. Then he will come forth to save them."

Bedwyr stared at the priest in astonishment.

"You had disappeared," he continued, "and I couldn't tell you what I intended. I traveled eastward as far as the Saxon holdings, then north. For years I passed through the land talking with the people, telling them the story. You needed to see their faces, Bedwyr, the look of hope when I told them. If I had not done it, I think they would have created the belief themselves." He stopped pacing and looked at Bedwyr for a response.

Bedwyr searched his own feelings. To his surprise he found no anger. After a moment he said, "I find no fault with what you did, for what man does not need some hope to fasten his life to? Perhaps if I knew such hope now, the years behind would not seem a waste of breath. And if it keeps the British from despair as the Saxon tide rolls over them, I think Arthur would have approved."

Cethrum looked relieved. "Even the Saxons believe it," he said, "for they are terrified by magic. They think everyone else's spells are more powerful than their own." He eased himself onto the pallet.

For a time there was silence, until Bedwyr brought himself to speak of Caliburn and his disobedience to Arthur's final order. "I seek the sword now," he said, "and to find it I need to find Constantine of Dumnonia."

"He's here!" Cethrum said, startled. "Though he prefers the name Custennin now. But he has never spoken of Caliburn to me, and I care for him daily."

"Then he is in fact ill?"

"He's dying. He clings to life desperately, as if afraid of what awaits him."

"Will he speak to me?"

The priest tugged on his earlobe. "Possibly, since he once knew you. But I fear you will get no profit from it."

"Why?"

"He's unhinged, Bedwyr. I seem to be the only one he

responds to, perhaps because of the old days. Sometimes, when I can persuade him to take a bite or two of food, he's almost normal. Then I tell him stories of the good years and he smiles. If you like, you can come with me in the morning when I take him his breakfast. He's clearest in his head then. But do not expect overmuch."

SEVENTEEN

The crow of a rooster awakened Bedwyr. As he sat up, groggy, the door flap lifted and Cethrum entered, looking annoyingly cheerful, a steaming wooden bowl in his hand.

"I go to feed Custennin now. Do you wish to come?"

Bedwyr pulled on his boots, looked at his sword, thought better of it, and followed the priest out of the hut. The dawn felt chill and clammy, with only a gray, shadowless light to tell him the sun had risen.

Constantine's cell looked identical to the other huts, and as Cethrum ducked through the opening, Bedwyr followed. The sour smell of death hung in the air. On a cot lay a man whose gaunt form barely disturbed the blanket and whose breath labored harshly in his thin chest. Long hair the color of cobwebs framed a face that fell in sharply around his cheekbones. His eyes were open but they had the wandering blankness of a newborn infant.

As they entered, Constantine's gaze passed over Bedwyr without recognition and stopped on the priest. His face cracked into a ghastly smile.

"Good morning, Brother Custennin," said Cethrum cheerfully. "I bring you breakfast."

He set the bowl on the ground and knelt, lifting Constantine's head and cradling it in his arm. "Try to swallow some broth this morning, brother. There's much to do and you need to get well."

He put a spoonful of the warm liquid to Constantine's lips. The dying man opened his mouth and swallowed feebly, most of the broth trickling down his cheek. After a few spoonfuls he coughed and waved the priest away irritably.

"You'll drown me." His once-strong voice was no more than wind blowing through reeds. "I'll die soon enough, anyway. Who is that?" His watery gaze focused on Bedwyr.

"I'm Bedwyr ap Gruffydd." He stepped to the bed and squatted beside it. "I fought with Arthur. Do you remember me?"

A glimmer of recognition flickered in Constantine's eyes, and for the first time his face showed interest. "Did Arthur send you?" he whispered. "Tell him I'm doing my best."

"Arthur died," said Bedwyr.

Constantine's face fell. "Yes. He did, didn't he. I am High King now." He shook his head, trembling with the effort that memory cost him. "No, that's not right, either. I was High King but I abdicated to serve God." His gaze clung to Bedwyr's face like that of a drowning child. "I did right, didn't I? I had to, you see, because I . . . sinned. So I came here to live. I'm Brother Custennin now."

"You did rightly," Bedwyr said. "Constantine, do you remember the sword?"

"Brother Custennin. What sword?" He looked confused.

"Caliburn. Arthur's sword. Do you remember it?"

"Caliburn?" Constantine turned the word over in his mouth and spoke it again. "Caliburn. I remember a sword. A beautiful sword. But it did terrible things. It seemed good when I found it, but it turned evil. So I buried it."

Bedwyr swallowed. "Where did you bury it?"

But Constantine was suddenly on his guard. "I didn't truly bury it." He motioned for Cethrum to bend down. "Why does he want to know?"

The priest glanced at Bedwyr, who said, "Before he died, Arthur asked me to destroy Caliburn."

Constantine frowned and tried to speak, but instead coughed, a harsh, tearing sound with not enough breath in it. When he recovered, he wheezed and wiped his nose, peering at Bedwyr with eyes that glinted between half-shut lids. "I have already seen to that. Tell Arthur it will never be found. I did my best." His eyes closed. "Never be found." His lips continued to move but no more sounds came from them.

The words rang in Bedwyr's head like the tolling of a church bell. "Custennin?"

Constantine's eyes remained closed and his breathing grew regular. He slept.

Cethrum picked up the bowl and backed out of the hut, but Bedwyr remained by the cot, biting his lip in frustration.

"He will sleep now for a few hours," said the priest gently from the doorway. Finally Bedwyr rose and went outside.

"I'm sorry, Bedwyr," Cethrum said, as they walked back up the path. "I'm surprised he spoke of Caliburn at all. He had never done so before."

Deep in thought, Bedwyr stopped abruptly. "Cethrum, could Constantine have had the sword with him when he came to Ynys Afallon?"

The priest thought for a moment. "I don't think so. I came here after him, but there's no place on the island to hide something like that. Anyway, if he'd brought a sword as magnificent as Caliburn, someone would remember. There are no secrets here, as you can imagine. If someone saw it, I would know."

"May I speak with him again when he awakens?"

Cethrum looked doubtful. "I would suggest you wait until tomorrow morning. But don't hope for much. Come, we'll be late for matins."

Bedwyr spent the rest of the day with Cethrum, doing his best to stay busy and avoid thinking of what he would do if Constantine refused to speak to him. Between visits to the dying man the priest worked in a small chamber in the abbey, cleaning sheets of parchment for reuse.

Moving without haste, Cethrum soaked the sheepskin pages in a tub of meal and warm milk to soften them, then scraped them gently to erase the old ink. He paused often, as if the day were certain to be long and the task may as well be spread out. Bedwyr helped rub the softened parchment with a pumice stone.

"This is not warrior's work," Cethrum protested.

"Warriors would do well to put their hands to useful work when they're not fighting," Bedwyr said. "We have become like the Saxons, loving war as a sport and an end, and honoring warriors above men who perform other tasks or make beautiful things."

At dawn the next morning he returned with the priest to Constantine's cell. As they entered, the dying man opened his eyes and whispered to Cethrum for a drink of water. With the priest holding his head, he sipped from a wooden cup, then fell back, staring about him.

He saw Bedwyr and his body went rigid. The stretched face mottled with color. "Get out! Get out!" Spittle flew from his mouth. "It's Lucifer. Brothers, help me! Help!"

Bedwyr stood in shock as Constantine raved. Finally Cethrum looked at him helplessly and motioned for him to leave. He stepped from the hut, leaving Cethrum talking softly to his patient, calming him, until his raving became mumbling and then died away altogether.

When he was silent the priest emerged. "Forgive him, Bedwyr. When he becomes like this he's beyond reason."

"This has happened before?"

"When something upsets him, yes."

"Might he not forget about it in a day or two?"

Cethrum looked glum. "Not likely. Last winter he got it into his head that Abbot Worgret is the Antichrist. He still goes wild at the sight of him. I believe he has let his mind become possessed so he won't have to think about things that are very painful to him."

"I have no choice," Bedwyr said, "but to stay near him in the hope he will one day speak to me. I'll ask Worgret if I might stay."

"The abbot would no doubt let you. But he's not the one you must speak to. We Christians are guests on Ynys Afallon, and we abide by the wishes of the priestess of the old religion, for she has been here much longer than we."

Bedwyr's heart sank. Morgan. He had no desire to face Arthur's sister. There was something remote and forbidding about her.

Following Cethrum's directions he climbed to the top of the tor and passed through a tall grove of oaks, trunks gray with moss, whose branches swayed and creaked as if the trees whispered among themselves. It was a place where he felt the presence of the dark, strong powers of the earth.

On the far side of the grove a meadow lay green and glistening in the sunshine, and in it a woman supervised three brown-robed girls collecting herbs. As Bedwyr watched, one of the acolytes, a girl with a face as pale and round as a moonrise, brought the woman a plant with pinkish flowers on a long stalk.

"Yes," Morgan said. "Sanicle. See the five-pointed lobes?" Her voice held a rich, earthy warmth that seemed to rise from the center of a great stillness.

The girl nodded and went back to the place where she had found the plant.

Morgan gazed off eastward. Although Bedwyr could see nothing through the haze but sky and heather, wet mist and grass, she seemed to be watching something far in the distance. For a moment he stood silently, then he cleared his throat.

"The Goddess's greeting to you, Bedwyr," she said without turning.

"My pardon, lady, for disturbing you. You knew I was on Ynys Afallon?"

She turned, looking at him with dark eyes full of cold, dancing light. The sun caught the side of her face, so that she seemed to be a creature half of shadow, half of light. Although she did not smile, there was welcome in her eyes. "I knew," she said. She drew back the hood of her green cloak to reveal long, black hair with enough gray in it to prove wrong those who said Morgan never aged. "I see you have not fared well since we last met."

Disconcerted by her gaze, Bedwyr looked away. The defenses that shielded him from everyone else had never protected him from Morgan. He felt as if she could see directly into his heart. "There's been little enough reason for joy since my King died."

"But he was never yours, Bedwyr." Then seeing his confusion she added gently, "All things change. It is as it must be."

All at once his bitterness boiled over. "Easy words for someone whose life has not been squandered on a foolish dream." Instantly he regretted his outburst. "I apologize, lady. I do not mean to sound ungrateful for your help in years past."

Morgan's gaze searched his face. "Perhaps the pain of loss has not been less for me than for you. You believe that Arthur's life and yours were wasted?"

"How not? Look about you. Your island is surrounded by darkness."

"Yet darkness is also part of life. The fact that my brother died does not diminish the value of his living, Bedwyr. Or yours. Arthur's life was a promise, not that light will triumph over dark but that—" She paused, as if trying to find words for a thing that had no words. "—that the *becoming* will continue."

"The only becoming I see," Bedwyr said shortly, "is the world becoming a darker place."

She smiled sadly and touched him briefly on the chest. He felt a tingling warmth. "The becoming is in here, my friend."

Another acolyte approached timidly and presented an herb for Morgan's approval. "Shepherd's purse," Morgan told her. "You should know that. See the pods?"

When the girl had gone, she turned back to Bedwyr. "You seek Caliburn?"

Startled, Bedwyr stared at her. "You knew of that also?"

"I guessed. I have long felt that Caliburn has not been surrendered to the lake."

"It's true. For that I'm sorry."

"You owe me no apology, Bedwyr. It was not I who gave you the command. Yet perhaps you've been unable to accomplish your task because you've never understood why Arthur wanted the sword cast into the mere."

"I understand the sword has a great capacity for evil as well as good, lady."

"As do men. But there is another purpose. Look you, Bedwyr: Arthur tried to create a new order based on reason and strength. He was doomed to fail, for strength has limits and reasonable men differ. He understood that at the end."

Bedwyr was taken aback. "How, then, does one fight, if not with strength and reason?"

Morgan did not answer. Instead she gazed eastward again, toward Camelot. After a moment, she said, "Perhaps you keep your life too tightly reined, Bedwyr. Do you seek the sword here?"

"I did. I was told that Constantine possessed it. But he's hidden it and will not disclose its location. For that reason I've come to ask permission to stay on the island, near him."

"For how long? Until he dies?"

"It may be."

She looked at him thoughtfully and hard. Bedwyr lowered his eyes to avoid her gaze. "In other circumstances you would be welcome," she said. "The Isle is for the sick and wounded, and though your physical injuries have mended, it's plain you are in need of healing." She hesitated, then shook her head. "But your quest, I feel, cannot be accomplished here."

"You will not let me stay?"

"No. I'm sorry."

Bedwyr felt as if he had stepped off the bank of a deep river and the water was closing over his head. "Then have you any counsel as to where Caliburn might be found?"

"I am a healer, Bedwyr, not a seer," she said softly. "I do not know the sword's location. My only counsel is to go where your pain is, for there also is your life."

The moon-faced girl appeared at her side again, waiting to be recognized. Morgan smiled in apology to Bedwyr. "Forgive me, please. There is so much for them to learn, and the need on the island is great. Be well, Bedwyr." She walked away.

EIGHTEEN

Bedwyr left Ynys Afallon in a mist of despair. He rode slowly, making no effort at concealment. At some point he became dimly aware that darkness had fallen, and he stopped. He dragged stones into a circle and tried to set a fire burning in them, though he felt no cold. Spark followed useless spark until the tinder caught at last, and a small, clear tongue of flame sprang up. Around him the forest became a flickering green wall.

He lay down and closed his eyes tightly around the pain in his mind. Later he slept a little, but it provided no comfort, the interval of darkness providing only a brief interruption in his despair.

He rose at dawn. At a nearby stream he scooped water into his cupped hand and drank. Then he rode on.

The air grew warmer. Near midday the sun escaped from the clouds and poured down in a sudden dazzle of gold. Bedwyr's mind eased a little, and for the first time since he had left the island he became aware of his surroundings. He saw with surprise that he had covered most of the distance to Elyn's villa.

Beside him Fergus stopped and lifted his muzzle to scent the wind. At the same time the stallion snorted, tossing his head. Bedwyr could smell nothing, but as he rode over the lip of a hill he saw plumes of dark smoke rising above the trees. He urged Ariant to a gallop and they hurtled down the rise into the valley of the abandoned villa. It stood untouched.

Fear ran in him, drying his mouth as he galloped along the winding track toward the *dun*. At the edge of the clearing he reined the stallion back on his haunches and stared in horror at the palisade.

Bodies twisted in their death throes sprawled across the slope, many with the red horse of Ceawlin visible among the darker smears of dried blood. From within the walls smoke writhed upward. On the hillside nothing moved save for the fluttering of clothing and the flapping of ravens' wings. Ariant shattered the silence with a peal of challenge, answered only by a harsh croaking of the carrion birds as they hopped clumsily from their meals and then settled back to feast once more.

Bedwyr rode slowly up the hill toward the splintered remains of the gates and dismounted. Stepping among the bodies, he read the story of the assault. The main attack had come at the gates, where most of the defenders fell. In the end they had turned to face a new attack from their rear, inside the *dun*. At one place near the wall another group of fallen defenders told where it had been scaled. There had fallen Cas, Elyn's captain. Near him lay Beric, the young archer, a jagged rent in his chest.

The log hall still smoldered, with most of the bothies pulled down or torched. Bodies of women and babies and old men lay scattered across the enclosure. Fergus stalked through the wreckage with bared teeth, a low growl rumbling in his throat.

Bedwyr closed his eyes. How had they found the *dun?* Had he been followed after all? Heart in his throat, he walked over to the remains of the mead hall, searching through the still-warm ashes for a body he did not want to find. Something flashed in the debris. He reached down and picked up a broken shard from a looking glass, then hurled it away. Although he searched the rest of the *dun*, he found nothing else living, and no sign of Elyn.

As he walked out through the broken gates he saw a movement. Midway down the slope a raider stirred and groaned, then began crawling down the hill, making an odd, strangled sound, calling for water.

Rage overcame Bedwyr. He seized a nearby spear and ran down the hill. The man, a copper-haired Saxon, looked up, eyes pleading. Bedwyr thrust the spear hard into his back, shutting out the man's screams. Again he thrust, and again, until the Saxon was quiet. Then he drove the spear with all his force into the ground and leaned on it, forehead against the shaft.

Sickened by his own brutality he fought for air. Finally he slid to the ground and sat with his elbows on his knees, weeping openly.

Shadows lengthened and still he sat. At last he stood and drew his sword. He turned the blade slowly, examining its point, its razor edge, the blood gutter running the length of the blade. How well designed it was, a tool made for only one thing: murder. And he was a master of it. Once he had killed only to preserve civilization. Now he killed for any cause. How was he different from the Saxons he hated?

He gazed upward toward the ruined palisade. Again he had survived while the innocent died. Worse, by coming here, he may have brought death to them.

Bedwyr turned the sword so that the point rested on his stomach. No more. He could now handle no more pain and guilt. Like some parasite that bored deep within him, it had eaten through his spirit itself. There was only one escape.

Somewhere the wolfhound was barking. Although Bedwyr ignored it, the sound would not go away. Irritated, he finally glanced toward the gate and saw Fergus digging frantically atop a pile of bodies. The dog pulled aside a stiffening corpse, then paused and barked again at him.

Curiosity dragged him from his misery. He sheathed his sword and walked up the hill. Bending, he pulled away one body, then tumbled another from the pile, working his way through the grim carnage. At the bottom, curled into a ball, lay a boy. It was Brys, wild hair matted, dimpled cheeks bloody and begrimed, but alive.

Bedwyr lifted him and carried him down the hill, away from the battlefield, and, laying him down, felt for injuries. Save for a purplish lump on his forehead he did not seem hurt.

In a nearby stream he soaked a rag and with it bathed the boy's face. Brys's eyes opened, blank with shock. For a moment he stared around him, then he recognized Bedwyr. With a sob he threw his arms around his neck.

"You came back!"

"I came back. It's all right."

"Did we win?"

Bedwyr shook his head.

"My brothers?"

"No. I'm sorry."

Bedwyr held the boy while his small body shook with sobs. After a time Brys drew back, dragging a dirty paw under his nose. "We would have beat them but they scaled the walls and snuck up behind us. Dirty bastards!"

"I know. Do you hurt anywhere?"

Brys felt the lump on his forehead. "A little. Can I have a drink?"

Bedwyr filled his flask from the stream and carried it to the boy, who drank greedily.

When Brys finished drinking, Bedwyr said: "Know you what became of the Lady Elyn?"

Brys looked confused. "I don't think so. I was at the gate fighting with the warriors." He glanced at Bedwyr for approval. "I heard shouting behind us and I looked back and they were in the *dun*, running all through it, killing. But some they caught and didn't kill. They gathered them into one place, mostly girls and women. Then I didn't know anything until I opened my eyes and saw you." The child's warriorlike demeanor dissolved once more and he buried his face in his hands to hide the crying.

Bedwyr stood. Until now he had not dared to hope that Elyn still lived. If she did, she likely had been taken as a thrall to Ceawlin's steading, Camelot.

He looked around him. All this destruction, all of Elyn's suffering, was his fault. Everything he did seemed to turn to ashes. He deserved to die, but before he did, he owed it to Elyn to try to find her and free her. The thought was daunting. If she was being held in that fortress, there could be no hope of rescuing her alone. It would take the help of all the British. He thought reluctantly of Irion ap Medraut's plea for help in uniting the clans. As hateful as joining him would be, Bedwyr could think of no other way. It was Elyn's only chance.

He put his fingers to his lips and whistled. Fergus came bounding back from the stream. "Here's a survivor who needs attending," Bedwyr said to the dog. "Stay here and look after him while I see to things in the *dun*."

He left Fergus with Brys and went up to the stockade, where he gathered unburned scraps of wood and logs into a pile. Onto it he dragged the bodies of Elyn's people, leaving the dead raiders for the crows and rats to pick clean. He lit the pyre and, turning his back on it, went to find the stallion, then led him down to Brys.

"I think Ariant will consent to carry us both," he said. "Will you ride with me?"

The boy's eyes shone. "We go to Camelot to kill Ceawlin?"

Bedwyn picked the boy up and set him on the horse. "No. Not yet."

"Then let me go!" Brys shouted. "I won't ride with a coward. I won't! Run! I'll kill him myself. I'll show the Saxons there are still men in Britain."

Bedwyr sighed. "What would you have us do, minnow? Can one man and a boy overcome two thousand warriors?"

"We can die!"

"There's been too much dying. Britain needs live defenders, not more corpses." He tugged on the boy's foot. "To die takes courage, that's true. But sometimes it takes more courage to live when living is unpleasant. Have patience. There will be time enough to fight."

Brys paused in midshout, surprised. "Then you will help us?"

"I'll help."

PART FIVE

Camelot

NINETEEN

On the Isle of Môn, gulls wheeled over the ramparts of Aberffraw. Beyond it—nothing but sea. The emissary reined in his pony and looked long at the fortress, for he had been two years away as Maelgwn's ambassador to Gwent. A sprawling timber stronghold, it held many thatched balls, hazed over now with the smoke of cooking fires.

A half hour later guards passed him through the great gates and into a high-peaked hall, swimming in smoky torchlight. Dogs sprawled among the rushes and, against the walls, warriors lounged on rough-hewn benches. In the center of the hall a bright fire of pine logs burned on blackened flagstones, sending curls of smoke writhing upward like snakes toward the roof hole far above.

The emissary strode past the fire, heading toward the far end of the hall, where a larger blaze crackled in a deep fireplace three times the height of a man.

A woman walked toward him in a gown as fine as moth wings, which the flames painted in wavering colors. The new queen, then. How very beautiful. He understood now why Maelgwn had risked the censure of his clan to marry her. As she glided past, he smiled and bowed, but she had eyes only for the ornate gold bracelet on her wrist.

Inside the rim of the great hearth, stone benches sat opposite each other. On the left bench, staring moodily into the fire, hunched Maelgwn, the Dragon of the Isle, a horn of mead in his fist. For a moment he ignored the emissary, who studied him silently as he waited to be acknowledged.

The king had aged in two years. He looked small, with a face ruddy and narrow under a red beard. A ready smile, but it never quite masked the watchful calculation in his eyes, nor the temper which often flared and subsided before anyone could adjust to his mood.

At last he looked up. "Does my health meet with your approval?" His voice was the bark of a fox.

The emissary bowed. "Honor and praise to you, my king. Indeed, you look fit. May I add my blessing to your marriage? The queen is very beautiful."

Maelgwn glanced at him sharply, searching for hidden meanings. "She was a widow," he said defensively. "My nephew died of a fever. So did my wife. The marriage was perfectly legal."

The envoy nodded, his face, he hoped, expressionless. It was common knowledge that Maelgwn had put his first wife and nephew to death so he could marry his nephew's bride. Best to turn the conversation in another direction.

You've been most faithful in observing our laws, my king. It's of events beyond Aberttraw that I would speak."

Maelgwn looked away. "Speak, then. What's so important that you must deliver news of it yourself?"

Uninvited, the envoy sat on the bench opposite the king, the heat of the fire stinging his right cheek. "Gwent seeks an alliance with you against Ceawlin Cerdic-son."

"Annwn's Hounds, man. Gwent has bedeviled me for years to join its campaign against Ceawlin. You came all the way back to tell me that?"

"This time there is a difference. Arthur's Companion, Bedwyr Mawr, has returned to Britain."

Maelgwn gave him a quick, startled glance. "He is dead."

"He is very much alive. And he has offered his leadership to unite the Cymry against Ceawlin."

"Offered to whom? Gwent?"

"To Gwent and the Cornovi."

Maelgwn scowled. "Owein of the Ravens always was Arthur's ally. But why would he aid Medraut's son?"

"Irion ap Medraut has been removed as war leader. Brennus has offered command of the troops directly to Bedwyr."

Maelgwn took a drink of the mead, watching the envoy as he drank. When he finished he said, "Think you they will succeed at this alliance?"

The emissary knew the feel and balance of statecraft as well as he knew the feel of his own cloak. He said, "They will, now. Bedwry will lead it. Already support has come from Demetia, Builth, and Rheged. And Glevissig, of course."

"Rheged, too?"

"Aye."

He saw that Maelgwn grasped the implications. If the allies gathered a force large enough to defeat Ceawlin, the leader of that force would be in a strong position to renew the title of Count of Britain, the commander of all British armies. Arthur had held that rank and he used it to become Pendragon, the High King, forcing Maelgwn to yield to him.

They sat in silence. Finally the king spoke, slowly, thinking the thing out as he went along. "So. If I do nothing, sooner or later I will likely face the choice of yielding to the authority of another High King, or fighting him. Ceawlin must be dealt with someday, in any case. If I join their alliance I will have the largest war band, and the best claim to be Count of Britain."

The emissary nodded in approval of the king's reasoning.

Maelgwn kicked a smoldering log on the hearth, watching the sparks fly. Finally he stood, indicating the audience was at an end. "Rest here tonight. Tomorrow you return to Caerwent with our agreement of alliance."

TWENTY

And so the Cran Tara, a charred oak staff dipped in blood, went out to the kings and chieftains of the Cymry summoning them to war. A message went with it under the name and authority of the Emperor, bidding them to gather as soon as may be in Caerleon, and there take council. The summons bore the name of Justinian, but Bedwyr ap Gruffydd had sent it, and it was his name and his authority that brought the clans to Caerleon.

Before the first warrior appeared it became clear to everyone in Gwent that something unusual was afoot. Messengers rode to and from the fortress with obvious urgency; smiths and armorers worked late into the night. Then, one by one, the war bands marched or rode into the great Fortress of Legions, filling it as it had not been filled since the time of the Second Legion Augustus.

Gereint of Demetia brought a force of six hundred, the largest of the contingents save Maelgwn's. He also brought his queen, Erim, who insisted upon quarters in a luxurious villa outside Caerleon. She persuaded Gereint to come, some said, by reminding him that a victory would bring glory to King Jesus. Most felt Gereint had his own glory in mind.

Arthur's old ally, Owein of the Ravens, strode into the fortress at the head of three hundred kilted Cornovi warriors, pipes skirling. His long hair and beard blazed the color of a turf fire and on his right shoulder perched a huge raven, black eyes glittering. A white streak of bird droppings decorated the back of the man's black and red plaid cloak. Whether it was the bird, or the fact that he called his warriors Ravens, no one was certain, but the chieftain had never been called anything but Owein of the Ravens.

He greeted Bedwyr with a bear hug and a wicked grin. "What a land to loot!" he said, waving his arm around him. "A pity I'm on your side."

Marcianus and Gwynllew, brothers who inherited the divided kingdom of Builth, rode through opposite gates on their hill ponies, each leading two hundred clansmen. Neither would speak to the other, and they were assigned quarters in widely separated barracks.

Finally came Dunaut of Rheged, with a war band of four hundred, grim fighters with iron helms over hard eyes. Their wolf-head standard had not been seen before in Gwent and a workman called to Bedwyr as they rode in, asking nervously if the fortress was under attack.

The pace of preparation quickened and Caerleon clattered with activity. Man shod horses; repaired armor; cut, stitched, and replaced belts, straps, and harnesses. Wheelwrights pulled metal rims from wheels, shrinking leather strips onto the rims to replace them, for the iron foundries glowed night and day to meet the demand for horseshoes and tools of war.

Nor were the warriors allowed to idle while they waited. Bedwyr drilled them hard. As strict as a Roman general, he molded them into a single fighting force, to the grumbling of some who were unused to such discipline. But at the end of each day, as they rode or marched back into the fortress covered with sweat and dust, each warrior held himself a little taller with earned pride. After two weeks there was not a man who did not know the tactics and trumpet calls, and what was expected of him with each.

As hard as he worked them, Bedwyr worked himself hardest of all. He lived on the same bare rations as the troops, and after drilling all day, worked on at his table by lantern light, poring over dispatches and supply lists.

As he served in the war band under Bedwyr, Irion studied him. The Companion seldom raised his voice, never shouted. He listened patiently to the opinions, sometimes strongly expressed, of each king and chieftain, making those around him feel larger and more worthy in his presence. He treated everyone with the same dignity and importance, and he brought out the best they had to give. How could Arthur have been greater than this man? Irion wondered.

But Bedwyr avoided Irion. His relief when he discovered Medraut's son no longer commanded the warriors of Gwent was obvious. When he could not avoid him, he treated Irion with a stiff formality that did little to hide his abhorrence. Although Irion went out of his way to offer friendship, there was no breaking through the barrier of Bedwyr's cold courtesy. Ignored by most of the clan chieftains, Irion felt keenly his own isolation.

It was Gwythur who advised Bedwyr of Gwent's spy in Camelot. At Irion's insistence Gwythur did not mention that the plan had been Irion's. Bedwyr listened with interest as the little captain told him of Kylan, and when Gwythur left, Bedwyr was deep in thought.

When all had arrived but Maelgwn, who would join them at Glevum, the leaders gathered in the senior centurion's house for a council of war. Though the night felt warm, Bedwyr ordered the windows closed and posted guards around the house against the risk of spies. The chieftains sat on benches around the walls, their faces serious.

"You all know the condition of Britain," Bedwyr said, "and I will not weary you with a litany of grievances against Ceawlin. In Arthur's time, Saxons knew little of the uses of hill forts. Now Ceawlin, at least, has learned their advantages. He holds Camelot with no less then fifteen hundred men. While he squats on that hill like a toad on a rock, no Briton is safe. Urgency in what we do here is lent by what we have learned from Owein's scouts."

The huge, flame-haired chieftain stood, his raven flapping its wings for balance. "Ceawlin goes to meet Cynric and the Jute Wibtgar witin the week, seeking alliance with them. It's in my mind he'll get it, for Cynric ages, and he his being squeezed by two young kinsmen who speak for those newly come from Germania. Immigrants are swarming over the Saxon sea, thick as gnats in a swamp, filling their lands till they press on our borders. He must give in to their demands for war, or yield as *bretwalda* of the Saxon folk."

"But why should he join Ceawlin?" asked Dunaut of Rheged, a stocky, sword-scarred man with a broken nose so crooked it gave him a sinister appearance. "There's been bad blood between those two for years."

"Because Camelot blocks his advance to the west," Bedwyr said. "That was why it was built. Lords, it is only the Saxon quarrels that have spared Britain for the past eleven years. When they unite there will be war. The only question is how best to fight them. That is the reason for this council."

Dunaut snorted. "That's easy. We decide on a place where the terrain favors us and we attack them. How else is there to fight?"

"We have two thousand warriors," Bedwyr said. "Four thousand with Maelgwn. We'll likely be outnumbered two or three times by the Saxons. Those are not odds to be faced by choice. Therefore I propose a plan to lessen the odds: We will recapture Camelot."

The chieftains stared at him as if he danced before them naked.

"Man, you're mad," said Dunaut. "That fortress has never been taken. With fifteen hundred warriors Ceawlin could hold out till the Second Coming. You, of all people, should know that."

"Aye. But understand me. He will not have fifteen hundred. Within the week he will journey to Cynric's steading and he will not go alone. Were I him, I wouldn't go there with less than four hundred warriors."

At the back of the room Marcianus spoke for the first time, his voice a chronic whine. "To a council with another Saxon? What sense would that make?" Here was the only person he knew, Bedwyr reflected, who could give offense simply by saying good morning.

His brother, Gwynllew, growled, "Because, unlike you, Ceawlin is no fool." Marcianus's brother was a small, gnarled man with no need of tolerance and none in him for others.

Marcianus gave Bedwyr a blank look.

"To us," Bedwyr explained, "a Saxon is a Saxon. But there is no love between the West Saxons and the Jutes. To win an alliance with Cynric, Ceawlin must show enough strength to make it dangerous to refuse him. For that reason Ceawlin will take as large a force as he dares, without leaving Camelot defenseless. I think there will be no more than eleven hundred remaining in the fortress."

"Even so," said Gereint, "eleven hundred men behind those walls could resist long against us."

"The Demetian is right," Owein said. "And we have no siege engines, nor time to build them."

"What you both say is true." From beneath the table Bedwyr lifted a wooden bucket filled with wet sand. He turned the bucket over on the table and pulled it away, leaving a round, steep-sided mound of sand. With his hand he molded the contours of the mound until it looked roughly triangular, then pushed the top up slightly so it slanted toward a ridge near the center.

"Camelot hill," he said.

With his dagger he gouged out four deep trenches around the sides of the mound. "These are defensive ditches, with the dirt from them thrown down into dikes below each. Around the crown of the hill runs a stone-and-timber rampart fifteen fast high, with gates on the southwest corner, here, and on the east side, here and here. Roads squezze through the ditches up to the gates, but battering rams cannot be brought effectively to bear: It's a climb for goats."

The chieftains peered at the model, mystified.

Owein's eyes bulged. "Let me grip this business one handle at a time. You ask me to lead my clan, without siege weapons or battering rams, against the strongest fortress in all Britain, defended by a vicious war band allied with half the Saxon nation? Is that a fair summing?"

"Aye."

A slow grin spread across Owein's face. "Who could resist an offer like that?"

"We shoud need neither rams nor siege engines," Bedwyr said. "Gwant has a man in Camelot who has access to the walls. When we are in place around the fortress, he'll lower a rope over the wall at night. A company of one hundred picked warriors will go up over the wall and open the gate for the rest."

There was silence for a moment, then the leaders all began to talk at once.

Owein slapped his hand on his leg. "As easy as kiss your hand. By Thor's thunderous farts, it might work!"

Bedwyr held up his hand for silence. "With the fortress ours, our position is strengthened many times over. If we have even two thousand men and sufficient stores, the Saxons cannot take us. Neither can they afford to bypass us and leave a hostile army behind them. They'll have to fight. On our terms."

Gereint stood, brushing at his crimson silk tunic. The intricate designs embroidered in gold thread shimmered in the lamplight. "This spy," he said. "Have you seen him, or do we have only Gwent warrior's word that he's there?"

Gwythur flushed, and leaned forward to stand. By his side Owein put his hand on his shoulder.

Bedwyr frowned. "I've not seen the man, but I have seen a message he sent. There's no reason not to believe he is inside Camelot."

"How will we know when Ceawlin leaves, and how many warriors he takes?" asked Owein. "Your spy?"

"No," Bedwyr said. "We'll not risk him for that. We have scouts who watch the fortress day around. The morning he rides away, we'll know by nightfall."

They spoke long into the night of weapons and stores, levies of men, and strategy. Gereint alone showed no enthusiasm for the plan. He was a man, Bedwyr decided, who preferred options to decisions.

"It feels chancy to me," Gereint said. "What if your spy is discovered?"

"There are no promises in war," Bedwyr said patiently. "There are always things we cannot control. We can only weigh the odds and make a decision."

When the last objection had been addressed and the details shaped, the council voted, and adopted Bedwyr's plan. The next few days the Cymry worked feverishly to ready the army for marching.

The morning after the war council, news came by way of Caedmon the Crosser that the Roman General Belisarius had been recalled to Constantinople. Rome had fallen again to the Goths. Bedwyr said little that day, unable to shake the feeling that they were alone, a solitary island of civilization in a sea of savagery. Night was falling.

The following evening, as the gates of Caerleon drew closed, a scout slipped in with word that Ceawlin had marched out of Camelot, five hundred warriors at his back. Bedwyr issued the order to ride at daybreak.

TWENTY-ONE

The British rode out of the Fortress of Legions toward Glevum crossing to join with Maelgwn's forces. Leaving his position at the head of the column, Bedwyr guided Ariant to the top of a nearby hill. Two small boys, barefoot and dusty, left their herd of goats to pelt up the hill behind him and gape at the warrior on the tall, white horse. Fergus trotted over to cadge a pet. Bedwyr smiled at them, thinking of Brys, who was very angry with him because he'd been left behind.

Bedwyr tried not to think of Elyn, for the chance that she still lived dimmed with each passing week. And even if she lived, he knew the odds of recaputing Camelot were against them. Still, he thought grimly, what choice did he have?

Below him rode the cavalry, clan by clan, in their reds and blues and plaids, followed by the remounts and pack strings, then the infantry and supply wagons. They passed with a clanking of iron, a rumble of wagons, and an occasional shout, lifting a pall of dust above them. When the last ox wagon grumbled by, Bedwyr galloped down the hill to rejoin the column.

Spring had given way to full summer. The day was pearled with haze and larks sang high in the warm air. Around them all grasses swayed in the wind like a restless sea.

Bedwyr marched them hard, taking full advantage of the long summer day. Hywel's infantry set a mile-eating pace, none the faster for the gibes of the cavalry, none the slower for the twenty miles they had already marched that day. By nightfall they reached the Sabrina at Glevum.

There was no sign of Maelgwn.

They camped above the river, and soon soldiers were scattering to look for firewood while others were pitching tents, packhorses were rolling in the dirt, and infantrymen with sore feet were taking off their sandals and boots. Bedwyr knew this was the most vulnerable time for an army on the march. While half of the warriors made camp, the rest remained on watch.

He had organized them in the Roman manner, with eight men sharing a tent and cooking fire, drawing bread and beer from central stores. Fires would go out an hour after sunset, and there would be no noise until the trumpet blew at dawn.

The chieftains met for their evening meal in Gereint's tent, chosen for its size. Bedwyr had watched in fascination as the Demetian's servants struggled to put up the enormous structure, with its two rooms, high center peak, and gaudy stripes of red and yellow. Inside, silver-gray wolfskin rugs covered the floor, with ornate stools set out in a circle. Even Belisarius had not campaigned in this opulence, Bedwyr thought.

Behind Bedwyr, Owein entered and stopped short. "What manner of palace is this?" he thundered. "If I put food in all the wagons this thing takes up, I could feed my entire war band for a week."

Gereint ignored him, turning to Bedwyr. "Maelgwn has not come. Will he keep faith, think you?"

Bedwyr sat on a stool and accepted a cup of wine from Gereint's servant. "He's shrewd and has his own interests at heart. But once committed, he will not lightly break his word."

"I wouldn't trust the man two weeks after I buried him," Dunaut said, scratching his twisted nose. "He'd sit back if he could and watch this race, then praise the winner."

"We'll wait for him here another day," Bedwyr said. "Tomorrow I'll send riders north to find him."

The next afternoon the riders returned with a company of fifty horsemen wearing the blue and white of Maelgwn's kingdom of Gwynedd and riding the tough, shaggy ponies of the northern mountains. A rider escorted their leader to Bedwyr.

"We found them seven miles or so northward, lord," he said. "This is Dafydd, their captain."

He indicated a cheerful-looking youth with one blue and

one amber eye, who flashed Bedwyr a crooked grin and a genial salute. "Well met, lord. I've heard much of Bedwyr Mawr but never thought to fight with him. My king, Maelgwn of Gwynedd, sends you his apologies. He's been delayed. As we readied to ride south, word came that a Pictish raiding party had landed near Deva. The king was forced to turn aside and deal with them."

Dunaut of Rheged, who had come up to listen, said skeptically, "They must be bold indeed to land so near to the Dragon's Isle."

"Aye," said Dafydd. "The more reason to rap their knuckles, so they're not so bold twice."

Bedwyr studied Dafydd's face. "How many raiders?"

"Reports put their numbers at several hundred, landing at two different places." The youth met his eyes frankly. "The king is confident he'll need no more than three days to route them. When they're destroyed, he'll join you with all haste. He sent my company and me as a token of his good faith.

Bedwyr nodded. "You and your company are welcome." To Dunaut, he said, "Notify the princes. We'll take council in Gereint's quarters."

The leaders listened silently in the hot tent as Dafydd repeated his message. When he had finished and left, Bedwyr said, "So. That's the way of it. The question before us is whether to bide here for Maelgwn or to march on to Camelot without him."

"For my part," Gereint said, face troubled, "I'd wait. Maelgwn will bring two thousand spears, half of our strength. It would be unwise to move on without him."

"Witless, rather, to stay here," Owein said. "I'm for Camelot. We're on the border of Dumnonia. The longer we bide here the more chance one of Ceawlin's spies will see us and scuttle back to tattle. If the plan will work at all, it will work with our present strength. We still have two thousand to their one."

"There's another thing," said Gwythur. "The Saxons are hosting. If we wait here and Maelwyn is delayed overlong, we may find the entire Saxon host waiting for us instead of an underdefended Camelot."

Dunaut frowned. "Think you the story is true? To me it smells of trickery."

"Dafydd's story has the ring of truth," Bedwyr said. "I believe him."

"Then let's wait for Maelgwn," Gwynllew said.

Marcianus sneered at his brother. "Why? You can turn and run home as easily without him as with him."

Gwynllew colored and reached for his sword hilt. "If I die in battle it'll be facing forward."

"Peace, cousins," Bedwyr said. "It's in my mind that we would gain nothing by waiting here. We'll ride south at dawn. I'll send a courier to Maelgwn, telling him of our decision and urging him to join us at Camelot as quickly as may be."

Kylan stood on the rampart of Camelot and looked across the open land rolling out below him. To the west, the River Cam curled around the foot of the great hill and ran away to the north through the marshlands of Gwlad-yr-haf, the summer country, on its way to the Sabrina estuary. In the center of the marsh to the northwest, he could pick out Ynys Afallon rising from its lake. Out of the northeast, the Roman road from Aquae Sulis plunged past Camelot, skirting a circle of ancient standing stones before it ran spear straight toward the south coast. But it was what he saw on that road now that interested him: a long column of tiny figures, growing steadily larger—the army of the west.

Kylan had found a place in the Saxon war band more easily than he'd expected, perhaps because of Ceawlin's departure with five hundred warriors, leaving the fortress undermanned. He had worried about his great bow drawing suspicion, for Saxon bows were much shorter and less powerful. But when questioned by Dungarth, he bragged loudly about the Briton he'd slain to get it, and pulled from his pouch Guthwine's knuckle-bone dice, stolen from the sleeping Friesian during the night, as proof. He had given them to the envrious Dungarth to win his favor.

Beside him barbarian warriors lined the ramparts, laughing and jeering at the approaching army. He could hear the jangle and clank of iron and the rumble of the approaching wagons.

Just out of bowshot the column stopped and waited, while the dust it raised drifted away to the west.

Kylan watched their leader, a man on a white stallion with a wolfhound at his side, as he gave a command. A trumpet blew. The column split into squadrons of footmen and horse, each moving away toward a different position. The British war band was small. Too small, Kylan thought. They had not enough men to completely encircle Camelot hill and he watched anxiously to see what would happen.

A company of footsoldiers blocked each of the three roads leading to the gates, with squadrons of horse and infantry placed at intervals between them. Each stood within sight and quick aid of the other, and they effectively sealed off the fortress.

A shout from behind him interrupted his thoughts. He turned to see a tall Saxon climbing the ladder. The man's head was shaved smooth, save for a long blond horsetail, and he wore an enormous mustache. Kylan recognized him as Ulfang, the thane Ceawlin had left in command of the fortress. Kylan shivered. The Saxon's voice made him think of a serpent hissing in the grass.

"Ye three!" Ulfang pointed at a group of spearmen. "Come with me. I have a special welcome for the Welsh leader."

Kylan watched as the warriors made their way down the ladder and disappeared, then turned back to the British army below.

A shadow passed overhead and Bedwyr looked up to see a thick, black cloud trailing it. Behind it came other rain-promising clouds.

"Cover those grain wagons," he called to Huw, the master of the supply company. He had placed them on the east side of the hill, under the protection of the largest squadron of infantry.

Gwythur galloped up. "All squadrons in place, Lord Bedwyr."

Bedwyr untied his helm from Ariant's saddlebow and strapped it on. "I think it's time to announce our presence."

"You think they don't know we're here?"

Bedwyr laughed. "Aye. They know. Now they'll know *who*

is here. And I'll learn who commands them. Cut me a branch from that bush. Then tell the princes I go to talk with our enemies."

A track plunged straight up the slope to the southeast gate. Holding the green branch high to show he came in peace, Bedwyr rode slowly, looking up at the sky-sweeping walls. It felt strange that the great gates should be closed and barred against him; worse, that barbarian faces peered from the square gate tower. For an instant he had the absurd urge to share a drink with the Saxon chieftain and talk about Camelot's defenses, to show him the gouges in that mead-hall pillar he'd made testing a sword.

He halted below the tower and called out in Friesian, "Summon your chieftain. I will speak with him."

A sentry leaned out, scowling. "Get ye gone, before my spear finds your belly and lets the cold wind in behind it."

Jeers and hoots of laughter erupted on the walls.

Bedwyr pulled his helm from his head and lifted his face to the tower. His voice cut through the jeering like a dagger through cheese. "I am Bedwyr ap Gruffydd. I have returned to claim this fortress in the name of Arthur Pendragon, High King of Britain, and your ruler."

The laughter died. Astonished murmurs and the name Bedwyr swept along the walls. Then there was uneasy silence.

The sentry muttered, "Wait there. I'll get Ulfang."

There was a long wait. Finally, he heard a stir in the tower and a rumble of voices, then Ulfang's shaved head appeared.

Ulfang spoke Celtic in a rasping whisper, and under his mail hauberk, Bedwyr's skin crawled. "Bedwyr ap Gruffydd. Permit me a moment of surprise. I didn't think you had the courage to come here after you fled our patrol at Isca. Why do you attack us with these leavings of Rome? We are peace-loving men."

"In the name of Arthur, we offer you one chance only," Bedwyr said. "Open the gates and march out of Camelot unarmed, and you m ay depart in peace."

Ulfang's face crumpled into silent spasms of mirth. "Arthur is dead and rots in his grave. Soon you will too, and there will be one less Roman strutting under the sun. But before we kill you I have a gift for you—something we found in one of your old steadings. Come and take it."

He gave a signal and three warriors appeared on the wall to Bedwyr's left. They lifted something onto the rampart, a cage made of poles lashed to a plank floor and roof, with a rope tied to its top. The barbarians lowered it over the wall.

In the cage crouched a woman, unable to sit upright, her hands clutching the bars. Elyn!

TWENTY-TWO

Five feet from the ground the cage stopped. Elyn stared about her in confusion. She saw Bedwyr and her hands flew to her mouth.

Ulfang snickered. "If you don't like my gift I'll take her back and find other uses for her."

He signaled and the Saxons began to draw up the cage.

Bedwyr cried out in rage, drew his sword, and spurred Ariant along the narrow ledge next to the wall. At the same time the gates opened and a swarm of Saxons boiled out in pursuit.

The war stallion lashed out with his deadly hind feet. The heads of two pursuers turned to a froth of blood and brains. Fergus hurled himself at another's throat, knocked him backward into the rest, and they rolled down into the ditch, a snarling, struggling knot of teeth and screaming men.

Bedwyr reached the rising cage, clambered to his feet on Ariant's back. He swung his sword at the rope, could not reach it. Quickly he sheathed his sword and seized a bar with his hand. The cage drew higher, lifting him from the horse.

In the cage Elyn's face had gone white. Her eyes pleaded and she mouthed some words, but he could hear nothing above the shouting and screaming of men.

Above him a barbarian lifted a rock over his head and heaved it. Bedwyr threw up his shield arm to ward it off. It caromed off the rim and crashed into his head. The cage slipped from his grasp and he fell to the ground, rolling down the steep bank to the bottom of the ditch where he lay stunned, colored sparks dancing before his eyes.

He forced himself to his knees, a hollow roar in his head like the sea in a shell. His sight was blurred, blood ran into one eye, and he couldn't think.

Above him he heard a war cry. Squinting, he saw a Saxon plunge down the embankment. The man raised an ax over his head and grinned. Bedwyr groped for his sword, couldn't find it. Then a spear took the man in the throat and he fell forward onto Bedwyr, kicking and gurgling.

Someone flung the body off of him and an arm reached down and lifted him to his feet. "Quick!" Irion said. "Put your feet under you. Here. Lean against the bank."

Bedwyr took two steps and sagged against the ditch bank. Slowly the ground settled into place. He looked up to see Irion watching him anxiously, sheltering them from arrows with his shield.

"Come," said Irion. "We can't stop here." He handed him his sword. "Ariant is behind you."

He shook the last of the fog from his brain and mounted. Fergus loped down the bank, his teeth shining red. Bedwyr glanced at the wall. Elyn was gone.

Below the gate a sharp battle raged as a company of infantry fought their way up the hill. Gradually the barbarians retreated into the fortress and the gates swung closed with a hollow boom. A few enemy stragglers did not reach the gate in time and the British cut them down. Arrows hissed from the walls.

"Back!" Bedwyr called. "We'll be cut to ribbons here."

The warriors turned and retreated down the hill, out of arrow range. Behind them rode Bedwyr and Irion.

As they neared their lines Bedwyr saw columns of smoke rise from the supply wagons. He cursed and galloped over to them. Nearly all were in flames. Men frantically pulled the few that were unburned away from the rest. Some beat vainly with cloaks at the burning grain.

"Huw!" Bedwyr shouted. "Where are the guards I left here?"

The supply master dropped the tongue of a wagon and lumbered over, his florid face a mask of apology.

"Oh, Lord Bedwyr. It's all my fault. They took us by surprise completely. We be watching the fighting up there and suddenly they was behind us. I don't know where they came from. A dozen of them, only, but they had torches and before we knew what hit us the wains was burning, what with them so dry and all. We killed them, all right, but by then the damage was done. I'm sorry."

The man looked so miserable that Bedwyr's anger cooled. "You didn't see them until they were at the wagons? Where did they come from?"

Huw looked puzzled. "Well, sir, I don't know. Except they couldn't have come from the southeast gate. It may be they crept out of one of the other gates and came at us from behind."

"That's likely," Gwythur said as he rode up. "The Demetians you left to watch the southwest gate got excited in the skirmish and galloped over to help. Their gate was unwatched."

"Wherever they came from," Bedwyr said, "it's obvious that the sortie was meant to divert us from the supply wagons. And it worked very well."

The flames were finally put out, but relatively little of the food in the burned wagons could be salvaged. Some of the salted meat, though charred, was edible, and a few kegs of ale were intact. Bedwyr estimated they had lost three-fourths of their food. Gloom reigned in camp that night.

Bedwyr sat patiently while Gwythur fumbled at cleaning the gash in his forehead. The rock had left a purple bruise and a flap of skin hanging loose.

Finally the little cavalryman threw down his rag. "This is no good. You'll be needing a medicus to stitch this closed." He stumped out of the tent.

As he left a few drops of rain pattered against the roof, then thunder rumbled and a gust of rain blew sheets of water against the tent wall. Bedwyr grimaced. An hour earlier and the grain would not have burned.

Gwythur came back leading a thin, dour old man with a medical pouch at his waist. "Our best surgeon," he announced, "nothing against Gwylum and Netio. This is Catullan out of Caerwent. He has the touch."

Catullan eyed the rent in Bedwyr's head. "Whose brilliant idea was it to charge the fortress?"

"We were not charging the fortress," explained Gwythur.

"They violated our branch of truce. Lord Bedwyr, here, was hurt trying to save a lady they dangled from the wall in a cage."

Catullan grunted, unimpressed. From his pouch he took a curved iron needle and a pot of salve. He plucked a long, white hair from his head and threaded it through the needle.

"Then Irion saved Lord Bedwyr's life," Gwythur continued, "when those devils came at him out of the gate. You should have seen him, Catullan, you would have been proud."

The surgeon said nothing. He smeared salve on the wound, closed the flap of skin and began stitching it together with the needle.

A guard stuck his head in the tent. "Irion ap Medraut to see you, my lord."

Bedwyr frowned. "Now?" He sighed.

Irion ducked under the tent flap. When he saw Catullan and Gwythur he straightened in surprise. "I can come back. . . ."

Gwythur brightened. "Come in, come in, lad. We were just speaking of you. All of us owe you thanks for saving Lord Bedwyr's life. He'll be wanting to thank you himself, I'm sure."

There was an awkward pause.

Why couldn't it have been anyone else? Bedwyr thought. In truth the boy looked more like Arthur than Medraut, yet every time he looked at him he thought of the traitor. At last, he said, "He has my thanks."

Irion's eyes showed hurt at the coldness of his tone. Catullan glowered.

"That's all?" Gwythur looked confused.

"I said he has my thanks," Bedwyr snapped.

"He has your thanks. As if he had just brought your supper," Gwythur said. "I don't understand this, Bedwyr. When we fought together in the old days you knew the meaning of gratitude." He closed his mouth, opened it again to say more, then turned and stalked from the tent.

"Is there anything else, ap Medraut?"

Irion hesitated, then blurted, "Lord Bedwyr, who is she?"

Bedwyr knew who he meant, and Irion's face told him he already suspected the truth.

"She is Elyn ferch Caradoc. She is your mother." He winced as Catullan drove the needle into bone.

Irion sank onto a stool. "I remembered her face. All these years, she's been alive. Why didn't she let me know? How—how do you know her?"

"I knew her before she married your father. You have a right to know that much. I met her again on business of my own in Dumnonia this year, and I was several days at her *dun* before I left to finish my task. When I returned, Ceawlin had burned the *dun* and she was gone."

"Why did you not tell me?"

"Would it have been kinder to learn she had lived all these years only to die a few days before you found out?"

"But if she still lived . . ."

Bedwyr sighed. "I didn't know that. If we found her alive, she herself could tell you."

The medicus finished stitching the cut and stood watching them.

"I must have been a great burden to her," Irion said softly.

Bedwyr defended her. "She had good reasons for what she did. If she lives she will explain them to you."

"If she lives." Irion's voice was desolate. "I thank you, Lord Bedwyr, for trying to save her." He wandered to the doorway, his movements oddly vague and listless.

Catullan repacked his pouch and followed. "You'll be all right," he said over his shoulder, "if it doesn't take the wound fever."

The rain continued through the night and all the next day. After its initial flurry it fell with a slow and steady seriousness. The grass flattened and grew sodden, and the tracks were soon reduced to muddy memories. Mud oozed under the hoofs of the horses as patrols made their way between camps, the woolen cloaks of the riders soaked and clinging to their backs.

No cooking fires could be coaxed to burn. The troops, put on one-third rations, bolted their meager meals cold and went back inside their tents, though it was hardly drier there.

In the morning Bedwyr sent out two squadrons, under command of Dunaut and Gwynllew, to forage for food. They rode out dispiritedly, hunched against the rain.

There was no word from Kylan that morning. The sky

remained gray and heavy, clouds sagging onto the fortress walls, and the rain continued.

Bedwyr slept little that night. Rain soaked through the fabric of his tent and mud worked into his blankets. He felt as if he had never been dry in his life. Beside him Fergus slept restlessly, snarling occasionally and twitching in his dreams.

The next morning Gwythur returned from patrol and dismounted in front of Bedwyr's tent. Bedwyr looked at the grizzled captain for some word from the spy, but Gwythur took off his helm, his face mud-splashed to the helmet line, and shook his head glumly.

Irion slogged over. "Lord Bedwyr, there's a confession that needs making. If the spy fails, Gwythur should receive no blame. Any fault there is belongs to me. I chose Kylan for the task."

Bedwyr scowled. Had he known, he might have thought differently about hanging the whole campaign on the spy. He looked at Gwythur. "Do you still vouch for this man's reliability?"

"Aye," Gwythur said. "Kylan will come through, if any man can."

That afternoon the foraging parties returned with little to show for their efforts: a few sacks of moldy grain, a clutch of eggs, and one bony cow driven before them.

As Bedwyr splashed over to speak to Dunaut he heard cries from the sentries and under them the sound of a galloping horse. An outrider slid to a halt in front of him and threw himself from his mount, mud caked and breathless.

"My Lord Bedwyr—my lords," he said as the other leaders gathered around him.

"What's amiss?" Bedwyr said.

"The S-Saxons. They're moving. Ceawlin marches at their head."

"How distant?"

The scout wiped a hand across his eyes to clear them of mud. "Two days march from here and moving quickly."

"How many, man?" asked Dunaut.

"Who knows, lord? I could not see the end of them. Six thousand, at least. They move across the land like ants. I recognized Cynric's standard. He brings all his West Saxons with him, from the look of it. Behind him swarm many other tribes."

Gereint's face blanched at the news. "What's to be done?" he asked. "We cannot fight the entire Saxon confederation. We'll be caught between them and the walls."

The leaders were silent, exchanging glances. Warriors who had come over to greet the forage parties heard the fear in Gereint's voice and looked at Bedwyr, uneasy.

Bedwyr spoke, his attention on Gereint but his words loud enough to be heard by everyone around him. "Maelgwn of Gwynedd rides to our aid with two thousand horsemen. Combined, our armies are more than a match for a forest of Saxons. Until he arrives we'll send a squad of light cavalry to slow their march. By the time the Saxons reach us we'll be ready for them."

"Aye," muttered a warrior. "If Maelgwn reaches us in time."

"He will," Bedwyr said. "He knows the urgency of our plight."

Although some still looked fearful, most warriors seemed heartened by Bedwyr's words. Gradually they dispersed.

Dunaut volunteered to lead the light horse. Bedwyr ordered him to avoid at all costs being drawn into a pitched battle, for their strength could not be spared in the final struggle.

As Bedwyr watched them ride grimly out of camp Owein slogged over, the raven a wet, black lump on his shoulder remembering dry roosts. "This spy," he said. "How will he send word?"

"Simply," Bedwyr said. "He'll shoot an arrow at Gwythur's patrol. A near miss. The arrow will have the message."

Owein grunted. "Let's hope he sends it soon."

TWENTY-THREE

Gereint leaned back from his campaign desk and, laying down the quill pen, picked up the parchment to read the words he had written on it:

> King Gereint to Erim, most beautiful and faithful of wives: Best health and his love. Know for certain, beloved, that as this letter leaves me, I am safe and unharmed.
>
> Know, as well, that the princes have selected me as host of the nightly war councils, and that my advice is earnestly sought and highly regarded. The council having just met, I am safe in saying there is talk of abandoning the siege, for there has been no progress in the secret plan to breach the walls of the fortress. Time draws short, not for the sake of food only. Reports have reached us that the Saxons are approaching.
>
> All these matters, though serious, pale beside my regard for you. I bid you take care of the affairs of Demetia and treat the citizens with lenience as becomes you. Look for me when matters here have resolved themselves according to God's will.

Summoning a courier, he signed the limp parchment and sealed it. "Make haste with this to Maridunum."

When the man left, Gereint huddled at the door of the tent, staring out at the rain. Wet and cold, hungry and thoroughly miserable, he wondered where the glory had gone.

Kylan peered out over the east rampart of Camelot through a predawn drizzle. Although he pretended to watch for signs of a British attack, he had more interest in the Saxon activity on the west wall across from him, where the morning patrol relieved the night watch.

For three nights he had studied the watches, trying to discern a pattern that would give time for a squad of Cymry to scale the wall. But he had found no pattern, not since the siege began. In addition to the sentries stationed along the wall every fifty paces, a patrol of twenty men circled the rampart at random intervals.

Kylan did, however, observe something that gave him hope. When the new watch came on duty near dawn, its leader stopped to share a flask—undoubtedly pirated from the stores—with the leader he relieved. Both mornings before, it had happened along the west wall, and this morning as well. He could see them dimly, and he heard murmuring and laughter. There was no guarantee they would meet at the same place tomorrow, but this was the only chance he was likely to get. He glanced at the sentry nearest him, a hulking Angle who stared out over the wall. He would silence him when the time came.

Kylan put his plan into motion. Groaning loudly, he bent over and clutched his stomach.

The other sentry turned toward him. "You, there! What's the problem?"

Kylan groaned again. "The flux. Must have eaten some rotten meat. I'm for the latrine. Cover for me."

Without waiting for an answer he ran to the ladder and scrambled down it, then hurried, bent over, to the privy, a crude, stinking shed built over a pit. Once inside he pulled a candle stub from his tunic and set it alight. The latrine was deserted.

Kylan unfastened his belt and pulled off the quiver at his waist. Turning it over he dumped the arrows onto the floor planks and gave it a hard shake. Out fell a small bundle, a scrap of white cloth wrapped around a charred stick. Quickly he spread the cloth on the planks and drew on it with the stick, then wrapped the cloth round the shaft of an arrow just below the head. From the candle he dripped tallow onto the arrow until the wax glued the cloth to the shaft.

He had replaced the waxed arrow in the quiver and begun

picking up the others when torchlight stabbed through the doorway. His squad leader Dungarth stood above him, light winking off the gold torque around his bull neck. Kylan grinned sheepishly and scurried to gather the rest of the arrows.

"The flux," he said. He straightened and patted his stomach. "I was in a rush to get my belt off and my quiver got dumped."

Dungarth grunted, his pig eyes suspicious. "Get back to your post, worm, before I report ye for desertion."

Kylan ran out the door rebuckling his belt and climbed back to his place on the wall. On the west wall the old patrol had left. The new watch marched south along the rampart. That was well, for it would take longer to bring them around to him. He waited for dawn.

The rain finally stopped as dawn, faint and pallid, reached across the low hills pulling a warm breeze behind it. A short time later a mounted squadron of Cymry rounded the hill from the north, their horses' hoofs squelching in the muddy track they had worn. The British rode slowly, alertly, outside the farthest ditch and just beyond the range of barbarian arrows. Gwythur rode at their head carrying the red-dragon standard, shield hanging from a saddle hook.

Kylan reached into his tunic and pulled from it the leather pouch in which he stored his bowstring to keep the rain from softening it. The sentry next to him watched as he strung it to his man-high bow.

Glancing over at him, Kylan said: "I'll wager today's ale ration I can hit one of them."

The man gave a snort, but looked interested. "The Welsh bastards are too far away. It's a bet."

Kylan eyed the standard fluttering above Gwythur for windage. Then he plucked the waxed arrow from his quiver, fitted it to the bow, drew to his chest, and released, all in one fluid motion. The arrow sprang from the bow, arcing toward Gwythur. It chimed through the bronze boss on his shield and stuck, quivering, in the wood beneath.

Startled, Gwythur cursed loudly and fluently and galloped his horse out of range.

The sentry guffawed. "Ye owe me your ale."

"But I hit him."

"His shield don't count. Ye missed."

Kylan didn't argue.

A few moments later his replacement thumped him on the shoulder and motioned him to leave. Yawning, he climbed down the ladder and headed for the barracks and sleep.

As he passed the feast hall two guards stepped from the doorway and swung in behind him. At the far end Dungarth rounded the corner and stood, sword drawn.

Kylan's heart pounded against his ribs. There was no place to run. Ignoring Dungarth, he made as if to walk past him. The sword flashed up toward his chest.

Kylan tried to look surprised. "What is this?"

Dungarth grinned. "Looks innocent, don't he? I saw ye shoot that arrow, worm, and I think it had something on it. Take him."

Kylan reached for his sword, but a blow to his back drove him to his knees. One guard wrenched the sword from the scabbard while another picked up his fallen bow. As Kylan struggled to stand, Dungarth brought his fist down in a savage blow on Kylan's head. Pain exploded through him and he cried out. Then grainy darkness drove out the light.

"Impudent puppy!" Gwythur stormed, as Bedwyr examined the arrow. "If he'd missed, he would have spitted my horse, or worse."

"Kylan does not often miss," Irion said with a laugh. At Gwythur's insistence Bedwyr had started inviting him to the war councils and he basked in the success of his plan.

Bedwyr held the waxed shaft near a candle flame as the other leaders gathered around. When the wax dripped away he carefully unrolled the scrap of cloth and spread it on Gereint's writing desk.

Upon the cloth were scrawled two pictures. One was a crude diagram of Camelot, with a small arrow pointing to the center of the east wall. The other was a picture of the sun peering over the hills east of the fortress.

"Center of the east wall," Bedwyr said. "At dawn."

Owein struck his palm with his fist. "By the old gods! We have them!"

"Each of you pick ten of your best warriors," Bedwyr

commanded. "Owein will lead them over the wall. The rest of you stand ready to attack through the northeast gate. Tomorrow morning Camelot should be in our hands."

"Lord Bedwyr, I ask the honor of leading the raiders over the wall," Irion said. "The spy is Gwent's. The risk should fall on me."

Bedwyr glanced at him, frowning. "This task is critical to our success," he said. "It should fall to a tested warrior."

Irion felt himself redden. "I've been tried in battle," he said, "and passed the test. My warriors will tell you that."

Owein clapped Irion on the shoulder. "The lad is right. The plan is his. To him should go the honor of leading the assault on the wall."

Bedwyr hesitated, then nodded stiffly. "Very well. It's on your shoulders then, ap Medraut."

The remainder of the day dragged interminably. The rain stopped but the sky remained closed by pewter-gray clouds that seemed part of the earth. Soldiers finally succeeded in lighting cooking fires, the smoke struggling through the sodden air. To Irion, the time smelled of campfires and drying leather. He beseeched the gods of weather to keep the clouds overhead, for without them the short British summer night would not be dark enough to give them cover.

Evening finally came and the outline of the fortress dimmed above them. In the shifting lights of the fires the tents looked like crouching animals as the hours of night crawled toward dawn. And still they waited.

Finally, Irion rose and walked quietly to the staging point. Other warriors drifted in, their faces, like Irion's, blacked with mud and charcoal.

When they were all there he spoke to them in a murmur. "Wait in the bottom of the highest ditch until the rope comes. Then go up quietly. May your gods go with you."

At that moment the moon drifted through a hole in the clouds. White light clung to the walls of the fortress and spilled down the slope toward them. They waited with held breath until the moon was swallowed again by the clouds. Then Irion signaled them to follow him.

Like wraiths, they climbed the hill toward the east wall and slipped into the topmost ditch, pressing against the darkness of the steep bank. There they waited again as night wore thin. A flare of torches showed on the rampart above them and the heavy, monotonous tread of the patrol grew louder, then faded.

As he waited, Irion chewed on his fingernails and stared at the dim outline of the wall until it blurred, trying to make out anything that looked like a rope. He knew Kylan would not fail. He must not.

The sky had paled and the air carried the scent of dawn when Irion heard a rustling and saw a thick rope snake down the wall. Relief washed over him.

"Now!" he whispered. He rose from the ditch and sprinted toward the wall. Along the ditch others sprang out and followed.

On the wall above them Saxons appeared. A hail of spears and arrows rained down. The dawn erupted into shouts and curses. Beside Irion a warrior screamed and went down, impaled on a spear. Around him other men fell. Irion ran on alone.

He reached the rope and began to climb, heedless of the missiles flying around him. Laughter sounded on the wall. He looked up to see a Saxon lean over and chop at the rope with a seax. It parted and Irion crashed to the ground, stunned.

"Back!" someone yelled. "It's a trap!"

Gasping for breath, Irion scrambled back to the ditch. Bodies lay strewn around him. At the bottom of the hill, British archers loosed a flight of arrows at the wall. A few found their marks, and the rest of the Saxons on the ramparts stopped hurling their spears and took refuge. Under cover of the arrows Irion climbed from the ditch and ran down the hill.

When he reached the British lines he turned and looked back. Below the wall, bodies were heaped. He glanced around. Only a handful had made it back.

In a rage Irion seized a bow from an archer and fired arrow after arrow toward the fortress. They were met only with mocking laughter from the ramparts. Finally, his arrows gone, he threw the bow down and sank to the ground, covering his eyes with his hands. To his shame he had not even suffered a scratch.

TWENTY-FOUR

In Gereint's tent, the leaders of the British sat stunned. Gereint and Gwynllew urged them to abandon the siege and retreat, before they became trapped between the anvil of Camelot and the Saxon hammer.

"If Maelgwn is coming, where is he, I'm asking?" Gwynllew said. "We're out of food and my men are forced to eat their horses."

"Even if he does come in time," Gereint said, "there's no hope of seizing the fortress now. And without its protection we're doomed. I'm also for leaving this place."

But Owein growled, "I will not be frightened into bolting for home like a barn-soured mare, before even a blow is struck at me. By the Wolves of Annwn, I will stay!"

Irion sat alone with his head down, ignored by the others.

As the chieftains argued among themselves, Bedwyr said little, letting them choose their own course. He did not look at Irion, for he felt sympathy toward the youth, and that irritated him. He knew he should abandon the siege. There was no hope of succeeding, and he was convinced that Elyn was dead by now, in any event. A man with any wisdom would pack up and ride away. But what use was there? Where would he go? He had no home, no one waiting. And today he wanted nothing more than just to go home.

Stop feeling sorry for yourself, he thought. You have a fire, you have a bed. How much home does a person need? But he knew now that home was more than mountains and rivers and remembered landscapes. More than a horse farm on the banks of some quiet river. The rootedness for which he ached was not just a longing for place but for a self that had been buried with his past. He no longer knew who he was.

Later that morning, while the road remained open, Gereint packed up and rode away with all his following, toward home and his beloved Erim. Marcianus and Gwynllew, agreeing on something for once in their lives, hurried after, meeting no one's eye.

On the pretext of hunting, Bedwyr saddled Ariant and rode eastward out of camp, leaving Gwythur in charge. The wolf-hound had trotted away earlier to hunt his own food. Though Bedwyr had refused his day's small ration of barley bannock, he felt no hunger, only a deep ache he could not define.

He rode with loose reins, letting Ariant have his head, not caring in which direction he went. The land seemed empty, lying in a great silence, as if all life that had legs or wings had fled the coming battle. Around him he saw green, so deep the very air seemed emerald. As he rode, a mist crept up from somewhere in the direction of Ynys Afallon and thickened about him, swirling around the horse's legs.

Lost in thought Bedwyr was startled by an owl that launched itself from the branch of a withered oak and drifted silently across his path. For a moment he thought of Myrddin, with his strange dress and gruff manner. People had thought Arthur's adviser a sorcerer, a magician of great power who could transform himself into an owl because he was rarely seen entering or leaving Camelot. Bedwyr shook his head. Perhaps if he had truly been a magician, Camelot would not have fallen.

Ghostly in the fog, the owl skimmed low over the ground in search of prey. Ariant, curious or perhaps just bored, turned and followed it. Instead of flapping away in alarm the bird seemed to toy with them, staying just within sight.

The mist grew thicker and Bedwyr made his way through drifting whiteness. Dark shapes loomed and were lost. Suddenly the horse stopped. For a moment a breeze shredded the fog. To his right Bedwyr glimpsed a standing stone, then others on both sides. He shivered. He was not superstitious, but there were places that were safer left alone.

He was about to rein Ariant around when a quail exploded

from behind one of the stones and whirred past. From somewhere above it, the owl plummeted after, talons reaching. A nearby standing stone tilted to within two feet of the ground. The quail reached it inches ahead of the owl and disappeared beneath it. The owl banked hard and flapped away out of sight.

Bedwyr hesitated, then dismounted. Standing stones or not, the quail was food. He owed it to the starving warriors to bring it back if he could.

Crouching on his hands and knees, he peered beneath the stone. He could see little. He felt ahead for the soft warmth of the bird, then crawled further in, scraping his back on the rough stone, but he felt only the coldness of rock and damp earth. The space grew tighter and Bedwyr dropped to his stomach, wondering whether the quail was large enough to justify the effort. He reached as far as he could and his hand slid over gravel into . . . nothing.

Cautiously he crept forward. The air was cool and musty with the smell of earth. Bedwyr peered into the blackness of a hole no larger than a shield. Curiosity drew him on.

He turned and swung his legs into the hole, feeling for solid ground. Crumbles of dirt slid down around him. Half a spear's length down, his feet touched rock. And something else that crackled like dried parchment.

Groping, Bedwyr discovered a bundle of waxed rushes and, nearby, a worn flint and striker. He soon had one of the rushes burning and squinted against the sudden brightness.

The fire reflected dully from gray rock around him. He appeared to be in a natural vent which snaked through the mother rock away into darkness. Bedwyr felt a moment of panic. Caves were supposed to be doorways to Annwn, the underworld. Then he admonished himself. Besides, he cared little at the moment if he met Arawn, the Gray Man of Annwn, himself.

Quail forgotten, he picked up a handful of rushes and thrust them into his baldric, then set off cautiously down the tunnel. The rushlight carved a flickering hole in the darkness.

As he rounded a turn the walls of the tunnel swept outward and disappeared. On all sides the light showed only blackness. From somewhere ahead he felt a draft of cold, damp air and heard the trickle and splash of running water.

Bedwyr moved to his left, trying to find the wall. After a few steps the torchlight reflected glistening, wet rock, and keeping his shoulder near the wall, he walked slowly along it.

He stepped around a jutting rib of rock and stopped in surprise. Ahead was a lake, still and dark and silent in the feeble rushlight. "Black as a Saxon's heart," he murmured. High above him the ceiling of the cavern threw his words back at him. The unseen rock wall on the far side of the lake echoed them again.

Against the near wall a narrow ledge of rock skirted the shore of the lake. Seeing no other way around, Bedwyr followed it. He moved slowly, for the ledge was slippery and angled downward so that the footing was treacherous.

The ledge dipped below the surface of the lake and icy water lapped over his boots, sending ripples out onto the still surface. He was ankle deep, then knee deep, before the ledge leveled off and finally climbed. When at last he stepped from the water his legs were numb from the cold.

The rush sputtered and Bedwyr drew another from his baldric, lighting it from the dying torch. Ahead, the floor of the cavern sloped steeply upward. Holding high the lighted rush Bedwyr walked up the rough surface.

A short distance up the slope the flickering light cast into relief a line of runes carved into the stone wall. Bedwyr looked closer, then stopped in amazement. The runes were graven on an arched stone door, designed so that it fitted cunningly into the blank rock of the wall. He traced the marks with his finger. Runes such as these were used by Druids, and by the secretive Myrddin when he wished his words to remain private. Bedwyr could not read them.

He pushed against the door tentatively, then harder. For all that it moved, he might have been pushing against the wall itself. Myrddin had disappeared years before Camlann, Bedwyr remembered, and the peasants told a story that he had been entranced by Nimue, a young sorceress he had fallen in love with in his old age. She had sealed him into a chamber in a cave, so the story went, where he would remain forever, powerless to overcome the spell that bound him.

Bedwyr shivered. Probably the door only closed off some storeroom, perhaps used by Myrddin in long years past. Yet the cavern itself might provide a secret way into Camelot, for it explained how Arthur's adviser could come and go without being seen.

Bedwyr walked on. A few steps ahead the slope ended abruptly in a vertical wall of rock. His torch failing, Bedwyr lit another, then turned to the right and walked slowly along the new wall, his steps echoing faintly in the darkness.

Something clung to the rock ahead and he quickened his pace. A thick rope ladder soared up the wall into the darkness. Bedwyr held the torch as high as he could and peered upward, but saw only blackness closing around the rushlight.

He pulled on the rope and dust flew. Holding the rush in his teeth, he climbed gingerly onto the bottom rung of the ladder and bounced, testing its strength. The ladder seemed sound and Bedwyr began to climb, wrapping his left arm around one side rope as he gripped the other with his hand.

For what seemed an eternity he crept up the rock wall, blinded by the lighted rush near his face. He felt as if he were ascending from the very roots of the world. Once he missed a rung and the rope ladder bounced and twisted, but he clung grimly, sweating, then went on. The echoes of the sounds he made came more quickly now and he guessed that he had climbed into a narrow chimney in the rock.

At last he reached for the next rung and his hand found instead a dusty ledge. With a gasp of relief he climbed onto it and lay panting. When his breathing steadied he looked around. The ledge was narrow and no more than twenty feet long. Near his head a small opening showed black against the dull gleam of the rock.

Bedwyr thrust the torch into it and peered after, but could see little. He drew a deep breath and crawled in. His hand sank into moist, cool earth. The rushlight revealed a pit, on the side of which leaned another ladder, this one wooden. Strewn about its base were bundles of waxed rushes.

He started up the ladder, then hesitated. He had no idea where he would come out, perhaps in the center of the mead hall or the *brôch*, the circular stone tower Arthur had built for the Round Table. He pictured himself crawling out into the middle of a surprised Saxon council. He took a deep breath and began to climb. There was no choice.

As he went up, his back scraped the sides of the hole. The pit was not deep and a few steps brought him to the top of the ladder. Above him he found only solid rock. Fighting panic, he pushed against the roof with his back and, to his vast relief, felt it give.

Raising the rock slab a few inches, he listened. Light filtered into the pit but he heard no sounds beyond his own breathing. Bedwyr drew his sword, then thrust up hard with his shoulders and the stone lifted up and back. He vaulted out of the pit.

TWENTY-FIVE

Bedwyr stood in an empty room that smelled of dust and age. Light sifted through a high window to reveal debris heaped and piled at random: a stack of untanned cowhides, bags of raw wool, a sack of lime, several broken cart wheels leaning against the wall. Above him, sleeping bats that had been clinging head down to the thatch woke and jittered out the window with brittle squeaks. Nearby stood an altar made of stone slabs, defaced and stained with obscene pictures scrawled in what looked like dried blood.

He knew where he was, though he had not spent much time here. It was the building Arthur had used as his Christian chapel. A moss-grown, dry stone building, it was much older than Camelot, so old that it seemed to grow from the hill itself.

For the first time in days, Bedwyr felt a surge of hope. Here was their entry into Camelot. He was tempted to wait until dark, then look through the fortress for Elyn, but he knew that would be folly. He sheathed his sword and climbed back into the pit.

Darkness had fallen when Bedwyr emerged from the hole beneath the standing stone. Ariant greeted him with a soft nicker. To the west, between him and Camelot hill, he saw the flames of the British bivouac fires, blotted out at intervals by the black shapes of patrolling sentries. He picked one form and rode toward it.

"Who comes?" the sentry called.

"Bedwyr."

The sentry peered at him for a moment, spear leveled. Then he broke into a wide grin of relief. "Lord Bedwyr! We thought you ambushed and dead, begging your pardon." He passed him through.

To a hurried council in his tent Bedwyr called the remaining Cymry leaders. "There are left to us barely nine hundred warriors," he said. "Yet that may still be enough to take the fortress." He described what he had found.

The chieftains' faces lit with hope.

"By Lugh's shaggy eyebrows," Owein said. "Tomorrow night we'll sleep in Camelot."

They decided that Bedwyr, with Gwythur and Dafydd, would lead a hundred warriors back through the cavern to open the northeast gate. Owein would lead the army into the fortress.

Bedwyr left Fergus behind. The wolfhound, who had bounded up from the corner of the tent on his arrival to put his big paws on his shoulders, heaved a morose sigh and slouched back to the corner.

Within an hour Bedwyr found himself back in the cave at the head of a line of warriors, silent except for the soft tread of their feet. In the torchlight the dark surface of the lake mirrored the glittering hauberks of linked mail and the shields carried on their backs, and reflected faces grim and unsmiling beneath their helms. As they passed the rune-carved door many of the warriors made the sign against enchantment. The rope ladder remained where it had been, scaling the darkness above them.

Bedwyr waited until all had gathered, then said, "Let each man count five and twenty before he begins to climb, to avoid overstraining the rope. There's a ledge at the top which will hold eighteen or twenty men. When it's full those on it will go up into the chapel. What awaits there I do not know. May your gods go with you."

To leave himself free to fight, Bedwyr gave his torch to Gwythur, who would go up last. He began to climb into the darkness, the ladder stretching as it accepted his weight. Twenty-five counts later it bounced and creaked as the next man's weight was added to it. Rung by rung Bedwyr pulled himself upward until, reaching, he felt the rough surface of the ledge. He crawled onto it.

A torch appeared below as the next warrior made his way up. Kneeling at the edge of the rock shelf Bedwyr grasped his hand and hauled him up. Then, as each warrior appeared, he pulled him onto the ledge.

When the ledge was crowded Bedwyr signaled and they ducked through the hole and crept up the wood ladder. Beneath the opening he hesitated a moment, listening, but heard nothing save the hiss of swords loosening in their sheaths below him.

He sprang into the chapel. It was empty. But as he turned to give the all-clear signal the door to the building groaned inward. Torchlight glared on the surprised faces of a Saxon and two slaves.

The barbarian warrior saw him and sprang forward with a snarl. Bedwyr drew his sword and they met with the clang of iron on iron, like great dull bells. Other Britons hurtled up through the opening. Seeing them, the Saxon broke off the attack and fled through the door, yelling his alarm as he ran.

Bedwyr sheathed his sword, panting. As he did so muffled screams came from the pit. He seized a sputtering torch from the floor and flung himself down the ladder.

On the lip of the ledge clung Dafydd, his hands scrabbling for a grip on the rock. Relief bathed his face as he saw help coming. Bedwyr reached down and pulled him onto the ledge. A few feet below the lip the rope ended in frayed stumps.

"What happened?"

Dafydd shuddered. "We heard fighting, my lord. We all crowded forward to climb the rope. There must have been too much weight." He met Bedwyr's eyes. "My lord, I'm no coward. But to hang like that in the dark, without knowing . . . Thank you."

Bedwyr clasped the youth's shoulder and sent him above, then kneeled at the edge. "Does Gwythur live?" His voice rebounded in the rock chimney.

From the depths below a reverberating answer came. "I'm here, Lord Bedwyr. We lost six men in the fall. One more with broken legs. Can you get us more rope?"

"There's no time to find any. They've raised the alarm.

We'll try to force the gate with the warriors we have. Go back through the cavern and lend your strength to the war band outside."

"We'll be there straight," Gwythur called. "Save some of the bastards for us, look you." As Bedwyr scrambled back up he heard him barking orders at the troops below.

Bedwyr counted twenty-two warriors in addition to himself who had made it up into the chapel.

"Quickly!" he said. "To the gate. No lights. Don't stop to fight unless there's no choice." And he raced through the door.

Outside, the night was alive with shouts and scurrying torches. They ran. Behind them came yells and running feet and the rasp of drawn blades. Arrows hissed past them and a Cymry warrior beside Bedwyr stumbled with a gasp and went down.

Three barbarians ran out of a stable, fumbled for weapons, and went down before British swords. They ran on.

The glare of torches on the walls outlined the square bulk of the gate tower. From it warriors erupted and scrambled down the ladders to intercept them. They barred their path and the Cymry could run no further. As they slowed, their pursuers caught them.

The British gathered into a tight knot and hacked their way forward. But the Saxon numbers grew as more barbarians caught up. The shield ring grew ever smaller as one by one the British fell and died in the blood-stained dust of Camelot.

Their advance stopped. Around him Bedwyr could see nothing but wave after wave of tusked helmets and yellow heads. If they did not reach the gates within moments they would not reach it at all.

Near him Dafydd stumbled and went down. Bedwyr sprang astride him and took on his shield the ax blow meant for the youth. It clove the shield in two, numbing his arm. He jerked shield and ax aside and thrust his sword into the enemy.

Then he threw back his head and shouted a war cry he had nearly forgotten: "For Britain! For Arthur!"

His companions took up the shout, and the strength and force of it cut through the din of battle. For only an instant the barbarians hesitated, but that was enough. The Cymry surged forward and carved a path to the gate.

Bedwyr wondered where the British war band was. If they did not arrive as the gates swung out they would be too late, for he would not be able to keep them open. If they were already crowded against them, pressing inward, he would not be able to open them at all.

He glanced up. The gates were massive timbers hung on great iron hinges and battened closed by three heavy beams. Bedwyr and Dafydd sheathed their swords and heaved up on the lowest of the beams. Around them the Cymry formed a protective circle, while a killing hail of arrows fell from the walls. The beam lifted grudgingly and Bedwyr threw it aside.

The center beam stuck fast in its bracket and they could not move it. Another warrior sheathed his sword and sprang to their aid. With a squeal of splintering wood the beam lifted and fell away. The warrior cried out, spun around and fell, an arrow protruding from his back.

The top beam was just beyond Bedwyr's reach. In desperation he drew his sword and thrust upward with the point. Dafydd did the same and the beam inched upward. It fell with a crash.

With a shout of triumph they threw their shoulders into the gates. Slowly they gave outward, then swung faster until they crashed into the walls outside. The gates of Camelot stood open.

His back to the gate, Bedwyr turned to make his last defense. Of those who had come through the cavern with him, only Dafydd still stood, leaning with a bloodied face against the opposite gate. As Bedwyr watched, a spear caught him in the shoulder and he twisted to the ground in agony.

Enemies boiled out of the open gateway. A dozen hands seized the gate and began to pull it shut. Bedwyr staggered, felt himself falling, knew he would die if he did. He put out his arm to catch his fall and from the corner of his eye he saw the blow coming, the sword looping over and down in a slow, graceful arc, the face of his enemy distorted in a grimace of hate.

Then the face exploded and the blow went wide. He looked up to see Owein grinning hugely. A hamlike hand reached down, hauled him to his feet, and propped him against the gate. His ears were full of wild shouting: Cymry war cries. The gate went slack as the barbarians let go and turned to meet the army that was upon them.

"Sometime do you teach me that trick of fighting from your knees!" the Cornovi chieftain shouted.

"Well met, Owein."

Owein glanced impatiently into the fortress where the defenders had retreated, swept away by the flood of British through the gate. The battle lust was on him. "Are you well, Roman? I have enemies to kill!"

"Aye."

The flame-haired giant waded into the battle with a triumphant raving.

Bedwyr sagged against the gate, sword dangling from his hand. But there was no time to rest. Inside Camelot ox horns brayed to regroup the Saxons. He searched through the fallen warriors for a shield with leather straps instead of hand grips. He found one, a round buckler, bullhide over wood, slippery with blood. Tying it onto his handless arm, Bedwyr walked wearily into the fortress, toward the din of battle.

The British swept upward from the gates and drove the disorganized barbarians before them. Squads of British bolted onto the walls to clear them of defenders. Saxons stumbled from their barracks, half-dressed and buckling on their swords, to be met by thrusts of Cymry spears.

The enemies fell back to the ridgeline which divided the fortress at its widest part. Some of the mercenaries might have fled through the southwest gate but that way was shut and barred against them by Ulfang's personal guard.

Fighting grew fierce, building to building, doorway to doorway, a struggling of dim figures in a darkness spattered with orange fires. Swords struck gold and blue sparks as they met metal shields. A night fight was dangerous to friend and foe alike, for men hacked at any moving shadow.

Foot by foot the British ground their way up the slope. At the top of the ridge the defenders rallied and counterattacked. The armies seemed to draw apart for an instant, then come together like two rams.

Bedwyr found himself at the center of the ridge. To his right he caught a glimpse of Owein, tearing the night apart with his fury. In front he saw only a chaos of struggling shadows and wild eyes. The battle cries were over and men fought now like animals, silently. The bodies of the dead hindered the feet of the living.

For what seemed hours, the lines strained together, locked and immovable. Then slowly the British line wavered and bowed backward. Contesting every foot, they were driven back down the hill they had just won.

Bedwyr fought at the center, beyond weariness, numbed sword arm rising and falling in macabre rhythm, no thought but for the next parry, the next thrust, unaware even that the line was being pushed backward. Behind him someone called, the voice cutting through the fog in his brain.

"Lord Bedwyr! Watch out!"

He knew the voice was Irion's and he saw from the corner of his eye the Saxon working his way around to his back, but he was unable to prevent it, for his whole attention focused on the enemy in front of him, so close that Bedwyr gagged on the foul breath of his decayed teeth.

His concentration broken for an instant, he did not anticipate quickly enough, and he watched a sword slide into his thigh. He heard his enemy grunt with the exertion of the thrust and he felt the sticky warmth of his blood flow down his leg. He saw all this and felt no pain. With all of his remaining energy he brought his own sword up into the man's exposed chest, an unthinking reflex triggered by long years of experience. The man gasped in shock at his death blow and sank to the ground.

But the other Saxon saw his chance and his sword crashed into Bedwyr's helm. As he fell Bedwyr dimly saw the great wolfhound hurdle over him, mouth dripping blood, and heard a scream. Then batwing tatters of darkness reached into his mind and he knew no more.

Irion stooped over Bedwyr's body and dragged it away from the battle line. Quickly he ran back to the melee. The barbarians pushed the British back faster now, and Irion knew the retreat would soon become a rout.

Sword high, he charged the Saxon line. "To me!" His call rang clearly above the noise of battle. "Cymry! This is your hour! This is your fortress! For Camelot!"

For a moment the British retreat halted. But most warriors did not know him, or did not trust him. So the fallback began again.

Then Owein reached down and picked up a standard, torn and bloody beyond recognition of kingdom or color. He held it high and with a great roar of rage strode up the hill.

The British cheered and surged forward. They pushed the Saxons back until they controlled the ridgeline, then slowly drove them down the other side toward the southwest gate. Irion heard fighting at the gate and screams, and the sound of the gates swinging open.

Suddenly the resistance collapsed as barbarians took their chance to flee through the opened gates. Those who were left retreated into the tower and the iron door clanged shut.

To Irion the change from fighting to not fighting came as a shock. He looked around, bewildered. As the first light of dawn showed in the east, Camelot, save for the *brôch*, belonged to the British.

Bedwyr awoke from a comfortless dark in which he wandered through murky places. The air was heavy with the smells of vinegar and herbs, blood and sickness. His head throbbed and his wound was on fire. Around him men groaned or shrieked among the urgent murmurs of attendants. He dimly recalled a sharpening of the pain when the wound was tended. Then he began to remember more and, having begun, could not stop.

Turning his head he saw long lines of straw pallets under a thatched roof. All of them were occupied by injured or dying men. Soldiers fortunate enough not to be wounded hurried back and forth with hot water and salves for the surgeons. Outside he heard orders called and the creak of cart wheels, and from the roof, the blithe song of a goldfinch.

Someone cleared his throat and he turned back to see Gwythur standing above him, arm in a sling. He looked relieved.

"It's nice to see you back, my lord."

Bedwyr sat up, fighting the urge to vomit. "How long have I been here?"

"The best part of the day. It's near to suppertime."

[186]

"The fortress?"

"Ours. Except the tower. That horse-tailed beggar is holed up in there with a hundred or so men. We've tried to batter in the door but it's iron and too thick. We were losing too many men to their spears, so we gave it up."

He listened bleakly as Gwythur recounted the battle. More than three hundred British warriors had been killed, including Hywel, the giant infantry captain who had seemed indestructible. When the Cymry line had fallen back, Hywel had not yielded and was engulfed by barbarians. They finally toppled him, like a great tree ringed by insects.

Owein had survived, but lay weak as a newborn from loss of blood from a dozen wounds.

When Gwythur finished, Bedwyr said, "To whom do I owe my life?"

Gwythur scratched his head. "Well, the dog there, I expect, for one."

At the foot of the pallet Fergus stopped licking matted fur around an angry cut. He gave a whining yawn and thumped his tail on the plank floor.

"Last I saw him," Gwythur said, "he was prowling the edge of the battle, looking for you. Irion said he jumped over three people to tear the throat out of a barbarian about to backstab you. Then Irion dragged you to safety after that, so I guess he's to be thanked as well."

Bedwyr frowned and said nothing.

"With you and Owein both laid by, Irion has taken command, and doing a good job, too, sir." His pride was unmistakable. "He's got the fortress as ready as may be for them Saxons. They'll be on us tomorrow morning."

"Then Maelgwn had better reach us tonight," Bedwyr said. "Send a rider north on the fastest horse. Tell him that if he loves Gwynedd and Britain, make haste. Unless he makes Camelot tonight he'll find only smoldering ashes."

"It would be a waste of a man, sir."

"What?"

Gwythur hesitated, studying Bedwyr as if to measure his strength. "It's like this, lord. One of Gereint's captains, Ceredig by name, rode in an hour ago. I got to know him well enough during the last month and he's a decent sort, for a Demetian.

He was ashamed of running out like that, so he came back to help. Not that he'll be of much help now. He ran into a band of Saxon looters who had wandered north ahead of the main horde, and they stuck an arrow in his leg."

"And?"

"And he said King Gereint met Maelgwn on the road north. Gereint told him there was no hope for us; that even with Gwynedd's army we were as good as dead."

Bedwyr watched him, dread growing.

"Lord, King Maelgwn has turned back. There'll be no help from Gwynedd."

He sagged, numb. "How many warriors have we left?"

"Less than six hundred able to fight."

They looked at each other, both knowing that six hundred men had no chance of holding the walls against thousands of Saxons.

"Anything else to report, captain?"

"No, my lord."

Bedwyr held out his hand and, with Gwythur's help, struggled to his feet. When the dizziness subsided he said, "Call a council as soon as might be. And Gwythur—were any thrall women rescued alive?

"Aye. A few." Gwythur looked away. "The lady in the cage was not among them. Lord Irion already checked."

TWENTY-SIX

Irion stood near the gate, watching as the last of the horses were led into the fortress. All afternoon a steady stream of refugees had trudged past Camelot. Some sought shelter inside. Irion had discouraged them from staying, for it was safer for them to keep going west, though in the end there would be no safe place in Britain.

A soldier labored past under a double yoke of water buckets and Irion hailed him. The man eased down the buckets and unhooked a wooden dipper, filled it, and offered it to him. He drank deeply of the cool, sweet water, noting by its reflection the grime and dried blood that covered his face, wishing some could be spared to wash. He thanked the man and sent him on his way.

A commotion behind him made him turn. A sentry came toward him, pushing ahead of him a warrior, hands tied.

"What goes forward?" Irion asked.

"Caught him sneaking away, sir," said the sentry.

Irion looked at the deserter, a slightly built veteran with sharp eyes that would not meet his gaze.

"You know the penalty for desertion is death," he said. "Why did you risk it?"

The man stared sullenly at the ground. "What risk was there? We're going to die anyway."

"Shall I take him and hang him, Lord Irion?"

Irion thought for a moment. "No. Let him go."

Both men looked at him in shock.

"He's right," Irion said. "Without Maelgwn, there's no hope that any of us will survive. If Lord Bedwyr cannot resume command I intend to allow any who wish, to leave. I will send no man to a certain death."

Hands freed, the deserter ran through the gate and loped down the hill, snatching quick looks behind him as he ran.

Irion turned and walked toward the dressing station, feeling strangely content despite the desperateness of the situation. In the chaos of the battle it hadn't mattered who his father was, only who he was.

Catullan still tended the wounded, his face gray with fatigue. Dark blotches stained his tunic and blood and salve smeared his arms to the elbows. Irion watched him for a moment. As he worked he cursed. With each new wound he treated his swearing increased.

Irion touched the medicus on the shoulder. "All wounded who can walk," he said, "should leave the fortress immediately. Only death awaits them here."

Catullan nodded brusquely and continued wrapping a mangled hand.

"I will not order you, friend," Irion continued, "for you're not within my power to command. But I ask you to leave Camelot also, while the road is still clear. You can find a boat in Cornwall and cross the estuary to Caerwent."

The medicus looked up at him, exhausted beyong retort. "I cannot," he said simply. He waved his hand at the rows of pallets.

"Then you will likely die with us," Irion said. He reached for his dagger, intending to give it to the medicus for protection in the pillaging to come, for Saxons respected no one. But the dagger was gone, lost some time during the assault. And the surgeon, he realized, would not have accepted it, anyway. He clasped the old man's hand. "Your gods be with you, Catullan."

When he reached the makeshift council room Irion found Bedwyr alone outside, leaning on a crutch made from a spear shaft, his face set in lines of pain.

"How is your wound, Lord Bedwyr?"

"I'll live long enough. I understand I owe my life to you a second time."

"No, lord. It's your hound you have to thank." Irion stroked the wolfhound's head.

"Mm." Bedwyr was silent for a moment. "The others are

inside. I waited for you because I wished to speak with you. Alone."

Irion waited, bewildered, for an explanation. He knew of nothing he'd done to warrant a private reprimand, unless assuming command . . .

"Lord, if . . ."

"I'm sorry." Bedwyr's voice was quiet, drawn.

"What?"

"I have treated you badly."

"You owe me no thanks for my actions in battle."

"No," said Bedwyr. "Not that. Though you have my gratitude, and more truly than I expressed it before. I've wronged you because you're the son of Medraut, even though in your actions there is no resemblance to him. I should have seen that at our first meeting. Yet, because I needed a man to hate for my own failure, I hated you. In truth, you look more like Arthur, but I saw only your resemblance to your father." He smiled a wan smile. "I refused to see what was there to see, until now."

"Now?" Irion sorted through the things he had done but came up blank.

"The deserter. Arthur would have done such a thing as you did. Medraut would have had the man whipped before hanging him. Forgive me for being blind."

Joy spread within Irion. "There's nothing to forgive, lord. Come, I'll help you to the council."

The Cymry leaders, what remained of them, were already in the room slouched in chairs, lost in gloom. They looked up as Bedwyr entered.

Owein, who had been carried in on a litter, spoke, subdued for once. "Can we hold these walls?"

Bedwyr eased himself down onto an empty bench, stretching his wounded leg along it with a groan. "No, Owein. We cannot hold the walls. Not against that many. Not with six hundred men. Camelot was built to house a large army. Her walls enclose eighteen acres. Spread six hundred men along them to defend against six thousand and we'll be overwhelmed by a force massing at any point."

"Then our choice is simple," Owein said. 'We run or we die. If we stay behind the walls, we're cooked. If we fight them in the open, they'll eat us raw." He stared at the others as if hoping for contradiction, but no one disagreed.

"You're right," said Bedwyr. "And any who wish to leave, I now release, with honor. There is no disgrace in refusing to throw away your life for a cause without hope. I, myself, will run no further."

There was silence, save for the tapping of a moth against a lantern. The leaders studied the floor.

Finally, Irion said, "I will go and meet the Darkness with those who choose to stay. Perhaps we'll light it for a brief time, and men will yet remember us on the other side of it."

Owein looked at him for a long time, then broke into a sly grin. "Aye, all men die. I suppose in the end it's the reason for dying that counts. If it comes to that, I prefer a death on the battlefield surrounded by Saxons. I'll take a dozen of them with me to Uffern."

Gwythur spoke, picking his way through the words with care. "I've never wanted to grow old sitting in a chair and feeling my veins rust. But there is one thing: Me and the men have talked. We're cavalrymen, and we fight best from horse-back. If we must die, we would ride there on our horses, not be chopped inot kindling with the gates."

So it was decided. In the morning the Cymry would ride out of Camelot and meet the Saxons on the open plain.

"We'll fight such a battle that the bards will sing of it for a thousand years," Irion said.

"Well," said Bedwyr, "at least a few months."

TWENTY-SEVEN

Night came, the air like warm gruel. Soldiers sat in groups around small fires lit for comfort and light, rather than heat. They talked in low voices and laughed nervously, and did not speak of the other fires they could see from the walls on the plains to the east, tiny saffron flames that spread out for miles.

Though his leg throbbed and fresh blood soaked his bandages, Bedwyr limped from fire to fire, trading stale jokes, clapping shoulders, keeping the soldiers from despair. His very presence lifted their spirits, for rumors had spread wildly about his condition, and some said Bedwyr was dead.

As he hobbled into the circle of a bivouac fire a soldier elbowed his companions and the group fell silent, eyeing Bedwyr's leg.

"Lord Bedwyr," called the elbower. "How is it with you? We heard you was wounded near death by a barbarian sword."

"No," Bedwyr said. "His sword hurt me not at all. But he had a breath to melt the snows of Yr Widdfa."

Bedwyr found Owein and Irion sitting with Gwythur, and collapsed onto the ground. For a time nothing was said, each man thinking his own thoughts.

Somewhere an owl was asking its eerie question. Owein spread his fingers behind his back against evil spirits. "There's a soul crying in that voice," he muttered.

"You believe in the old gods then, Owein?" Irion asked.

Owein frowned, thoughtful. "I don't know," he said at last. "The bad things that are happening to Britain are a good argument for the old gods. But the more the country suffers, the stronger grow the Christ worshipers. They're a strange people. Always they excuse disaster by saying their god is punishing them for their sins. And they prattle of love and peace, but hardly ever follow their own teachings. Yet a god who has died and come back to life is not to be trifled with. A man cannot make up his mind."

"Perhaps it's best to be on good terms with whatever gods there may be," Irion said.

Owein studied Bedwyr. "You've been many places, and seen things few other Britons have seen. What gods do you follow?"

Bedwyr shrugged. "I've followed many, and I've been threatened with the hells of many others. The gods change from country to country, but men remain the same. Saxons kill for their surly gods. Christians kill for their one god. But still they kill. When a spear tears a man's life from his heart, he's just as dead, no matter what religion is behind it."

From an adjacent fire a flute began playing, its sweet song following the smoke into the clouds above them. A man's voice joined it, clear and untroubled. Bedwyr looked over to see Dafydd, his shoulder swathed in white bandages.

Other men joined him, then warriors from other fires added their voices, until Camelot itself rang with the music of hundreds of men singing in unison. A line of melody began above the first melody, then another rolled under it like a dark river.

And for no reason that he knew, Bedwyr wept. He realized that he would never carry out King Arthur's last order, but for the first time he forgave himself. He had given the best that was in him to give. His efforts, and those of the men around him, would be swept away, but they were not the less worthy for that, for all things must end.

And if there was an answer, he thought, perhaps it was simply this, that the lives of Arthur and those who believed in what he had believed were one great chord swept across the years, a song of beauty to catch men's hearts. And though the musicians would die, the music would live on in the imaginations of all who had heard it.

At dawn Bedwyr rose and, maneuvering his crutch under his arm, limped out of the barracks. Fergus growled a grumpy protest at being awakened, stretched, and followed.

The air felt heavy and still, with an oppressive closeness that made breathing difficult. Around him the fortress stirred into life as warriors saddled horses, checked straps and cinches, and laced on battle gear. Bedwyr walked to the picket line, where Ariant greeted him with a soft nicker, and he stroked the velvet nose.

The grooms had been sent away during the night with the wounded who could walk, and he saddled the stallion himself while Ariant snorted and fidgeted, knowing what was coming.

Irion walked up, carrying his saddle. "Outriders say the Saxons have broken camp, Lord Bedwyr."

Bedwyr nodded and fumbled in his saddle pouch. "Look you, Irion. If Elyn by chance still lives, and you should find her after this day's work, tell her for me that I . . . that she . . . Oh, Uffern's Fires, man! Tell her I love her still."

He pulled from the pouch a small looking glass of polished silver, with a corded gold handle. "Give her this for me."

Irion took the mirror. "Aye. If you will tell her the same for me."

Shouts sounded outside the fortress and the gates groaned open. Bedwyr looked out and saw the light cavalry flying toward them, Dunaut at their head, riders strung behind him like a storm-blown skein of geese. They dug their way up the slope and shot through the gate.

Dunaut rode over to them, his horse foam flecked and stumbling. He slid from the animal's back and Bedwyr welcomed him with an outstretched hand.

"There's six thousand irritated Saxons behind me," Dunaut gasped. Breathlessly he described their efforts to slow the horde. "They wouldn't listen to reason, though we left a trail of crow-ridden barbarians halfway across Britain. Give us a hint of that water."

He drank deeply from Irion's flask, then looked around. "Where is everyone?"

Bedwyr explained and Dunaut shook his head. "Gone home? What's to do?"

"Those you see," Bedwyr said, "have chosen to stay and fight. You already have done more than your measure. Don't deprive Rheged of their King."

Fear flickered in Dunaut's eyes for a moment, and he

turned away to look down at the green meadows over which he had just ridden, rubbing his hand over his sword-scarred nose. Then he turned back and shrugged his shoulders with a little laugh.

"In truth, kings are as common as blackberries. Better I should die now and be missed, than live long and let my subjects remember the uses for feathers and pitch."

He clapped Bedwyr on the shoulder and led his horse away to water it.

As Irion slipped his baldric over his head and settled it into place, Bedwyr saw tears slide down his cheeks. One by one the surviving warriors of Gwent came by to clasp Irion's hand or clap his shoulder in farewell.

The trickle of peasants fleeing the Saxons had now almost stopped. A lone figure plodded wearily toward them and labored up the slope to the fortress. Bedwyr shook his head. This morning the man would be safer nearly anywhere else in Britain. As he turned away something about the man's rolling gait caught his eye. He looked back, peering closely. Cethrum!

Bedwyr went to the gate and greeted the priest as he reached the top of the hill, panting. Cethrum stuck out his hand and Bedwyr pulled him up.

"What is it you do here, friend?" he asked the priest. "We are about to have several thousand Saxons for breakfast."

"I know," Cethrum panted. "I forgot . . . what a climb . . . this is."

He breathed deeply for a moment, then said, "We had reports at Ynys Afallon of what has happened. I thought your army priests might need some help." He eyed Bedwyr's leg. "Is it serious?"

Bedwyr shook his head. "The wound won't kill me. You're welcome here, of course, Cethrum. But there may be little more you can do than die with us. Why throw your life away?"

Cethrum looked at him reprovingly. "If you think giving solace to dying men is to throw my life away, then I see I have more work to do with you."

Bedwyr felt himself redden. "I only meant . . ."

"No, no, let be. I know what you meant. Bedwyr, there's another reason I came." He hesitated as Irion came up to report.

"He's a friend," Bedwyr said. "Irion ap Medraut of Gwent."

Cethrum nodded at him, then turned back to Bedwyr. "Constantine has died."

An image of the crazed man's hollow face flashed in Bedwyr's mind.

"He died as I talked to him at breakfast," the priest said. "I don't know if he was his true self or if he raved, but . . . he told me where he hid Caliburn."

Bedwyr felt an echo of the old resentment. "Your timing has been better. I can do nothing about it now."

"Perhaps you can. Constantine told me the sword is here. In Camelot."

"Impossible."

"Is it? You remember Camelot lay deserted for several years after Camlann. Constantine could have hidden it at leisure then."

"Ceawlin would have found it."

"Not likely, in this hiding place."

Bedwyr's thoughts eddied and swirled like blown smoke. Perhaps it was possible. He had not known about the cavern. He was beginning to think there were many things he did not know about Camelot. But even if it were here, of what use to find it now? Better it stay hidden than fall into Saxon hands. Better anything than that. Or was it too late? The road west might still be open, and he could escape with it to the mere.

"Where, Cethrum?"

"Come with me," the priest said, and trudged away toward the chapel. Bedwyr and Irion followed.

Cethrum pushed open the door and strode in, looking about him with dismay. "Heathens!" he muttered. "I'll thrash their backsides."

He led the way to the altar and hoisted his robe about his waist. With a grunt he climbed up on it, and walked to one end where he stood, frowning.

"Is something meant to happen?" Bedwyr said.

"Young man, come up here and stand," the priest ordered Irion.

He did so, but still nothing happened.

"More weight," Cethrum said. "Bedwyr, can you . . . no, I

see you cannot. Lift something onto this end of the altar, will you?"

Bedwyr grasped the first thing at hand, a fifty-pound sack of lime, and slung it onto the stone slab at Cethrum's feet. The slab lurched and the far end tilted slightly. The upright stone that served as the endpiece of the altar toppled backward with a crash. Dust rose.

Bedwyr limped to the end and peered in. The altar was hollow. As the dust settled, he could see inside it the outline of a large trunk, a clothing trunk, from the look of it. He reached in, found a handle, and pulled. With a rasping screech it slid out of the altar.

His heart pounded as he opened the lid. Folded neatly on top of a pile of clothing was a cloak of finest wool, imperial purple in color. He traced with his fingers the initials embroidered into one corner in gold thread: AI.

"Artorius Imperator," he said softly. "Arthur's cloak."

Beneath it he found a thin circlet of honey-pure gold, unadorned, which the High King had worn on occasions of state. Other items of his were there as well, but Bedwyr paid them little heed as he groped toward the bottom of the trunk. There was nothing . . .

His fingers closed around an oiled leather scabbard and he pulled it gently from the trunk. Smooth from wear, dark with age, Caliburn's scabbard.

Holding the sheath with one hand, he drew the sword. The keen, blue edge glinted, seeming to draw to it what light there was in the room. It was heavier than most swords, for Arthur had been a tall and powerful fighter, but it felt balanced to a hair, so that its weight was not noticed. Two gold serpents twined down the leather hilt. On the pommel the single amethyst, nearly as purple as the cloak, gleamed as if with a life of its own. As he held it the grip warmed to his hand until it seemed to become part of his flesh. The perfect weapon, he thought, almost with its own will to fight.

Spellbound, he rose, oblivious to those around him. Here was the end of his quest, the sole reason he had returned to Britain. The road west remained open. On Ariant, he could be at the mere by sunset. If he died here, Caliburn would someday be found, most likely by the Saxon inheritors. Of what use, anyway, to die for Britons who could not, would not, unite even to meet a common foe?

But even as he thought the words, he knew that he could not desert those who looked to him to lead them, if only to show them how to die. For good or ill, this was his place. He must disobey Arthur a third time. Feeling utterly wretched, he slid Caliburn slowly back into its scabbard and laid it on the cloak. Forgive me, my King, he thought. Then he closed the trunk and pushed it back into the altar, out of sight.

Raising his eyes to his companions, he said, "It must stay here, hidden, for another time. Do you stand on the stone and I'll lift the slab."

With an effort that cost a trickle of blood down his bandages, Bedwyr managed to lift the end stone into place, closing the altar. As he did so a trumpet blew from the walls, sounding the view.

"Come," he said. "It's time." With Cethrum he limped from the chapel.

Irion followed, but he paused at the door and looked back at the altar, deep in thought.

TWENTY-EIGHT

The warriors had mounted and stood waiting. The stillness of the air became intense, as above the fortress dark clouds built one on the other. Bedwyr and Irion went to the open gate and looked east.

Over the ridge of the horizon stole a shadow, a black line that shimmered in the heat and distance like a mirage. As they watched, it crept down the hill and spread toward them, a dark stain on the green land. The Saxon host.

Silent at first as a true shadow it came, but soon sounds could be heard: War horns, carried on the wind, clamoring for blood. Closer. And now they could make out tiny figures.

Only the battlefront kept to a line. At the ends and in the rear, far behind, barbarians swarmed like midges at the edge of a cloud.

Bedwyr could make out the standards, and he pointed them out to Irion. "There. The white horse. That's Cynric, son of Cerdic, who is *bretwalda*. And there, Wihtgar, his cousin, from the Isle of Vectis. There, under the red horse, Ceawlin, most dangerous of all."

On the host came, shouting and clashing shields. The noise grew until a roar broke over the waiting British like the thunder of breakers pounding rocks.

Bedwyr lowered his helm over his head and buckled the chin strap. He turned to bid good fortune to Irion, but he was gone.

As Bedwyr limped toward Ariant, Cethrum came over. "Whatever blessing I can give you," he said, "you have. God be with you, Bedwyr."

Not trusting himself to answer, Bedwyr clasped the priest's hand and pulled himself painfully into the saddle.

He waited at the gate while the Cymry rode proudly past him, saluting or nodding their heads. As jeers sounded from the *brôch* behind them, they filed down the slope and the great fortress emptied like an overturned cup. At the foot of the hill they formed up, cavalry on both wings. Somehow Owein had gotten out of his bed and now stood with his Cornovi warriors in the center, where in the old days the legions would have been.

Bedwyr rode out of Camelot, Ariant dancing as though he scorned the earth beneath him. At the top of the hill he paused. Fergus stood stiffly by his boot. His trumpeter halted beside him and put the trumpet to his lips. The call sounded, high and sweet and shining.

A long arrow's flight away, beyond the standing stones, the Saxon host drew up. Their standards hung close and heavy in the still air as lightning flickered and thunder grumbled in the distance. When they saw the numbers of the British they faced, they began to mock and taunt them.

Bedwyr waited a long moment. Then he raised his arm to signal the charge. Before he could bring it down, he froze.

At the edge of the standing stones, between the armies, a man stood where no one had stood earlier. Alone, he faced the Saxon confederation.

From his shoulders draped a mantle of imperial purple. A circlet of gold rested on the white hair. At his side hung a scabbard of oiled leather, dark with age, the amethyst of Caliburn flashing in the eerie light of the approaching storm. He stood silently, as if he had risen from the earth itself.

For an instant Bedwyr saw another scene, a young Count of Britain at his King Making, wearing that cloak and that sword, with Myrddin setting the gold circlet over his brow. The years dropped away and Bedwyr was a young warrior watching Arthur become Pendragon of Britain. Then the vision vanished.

Anger exploded from deep within him. "Fool!"

His trumpeter looked over at him in wonder.

"By what right does he take Caliburn? As well hand it to the Saxons on his knees!" So he had been right about him. This was the very son of Medraut.

He tensed to send Ariant plunging down the hill, to wrest Caliburn from Irion's hands, and to take flight with it if he could, or die in the attempt. At that instant a hand seized Ariant's bridle, and the horse started and shied.

"Hold!"

"Loose him, Cethrum!" Bedwyr raised his hand to strike the priest.

"Wait!" Cethrum gasped. "The legend. Do you not see? It's the legend!"

"It's the son of Medraut, and he is about to lose his life. Turn loose, I say!"

But the priest clung stubbornly to the bridle. "Bedwyr, think! Irion has seen it. The one chance we have. The Saxons may believe he is Arthur, for does he not sleep beneath Camelot, waiting until the need of his people is great? Arthur will need his war stallion. Take Ariant to him!"

Cethrum's words filtered through Bedwyr's haze of rage and dispelled it, leaving him blinking. A keen, cold thrust of hope knifed through him and disappeared. It could not possibly succeed. "What is his plan? Were you part of this?"

"No. I knew nothing of it. Nor did he, I think, until the moment of its unfolding. If we would preserve Britain from the Dark yet a while, we must follow."

Bedwyr stared down at him, his heart warring with his mind.

"Please, Bedwyr! As you loved the King, do this for him. For Arthur!"

Bedwyr drew a shuddering breath and nodded. "Loose me, Cethrum. We will play out the scene. Let us pray it's not a tragedy."

Cethrum dropped his hand from the bridle.

"Ewan!" said Bedwyr, dismounting. "Lend me your horse."

Bewildered, the trumpeter clambered off his mount. Bedwyr pulled himself up onto it and, leading Ariant, rode down the hill. The British lines parted for him to pass, and he trotted silently toward the figure in the purple cloak, who stood like a king, facing down the Saxon host.

The Saxons had seen Irion now. A murmur swelled in the battle line and swept back through the ranks. Many of them knew Arthur by sight, for they had fought against him at

Badon Hill, or at Llongborth, or at Tribruit, and he had defeated them at every hand.

Cynric watched this apparition, uneasy. As Bedwyr rode forward the Saxon chieftain turned toward him and stared at the Companion, and at the great white stallion.

As Bedwyr drew near to Irion, a puff of breeze stole along the ground and flared the purple cloak of Arthur. Beneath the cloak Irion wore no armor, only the rich linen tunic with the red dragon, stitched into the fabric by the hands of Gwenhwyfar, the High Queen. His face was the same white as the hair and Bedwyr was startled. How? . . . Then he saw a tiny streak on the temple where the white had been washed away by a trickle of sweat. Lime.

A drop of rain hit Bedwyr's face and he prayed: Let it hold off a few more moments! He dismounted and sank to one knee in front of Irion.

"If you would play King," he said under his breath, "you need a horse. Mount Ariant." In a loud voice, he called, "Hail, Arthur! Pendragon of Britain! King that was, King that will be. Your people welcome you, for they are in sore need."

Irion looked at him with gratitude and mounted the stallion.

By the Three! Bedwyr thought. He does look like Arthur!

Irion drew Caliburn and held it high in the air. Its blade glimmered and drew all eyes to it, like a beacon. At the same time a flash of jagged lightning ripped between earth and sky. There came a moment of intense, quivering silence. Then, while the white streak of lightning still hung like wrath before Bedwyr's eyes, the world shuddered at the crack and hollow boom of the thunder.

As the echoes rolled away, Irion spoke in the Saxon tongue, a voice that was Arthur's voice in anger. "It is short years only since we sat at Badon Hill and drew the terms of the treaty which set your borders! Why do ye break your word? Are the oaths of Saxons no more than the grunting of pigs rooting for acorns?

"I know ye, Cynric Cerdic-son. Why do ye risk my anger yet again? Three times have ye fought me. Three times have I forced ye to kneel before me. Yet ye bring your swarm to my very door. Your gods are angered by your witlessness!

"I know ye, Wihtgar of Vectis. Ye seek to replace Cynric and so lead your people into ruin with your pride. Get ye gone!

"And ye, Ceawlin, I know ye. Ye are hungry for spoils and the blood of my people. That I do not forgive. Turn now and flee to your borders before I call the furies that inhabit your forests, and loose them upon your *duns* and steadings. And when ye huddle at your hearths for safety, the Wolves of Annwn will appear like wraiths in the smoke of your hearth-fires, to tear your throats from your bodies!"

The Saxon leaders shifted nervously and exchanged glances. Some made signs to ward off magic.

Ceawlin turned crimson with fury beneath his flowing mustache. "This is trickery!" he shouted. "Spirits there be, but a man does not come back from the dead. This fake is flesh and bone and I will prove it."

He drew his sword and spurred his horse forward, reining it so tightly that its neck arched, and it fought openmouthed at the bit. Knee to knee with the apparition, Ceawlin halted, his face under the tusked helmet wearing hatred as cold and hard as metal. Behind Irion, Bedwyr watched, helpless to interfere.

With a snarl Ceawlin swung his sword at Irion's head. Caliburn came up and parried the blow with a ringing sound like the sting and shiver of winter bells. Ceawlin swung again and again the heavy iron met the steel of Arthur's sword.

Then with a slight smile Irion lowered Caliburn and held out his arms, inviting a thrust to his midsection. Ceawlin drove his sword into Irion's side. The youth made no effort to evade or parry the thrust, and Bedwyr winced as he heard the blade grind through the bones of his ribs.

Ceawlin screamed in triumph as he withdrew the sword. He turned and held it high so that the Saxons could see the blood of an ordinary man.

But there was no blood. The blade remained bright and unstained. A rustle, a sound like a deep breath being drawn, rippled along the battle line.

At that instant Irion swung Caliburn in a flat, singing arc of blue steel. It struck Ceawlin above his gold torque and sheared through his neck. The chieftain looked puzzled. Slowly the head tilted forward and rolled a bloody track down his hauberk, wedging itself upright against his saddlebow.

Freed of the rein pressure, the horse bolted and galloped along the Saxon line, headless corpse still on its back gripping the sword, neck spraying blood. Ceawlin's head stared out from the saddle, eyes flickering, jaws working.

Cynric's face went white as bleached parchment. He shouted guttural words of command, wheeled his horse, and rode south, wrapping as much dignity about him as his flight would permit. His thanes followed, fear and awe on their faces. Above them thunder crashed and lightning leaped from cloud to cloud.

With Caliburn held high Irion rode toward the wavering barbarian horde. At that moment Bedwyr signaled the charge and from the hilltop Ewan's trumpet crowed. The Cymry cavalry sprang forward, their battle cry a single roar. Above Gwythur the standard fluttered and spread, the red dragon seeming to open its wings. On the other side Dunaut's horsemen thundered down on the horde, clods of turf flying from their horses' hoofs.

Panic swept the horde. The great Saxon host began to dissolve and scatter like autumn leaves, as warriors threw down their weapons and trampled each other to escape Arthur's wrath. Only a few small knots and individual warriors held their ground to meet the onrushing cavalry.

Those who ran did not look back, and so did not see Caliburn waver in Irion's hand, nor see him slump in his saddle, then tumble to the ground. Bedwyr galloped to him and flung himself from his horse to kneel in the rain over him. Gently he opened the tunic to staunch the flow of blood. He stopped in surprise. Irion's upper body was bound tightly by wrap upon wrap of cloth, wound to a thickness of Bedwyr's arm. A rent in the cloth told where the sword point had entered. Smears of blood fringed the tear where it had been wiped clean as it withdrew.

"Medicus! Here!" he called, but Catullan was already there, two litter bearers behind him.

"Go," he said gruffly. "I'll handle this."

He examined Irion for a moment, then motioned to the

[205]

litter bearers. "Gently!" he snapped. They picked up the litter and carried him back toward the fortress.

The storm broke and rain fell in torrents. In an hour the battle was over. The sodden plain before Camelot was still again, deserted save for those killed in the crush of escape, and the debris left behind by the fleeing Saxons.

Bedwyr retrieved Caliburn and mounted Ariant, then followed the jubilant cavalry up the hill. As he neared the top, the sound of fighting erupted from inside the fortress. He rode through the gates to see a force of Cymry outside the brôch. Led by Dunaut they surrounded a dwindling knot of warriors wearing red-horse tunics. Other British pursued the few barbarians who had reached the gate.

The iron door of the tower stood open. Heart in his throat, Bedwyr slid from his horse and limped through it. The interior stood empty. He struggled up the stairs and peered into each chamber, but found them deserted.

Above him he heard a high-pitched scream, ending in a wailing gurgle. Frantic, he ran up the remaining steps into the highest room, the chamber of the Round Table.

Near the great circular oak table stood Gwythur, calmly wiping his sword blade. Ulfang's body sprawled across the table where he had fallen.

Something moved in the shadows of the far corner. Bedwyr squinted against a shaft of light shining into his eyes from the tiny window. In the corner crouched Elyn, face bruised, clothing disheveled.

He went to her, wanting to lift her, to embrace her with a massive, savage joy, to say a thousand things to her. Instead he said, "Can you stand?"

She nodded, and with his help, got to her feet. Then she embraced him, weeping.

"Did they harm you?"

"I'm alive." She drew back and looked at him, then held him again. "I was to be Ceawlin's woman. He knew me when Medraut and he were allies. While he lived, Ulfang did not dare kill me." She turned to Gwythur. "At the end he would have finished me before he fled with the rest, had not this warrior come."

"We owe you much," Bedwyr said.

Gwythur blushed and nodded.

"My son," Elyn said. "I must see him."

"Come. He saved the lives of us all."

"I know. They forced me to watch from the window. Does he live?"

"Narrowly." Bedwyr led her down the stairs.

Irion lay on a cot in the dressing station, eyes closed, face washed clean by the rain. Near him the other leaders waited silently.

Catullan stood at his side.

"How does he?" Elyn said.

"The wraps kept the bleeding small." The surgeon's voice was hoarse. "But the sword did much damage inside. He's dying, and I cannot save him."

At the sound of Elyn's words Irion opened his eyes. His lips moved as he tried to speak, but no sound came.

She knelt by his side and stroked his forehead. "Rest you. Don't try to speak." And then as if to herself she whispered, "Ah, Jesu, Irion. You have grown up well. Arthur would be proud of his grandson. Forgive me, my heart, for not being there to watch you grow. We have missed so much, you and I."

Irion closed his eyes again, his face relaxing into a slight smile.

Elyn stood and turned away, fighting tears. She lost her fight and the naked hurt flooded out in great, tearing sobs. Bedwyr held her, comforting her against a grief no medicine could heal.

"There is one who might yet help," he said. "She is a great healer who dwells on Ynys Afallon."

Elyn looked up at him, hope in her eyes. "I know of Morgan. If there is any chance for Irion, please help me take him there."

Shadows stretched toward them as Bedwyr and Elyn stood at the edge of the shallow lake. The litter bearers set Irion carefully down on the grass. He was gray with the pallor of approaching death and remained unconscious.

Across the glassy water a coracle made its way toward them. In the stern stood a man in a black hood, poling, while in the bow sat Morgan, hood drawn over her head. The boat drew closer, whispering through the reeds.

When it bumped the shore Morgan stepped out and, without speaking, went to Irion. Kneeling beside him she looked at the wound and felt the skin around it.

"He is far spent," she said, her voice faint and sad, as if coming from a far distance. "I doubt that my power is great enough."

"Please," Elyn said. "Help him if you can."

Morgan looked at her for a moment. "He must be long in my care." She signaled the stretcher-bearers and they carried Irion toward the boat.

Bedwyr knelt on one knee in homage. "*Ffarwel*, lord," he murmured.

"May I not go with him?" Elyn said.

Morgan shook her head. "The Isle is not for you. Your life is in the world outside."

Elyn watched the boatman pole the coracle out into the lake as the light faded. Clumsy with caring, Bedwyr drew her close and wrapped his arms around the pain in her heart.

"I will not see him again," she said, gazing after the disappearing boat.

"Irion has earned the right to sleep beside the High King."

She gazed up at him then, her eyes questioning. "Does Arthur truly sleep beneath Camelot?"

"Aye," Bedwyr said. "Arthur sleeps everywhere."

Epilogue

Wild swans beat up from the lake as Bedwyr approached. The moon had already risen, four nights from the full, and its light gave a moving sheen to the water. Nearby, a fox drinking at the shore raised her head at the sight of him and froze, her muzzle silvered with crystal droplets. The knife-thin cry of a bat pricked the dusk. In the shadow of the riven oak Elyn waited.

Bedwyr breathed deeply, inhaling the cleanness of water and grass and twilight. A breeze stole past him, swirling the fog that had folded in over the water. It has more of the west in it tonight, he thought. As he watched, the white mist writhed and thickened.

He turned away from the mere, grasping Caliburn's hilt in his hand. Then he spun and hurled the sword far out over the water.

It turned and circled in a high, lazy arc, drawing to it the moonlight. As it descended, the mist engulfed it, seeming to form for a moment the shape of a woman's hand. The hand received the sword and drew it into the water smoothly and without a splash.

At Bedwyr's side the wolfhound nudged him with a huge, friendly nose.